Also by Dimetrios C. Manolatos

*The Sons of Herakles*
A Short Novel of Bronze Age Greece

*The Assassin's Pitch*
A Novel of Sport, Love, Loss and Revenge

*47 Ronin*
*A Novella*

# Sparta

## Dimetrios C. Manolatos

The Warrior Class

Published by The Warrior Class

This work is entirely fiction. Names, characters, places and events are the result of the author's imagination. Any resemblances of actual persons, living or dead are coincidental.

All Rights Reserved

Copyright © 2012, 2017 by Dimetrios C. Manolatos
Book Design, Cover and Maps by Dimetrios C. Manolatos

ISBN 978-1549948442

www.dimetri.com

For Nick and Melinda

# Map of Sparta

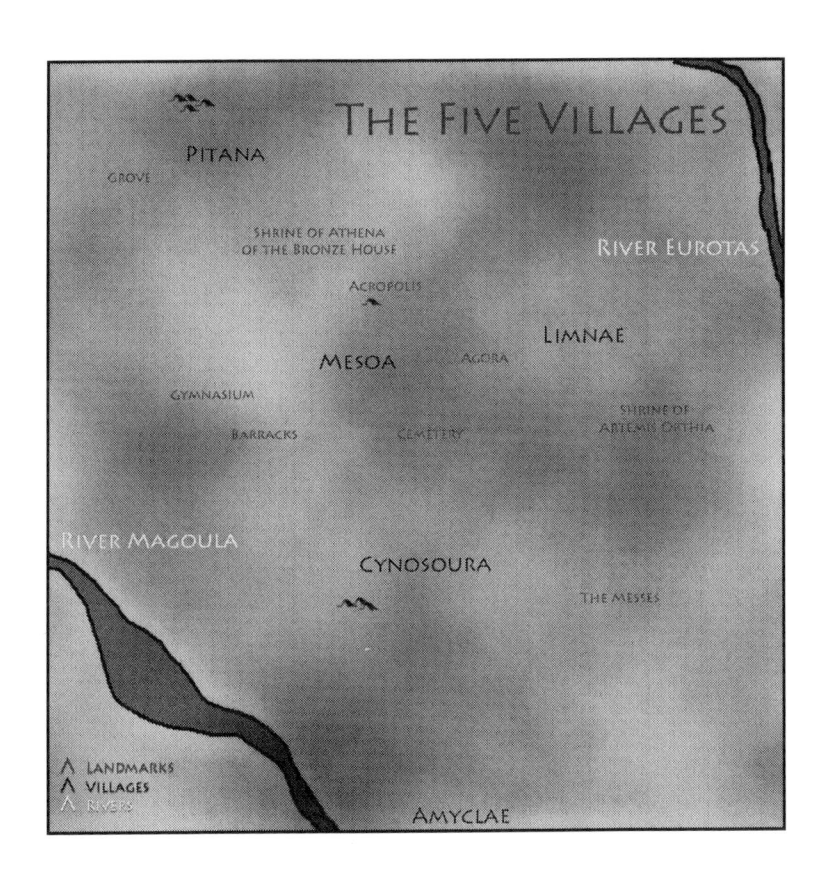

# Map of Greece and Asia Minor

# Map of the Persian Empire

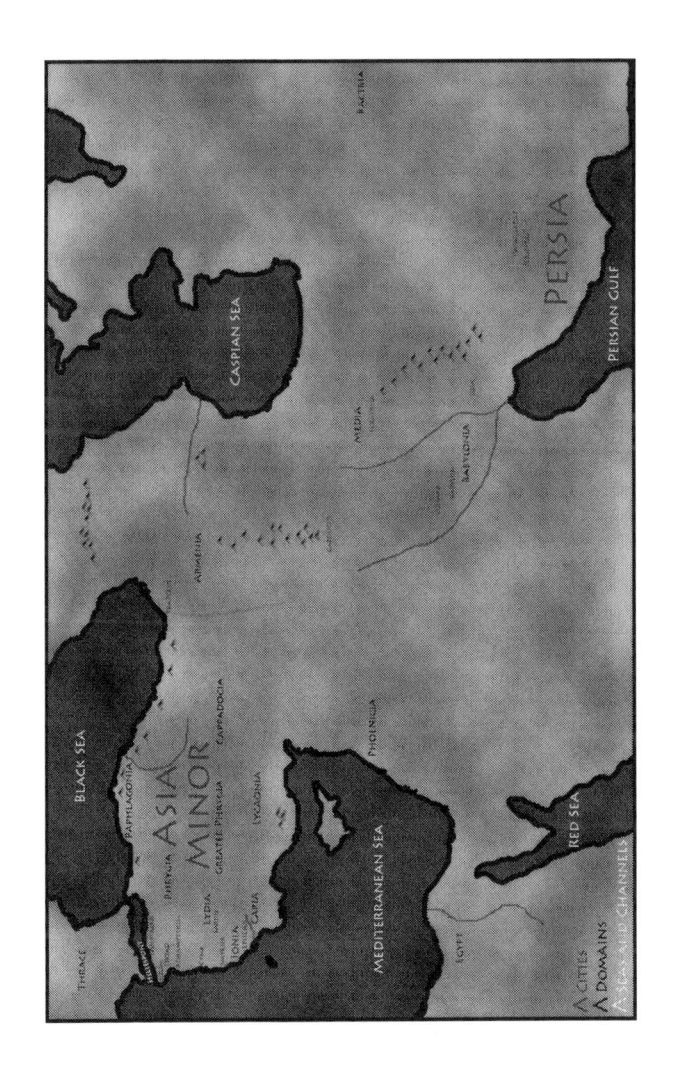

# Glossary of Terms

**Acropolis**   The highest fortified area of a Greek city, typically located on a hill.

**Agoge**   The Spartan education system that taught boys to be warrior men. Literally defined as "raising," "herding" or "man taming." There was also believed to be a comparable system for the girls.

**Agora**   A meeting place for the people in a Greek city, also used for trade and other activities.

**Amphora**   A ceramic jar or vase, sometimes with two handles near the mouth.

**Assembly**   A group of men who made up part of the governing body in Athens.

**Athlitika**   One area of Sparta's gymnasium that hosted machines used for strength training.

**Council**   A group of five hundred men who made up part of the governing body in Athens.

**Crimson**   Spartan slang for their crimson colored cloaks, also called *crimsons*.

**Eight**  Spartan slang for spear, also called *eights* or *ash*.

**Elders**  Twenty-eight male Spartan citizens over the age of sixty who were elected to serve as part of the governing body for life.

**Enomotarch**  An army officer that was one rank below the *pentecosters*.

**Enomotiae**  A contingent of Spartan *hoplites* within a *mora* that were commanded by an *enomotarch*.

**Ephors**  Five male Spartan citizens who were elected annually to serve as part of the governing body. No reelection was possible.

**Equal**  An adult, male, Spartan citizen who successfully passed the *agoge* and served as a *hoplite* until the age of sixty, also called *Equals*.

**Helen**  Spartan slang for a beautiful woman.

**Helot**  A Spartan slave.

**Hippodrome**  An arena used for equestrian performances and races.

**Hoplite**  A heavy armored infantryman.

**Knights**  *Equals* who were honored to fight alongside the king.

**Krypteia**  A secret order, consisting of *Equals* and *Youths* whose sole purpose was to kill *helots*.

**Lid**  Slang for a hoplite's helmet, also called *lids*.

**Lochagi**  High ranking army officers that were one rank below *polemarch*.

**Logos**  Greek for logo, a letter typically painted on a *hoplite's* shield to identify their origins.

**Lycurgus**  Ancient lawmaker who created the Spartan constitution.

**Mora**  A regiment of Spartan *hoplites*.

**Paean**  A joyous song of praise.

**Pankration**  A Greek martial art, consisting of boxing, wrestling and other combat movements. Literally defined as "all power."

**Peltasts**  Light armored infantrymen.

**Pentecosters**  High ranking army officers that were one rank below the *lochagi*.

**Perioeci**  Free non-Spartan people living in the southern Peloponnese who were subjected to Spartan law and also expected to serve in the military. Literally defined as "the dwellers round about."

**Pitch**  One area of Sparta's gymnasium that offered a flat grass surface that was intended for sprinting and javelin throwing.

**Polemarch**  The highest ranking army officer, just under the kings, who commanded a *mora*.

**Sands**  One area of Sparta's gymnasium that offered numerous beds of sand that were used for boxing, wrestling and *pankration* training.

**Satrap**  A governor of a Persian domain, sometimes they governed multiple domains.

**Skata**  Greek for shit. As in, you are full of…

**Skytale**  A device that Spartans used to send secret messages.

**Sortie**  A small contingent of infantrymen or cavalrymen used for scouting, stealth and other types of missions.

**Stade**  A distance of almost two hundred meters.

**Stadion**  Ancient equivalent of our stadium, a field the distance of a *stade* used for sporting events, typically running.

**Trek**  One area of Sparta's gymnasium that offered a long distance trail for running.

**Twenty**  Spartan slang for shield, also called *twenties*.

**Youths**  Spartan boys between the age of seven and eighteen, and undergoing the *agoge*.

# BOOK I
## ACCESSION TO THE THRONE

*She has been around for more than five hundred years, maintaining the longest form of government in Greece's history. Her laws are unwavering. She is incorruptible to gold. On her throne, sits a dual kingship, one from the Agiad Dynasty which is said to be the more dominant line, and the second, the Eurypontid Dynasty. After twenty-seven years of civil war, she defeated Athens and reigns supreme in the Greek world. Her victory was largely due to her Naval Admiral Lysander and King Agis of the Eurypontid, but it was not without consequence. Strife, now more than ever plagues her. She knows only one cure for her illness and that is through her strength of arms. But alas, her men are masters of war.*

# Agis

Agis, son of Archidamus, held the blade and made the sacrifice on Elean earth to Zeus and Athena. The she-goat fell between his legs, fresh blood warming his calloused feet. The *ephors* observed from a ways by the side of a vast regiment, three *moras*, all facing their king while he conducted the priestly affair. Agis was sixty this day and by Lycurgan Law he was ordered to retire this morning, not from his kingship, but from war. He reminded the ephors though, that he was born on the full moon and since last night was the final waxing, his day of birth was actually this night. The ephors agreed, neither daring to break the law, nor insult the gods. Either way, they both knew this was his last campaign, Agis's last war. As he lowered down to open the beast, he thought again, how retirement breaks the men from within and kills them. Twenty-seven years as king, and he watched many of the *Equals* fall deep into deadly sorrow. To Styx with that! Hades will sort me out, he would say to himself. So he made up his mind years ago, to go out of this world with his spear thrusting.

Peering beyond the thorny hairs and locks on his silver-white beard, which was styled in the old fashion, he pulled the liver out for inspection. The ephors watched a grin curl on his upper bare lip. They had accompanied him on all his campaigns over the last year and they could tell the signs were favorable. Agis looked to them to confirm, only nodding. This was the third sacrifice to Zeus and Athena, not counting those to Pythian Apollo, Artemis Orthia, Ares and his sons, Deimos and Phobos. The first was at home to determine whether they should embark on a campaign to make the Eleans see reason for their injustice. The second was at the farthest reach of Laconia, superfluous, but necessary to keep in line with the gods. All had been healthy, successful, and now he knew the ones he worshipped were in his favor. He carried the slippery organ with great ease to the fire brought by the fire bearer all the way from Laconia and set the dripping glop on the spit.

Agis turned and crossed back to his earlier position, eager as a youth on his first campaign, while brushing past one of his *polemarchs*. "Pipers."

The polemarch signaled the pipers with a pointed finger and they began playing. Then, he and the other two polemarchs barked out the order. The same exact order they always barked to their moras. "What are you looking at, you worthless dogs? Square your kits! Armor on! Get in file!"

All through the ranks, the Equals responded most lackadaisically by combing their hair and beards, laughing and joking, just another day's labor, while dirt and insects fell to their sides. The comb was their most precious possession next to their shield because if death should meet them, the Equals wanted to be as beautiful as possible, as an offering to those who judge their passing into the next world. While this was going on, the *helots* stepped in from the rear at the baggage train and attended to their masters. They brought them oil to anoint their bodies and other supplies, including their *aspis,* the dish-shaped shield the men called the *twenties*, or their *twenty*. It should have been called the *thirties*, or their *thirty*, but this was a wry way of dispelling its true weight, and one of the many things, the Equals loved to loathe.

Four furlongs behind Agis, the Elean army waited, tirelessly for battle. Since the sun rose, they have watched their enemy, the Spartans, ready themselves like performers in theatre through the slits on their lids. First their morning gymnastics, which was a grueling regiment of running around the edge of camp three times. This was followed by dashing from one edge of camp to the opposite side, down and back counting as one, until this was done three times. After that, the troops fell back into file and dropped to the ground, belly first. They placed their twenties upside down on their backs, and then began to push themselves off the ground with their arms while balancing on their toes, and then they lowered back down. This was done until it couldn't be. After the last man fell, they stood up, held their twenties out in front of them, and began to bend down as if they were going to sit on a chair and then stood back up. This was done until it couldn't be. Then, they dropped their twenties by their feet, bent over to pick them up, stood tall with their whole body while raising their twenties overhead, and then lowered them back down to the ground. This was done until it couldn't be. The last round consisted of something the Eleans had never seen before. Each Spartan paired with another of similar size. One stood, while the other lay on his back and locked his legs around the standing man's waist. Then they clasped each other's hands and the man standing, bent at the knees, and leaned forward just so. He then pulled his partner up to his torso, breasts almost kissing, and lowered him back down. This was done until it couldn't be and then they switched up. The Eleans thought it strange and compared it to a combination of rowing on a trireme and some deluded pederastic ritual that only the Spartans or Thebans would think of. When they were done with this, they broke down into age groups and the eldest Equals watched and cheered their younger peers, during countless rounds of boxing and wrestling matches. The Eleans couldn't see this from their position, but they did listen as their enemy's spirit soared to the heavens.

When the trumpets sounded, morning gymnastics ended and the moras gathered for inspection by their polemarchs. Then they ate a quick breakfast and here they are now, caring for their shields, the sheep's wool, meticulously bringing their twenties to a radiant shine. Each Equal then proceeded by reassembling the arm strap they kept on their person to the backside of their twenty. The prior removal of the band was done just in case their ungrateful servants decided to revolt, leaving their shields useless and the helots helpless. The tedious and distant observation of these masters of war greatly disheartened the Eleans. The Equals knew this of course. This was why they did what they did and continued taking their sweet time, showing no signs of fear or distress, as their wool caps were placed snug over their crowns and then topped with their gleaming lids that were scarred by countless days rendered on campaign.

With all three moras squared, the pipers stopped and the Equals commanded their helots to return to the baggage train and guard their property. The polemarchs then signaled the trumpets. The blow of the horns snapped the men into file. There were five hundred seventy-six Equals per mora. Each mora divided into sixteen columns, thirty-six men deep. A second signal and each column snapped three abreast, again and now six. The polemarchs gave orders to their *lochagi*, who gave orders to their *pentecosters*, who gave orders to their *enomotarchs*, who gave out the last command to their *enomotiae*, the contingent of Equals behind them.

Phobos radiated across the pitch, choking the Eleans. They began to question one another with stares, as they, a mob of seasonal soldiers were facing off against a square wall of highly organized bronze, muscle and iron spiked ash. Their desire to defend their political position had worn thin after so much time spectating, but it was too late. They, had committed.

The trumpets bellowed the final command. Agis and his *knights*, those Equals honored to fight alongside him, waited, as the troops shifted forward to fill in behind and to the left of their beloved king now positioned on the front right wing. Spanning down the line to the left of Agis were his moras, increasing their breadth to more than one furlong. Among them were the polemarchs, lochagi, pentecosters and enomotarchs. The remaining Equals were placed into their positions based on age. The eldest, those closest to sixty years of age were placed in the front rows, while the youngest, those closer to twenty-one, enforced the rear. All had their twenties strapped on their left arm and their spears, also called their *ash*, *eight* or *eights*, due to their height, stood tall on their right.

The king raised the ashen shaft of his eight. "Make these Eleans see reason!"

The Spartans unleashed their war cry, bellowing from the bottoms of their pits.

It sent shivers through the enemy's file.

Agis nodded down the front to his polemarchs, they to their lochagi, they to their pentecosters, and on down to the last enomotarch. The Spartans exhibited perfection in every aspect of warfare. Anyone who faced off against them and survived, swore they did this or that, some never before seen thing during an engagement. It was all a part of the Spartan plan. They are the masters of their craft. This is their way of life and they know exactly what war is, a means to an end.

"Forward!" the enomotarchs commanded to their columns.

The Spartans began singing Castor's Air as they advanced in a phalanx toward their enemy. All three moras moved as one in rhythm to their song. Smiles painted their faces. Their *crimsons* draped to their heels as they flowed in the breeze. They were beautiful and godly, marching under the sun.

The Eleans watched a shimmering bronze body of killers advance toward them. Phobos struck them harder. Deimos seized them entirely. Ares was laughing. Oh, the joys of war! Their untrained minds became polluted with muddled thoughts of retreat. Trickles of piss and shit sluiced down many of legs. It pooled and slopped next to their boots. By Zeus! What were they thinking? These are Spartans, proper!

"They've humbled Athens! How are we to—" one Elean said, as their trumpets signaled them forward to counter their invader's advance. They moved quietly, fluid and waste endlessly secreting. Their march had no rhythm, no joy, only fear.

Three furlongs away and a cloud of dust began to churn, sweeping up over the dry, grassy plain peppered with stones. Soon, the Spartan baggage train attendants, including helots, ephors, seers and doctors would be unable to view the battle. The same was true on the other side. Along the Spartan front though, jokes were being told and men were laughing as their song had come to an end. Two furlongs. Now one. Now three spears' length and Agis gave the command.

"Double!"

As a single body, every column shifted to their outside, loosening up their phalanx to spread the line and create gaps between them. The ranks positioned left through center-left, moved left, while the ranks positioned right through center-right, moved right. Then every other man in all columns took one step back toward the center, creating another column to fill those gaps. Lastly, all save the front line took a step forward to tighten up the phalanx, and there it was, that never before seen thing. In the blink of an eye, the Spartans had doubled their breadth, outflanking the Eleans' wings by an indeterminable margin, and by doing so, they crushed their spirits. The Equals greeted their enemy with smiles and cheers, as they watched them glance to each side, questioningly. Two spears' reach away and another command was given.

"Twenties!"

The Equals formed a wall of bronze.

"Take'em!"

They rammed the Eleans' front row as a single body. Shield clashed with shield and the Spartans overpowered them, throwing the Eleans into chaos. Agis, the man storm of war, a champion of the Athenian War, and now the pursuer of death, saw his opportunity and broke their most revered law in battle. He broke the line. Reckless, he stepped ahead of his knights, forcing his way into the second row of the enemy all alone. He was almost there, almost surrounded with no way out, as iron and wood seemed to evade him. If only he could keep his maddened pace and his men at bay for just a moment longer, his dream would be fulfilled.

Enemy eyes locked on to him, and in came the pointed shafts from the third and fourth rows.

"Kill me!" Agis yelled.

The Eleans accepted the challenge. It gave them hope amid the terror, but Agis was thrusting his eight. He had to or it would look like suicide, and this was something Sparta had not given the king permission to do. He, like all other citizens of Sparta were property of the state. He could only take his own life to regain his honor. If he threw his life away senselessly, it would be considered a crime against the state and his family's reputation would be tarnished for all eternity.

The king's knights became concerned, while Agis's polemarch had already issued their most sacred command. It was one that had rarely been used in the last seventy-five years, one that every Equal wished to be given, a command to unleash the wrath of Ares and shit on Tartaros if necessary. Thrust your eights. Lay down your life. *Do whatever it takes, damn you, and save your king!*

The command was relayed down the front and to the rear. Every *hoplite* shouted it above the din.

"Leonidas!"

The front line pushed forward, faster, catching Agis's pace, creating a momentary and vulnerable gap with the Equals to their rear by allowing the Eleans, fallen and alive, to breach their lines. They were just in time too, because Agis almost got his wish. A spear point got sliced off just below the head by a sword swing from one of his knights. It was a kiss away from felling him. The Spartans pushed harder, like a storm possessed to save their king. They ripped holes in their foe the size of melons, leaving them where they stood. The soil rapidly turned to stew. The Equals sank up to their calves, while bone fragments splintered their feet. They continued their rage and surpassed Agis, shielding him from death.

"Why?" Agis asked himself. "Don't they know? Don't they understand? What is life without war?" he screamed inside, as he pushed his way back into the front line and reunited with his knights. "Ahh! To Styx with it!" he resolved.

The Spartans cleaned out the enemy within their ranks and the file was able to quickly even out. Organization in the chaotic crush resumed on the Spartan side. Agis bore his twenty as he glanced left and right at his knights. His true desire was concealed from that moment on. Oh, the joys of war.

The Eleans had been halved and their wings flanked by the Spartan onslaught. They stopped their advance, praying for the skirmish to end or the gods to intervene on their behalf. The only thing separating them from their adversary was a polluted river of death. The Spartans however were not in a forgiving mood, so they pressed on.

"Twenties!" Agis ordered.

They were already raised. The white painted lambda on their faces, the Spartans' *logos* which identified their Laconian origins, was coated in muck.

"Take'em!"

The Equals charged with their king over the river of death and battered the Eleans with their twenties. The Spartans' back rows struck the fallen a second time, just to make sure as they trampled over them. Shield against shield, another shoving match ensued with the Eleans' sixth row now at their fore, but they were still inferior and quickly collapsed. Spartan spears plunged forward. They hit flesh and tore organs. The men of Elis were in disorder. Their cohesion, if they had any was gone. They fell into their rear ranks and pandemonium reigned supreme. Their center file was crushed. Bodies stacked and folded on top of one another. Seven rows down. Now eight. If Poseidon was watching from above, he just witnessed a massive wave of crimson and bronze, sweeping across a squandering mass of villagers. The Eleans were now reduced to six men deep.

Shield shove!

Spear thrust!

Forward advance!

The Eleans began their muted retreat. They could take no more. Not on this day. The last file back simply turned and ran for sanctuary in the hills. It was Deimos and Phobos, terror and fear. They made sure of it. Ares carried on laughing, while the remaining men followed in suit, leaving their unlucky sixth to slaughter.

"Hold!" Agis commanded. He and his front lines had annihilated all who remained. He watched the dying die and the dead lay, envious. "Another day I suppose," he thought. "Another day, I shall have my way." Agis raised his eight as he turned to face his men. "Nike!"

"Nike!" the moras responded, shouting their victory.

Λ

The victory trophy was raised. It was just a pile of rocks stacked into a small pyramid with a lambda painted on it. When the Spartans were victorious in more significant battles, they would erect a square monument cut from marble and engrave their victory in words, so that all who passed by would remember.

Meanwhile, the army remained in file as they waited for further orders, when a polemarch and six Equals escorted an Elean messenger over to Agis so that he could speak with him directly on the field of battle.

"King Agis, we Eleans now see reason and ask for a truce to collect our dead."

"Let me hear you say it," Agis said solemnly.

"There will be no objection to Sparta competing in the forthcoming Olympics."

Agis looked around, eyeing all the fallen. Not one of them was from Laconia. Then he returned his gaze to the messenger's. He was speechless, humbled, just like any other arrogant tribesman who wanted to test Spartan prowess. Agis shook his head at their foolishness. "Truce granted," he said, as if the whole ordeal was a complete waste of time.

The messenger departed without any delay, as his three polemarchs approached. "Are we to remain at camp, my king?" one of them asked.

"Olympia, then home."

"Yes, my king," he said, and excused himself as he barked out orders to the Equals. "Armor off you dogs! Marching kits only!"

# Cyrus

Cyrus, son of Darius, was recalled to his father's palace in Persepolis. The Great King was nearing his end and he wanted to proclaim which of his sons would be heir to the throne of the Persian Empire. Darius's palaces ranged throughout the middle region of his hard fought land from Susa to Ecbatana to Pasargadae to Babylon, but Persepolis was his favorite, and it was here, that he chose to die like the kings before him. His tomb had been prepared since the first day of his rule, just nineteen years ago. It was cut into the mountainside just to the north in Naqsh-I Rustam, where he would rest for all eternity with his forefathers, overlooking Persepolis and all that lies before it.

Of his many sons from his many wives, it was between Cyrus the Younger, the favorite among the people, and his brother, Artaxerxes. They both sat across from one another at their father's bedside, as Darius lay ill with death beckoning him this airless night. Across the polished red stone floor glowing with candle fire, Persian guards stood next to Tissaphernes, Darius's most trusted satrap, as well as Cyrus's good friend and escort on the way to the royal palace from Lydia. He was there to pay his final respects to the Great King and to witness the new successor. He watched as the brothers waited, while their father mustered up the energy to speak. There wasn't a shred of love between them as they both vied for the throne.

On the outside, Darius looked healthy. His complexion was strong, but his breath was wheezy and labored, and blood occasionally seeped from his nose. "Cyrus," Darius announced with a raspy voice.

Hopeful, he responded. "Yes, father."

The Great King strained to speak again. "Support…your brother," Darius's failing voice said. "In his…rule."

Devastated by the Great King's proclamation, Cyrus stared at Artaxerxes, envious and vexed. "Yes, my king."

Darius shut his eyes, nodding, while reaching out to clasp their hands, but time fell short and he passed on to the next world. Awkwardness lingered for Cyrus as he looked at the Great King, king of all the kings, king of all the lands of Persia from Asia Minor in the west, to the eastern boundary of the Hindu Kush, to Armenia in Colchis in the north, to as far south as Egypt, his brother, Artaxerxes, who was grinning arrogantly.

"Arrest him!" Artaxerxes commanded, stunning Cyrus.

The guards responded without hesitation and seized him, locking his limbs in chains. "Brother! How have I wronged you?"

"I will not have you, or anyone else, challenge my rule," Artaxerxes said, a kiss away from his face. Then he turned to Tissaphernes. "Take him away."

Cyrus looked pleadingly to his friend Tissaphernes who offered him a blank stare. Nothing angered him more than the falsehood of friendship, also known as Persian loyalty. He had been betrayed by his own blood and trusted friend, no doubt. Their eighteen day long procession in haste to Persepolis was nothing more than a ploy to make his apprehension all the easier, but was his father behind it? Cyrus couldn't be sure, but nor would it have been out of his character. As he was dragged out of the king's chamber, he eyed his brother. "I will see you flayed for your betrayal!"

Artaxerxes bowed his head confidently, mocking his brother and as soon as Cyrus was removed from the chamber, he snatched the ring off Darius's finger. The gold band was too big for his own, so he decided to hang it around his neck with a gold chain studded with ivory. The signet was of critical importance to Artaxerxes. It depicted his Achaemenid family crest which dated back to his forefather, Cyrus the Great. Not only that, it proved that he was king. The last obstacle he wanted to overcome during his first few moments as ruler was to dethrone an imposter who claimed to be him with a yearlong military campaign. It had happened before.

He began to loop the golden jewel around his neck, when it got tangled on his oily, black curls. Suddenly, two gentle hands were placed on his nape. He turned around, defensively, to see who it was and immediately relaxed his guard. It was Parysatis, his mother, wise as she was beautiful. She freed the necklace of its tangle and leaned in over his shoulder to whisper soft words in her son's ear. Artaxerxes listened without reproach and said, "Yes, mother."

# Xenophon

The *acropolis* dwarfed the city of Athens, while Phidias's wonder of the world, the Parthenon, sat upon the sanctified limestone surface. The temple, with its colored trim beneath the lifelike frieze depicting gods and men at their finest, shined brilliantly under the sun. It was an enduring symbol of the greatness of Athens, of what free men can do. It could be seen in almost explicit detail from the floor of the *agora*, where the city was always flocked with Athenian citizens and foreigners from as far as Libya and Lydia, conducting every kind of trade around. However this morning, majority of trade was interrupted and scattered because the Athenians were waiting in line to vote. The Thirty Tyrants had been banished and democracy swept back in like the tide.

Xenophon, son of Gryllus, a scrawny young man, who was nearly twenty-six years old, fought his way through the masses in the agora, utterly distressed. Finally making it to his preferred merchant, he bought some bread and wine, and as he offered the tradesman some coins, he became increasingly distracted by the mob of voters. "Thank you," he said with a raised voice, and forgot to take his goods with him. Xenophon scowled in frustration as he took a step back to grab his items and then he began to walk back through the voters. All of them were either holding a black or white marble clenched in their fist. White was for yes and the former was for no. "What were they voting on now?" he wondered, watching one of the men drop his marble in an *amphora*. The stone clanked as it hit the ceramic bottom of the jar. "This is the second day straight! When are they going to learn democracy doesn't work?"

"You there! Philosopher!" a voice called out to him.

Xenophon snapped out of his enraged trance and glanced across the way, spotting his longtime Theban friend of the same age. Proxenos was tall, handsome and was blessed with an arrogant expression at all times. They were both delighted to see each other after so long and met halfway with a handshake and a hug.

"Proxenos! By the gods! How are you, old friend?"

"Better than you. Hasn't your city learned its lesson with democracy?" Proxenos asked, as he motioned toward the voters, who were either debating politics in a heated fashion or just simply satisfied to have a say in matters.

"They vote incessantly and nothing ever gets done," Xenophon said at his wit's end. "Never mind that. What brings you to Athens?"

"To find you, Xenophon. To tell you that fortune is in your future."

Xenophon had a hard time believing that. Proxenos had always been out for himself and personal glory since childhood. "How so?" he asked.

"Cyrus builds an army to rid his territory of Pisidians. There will be much to plunder."

"Persia?"

"Yes, Persia Xenophon. Asia, Media, Babylon. It is the future of Greece."

"How do you know Cyrus's true intentions aren't to war with his brother for the throne?"

"Ahh! Well, we all have our ulterior motives. Do we not?"

"And what are yours, Proxenos?"

"The same as any Greek in our day. To get rich. Achieve fame and glory."

"I…I would enjoy that, but, I don't know."

"You can't stay here. Not with the Thirty Tyrants banished and democracy back on the ri—" Proxenos cut himself off. "I won't go there. Should you change your mind, we sail after the next moon. I'll be in Athens until then," he said, and then he began to walk away.

"Good to see you, Proxenos."

Proxenos patted him on the shoulder as he departed. "You too, old friend."

Xenophon watched him vanish in the throng and then he headed back toward the men voting. As he passed by all the varying emotions of the Athenians, his own distracted him, and he bumped into someone much bigger and much less reasonable than he.

"Watch it dog!" the passerby said and he continued on his way with an evil eye aimed at the philosopher.

Xenophon felt helpless, and for the first time, disconnected from his place of birth. Athens was a city he once loved until this moment, facing that stranger, who was giving him that cold stare. "Why didn't I insult him back? Because your face would've looked like minced meat. You're a philosopher, not a soldier. Hades's cock! That's going to eat at me all day!" he contemplated.

Xenophon headed down a ways, turning into a narrow alley and then another one, and knocked on an old battered door.

"If it's not locked, then it's obviously open!" a grumpy voice shouted from inside.

Xenophon rolled his eyes, further frustrated. He then attempted the door, found that it was indeed unlocked, and entered.

He shut the door behind him and faced his aging teacher. Socrates was sitting at an empty table that was more worn than his hideous, broken appearance and filthy, ragged tunic. He never cared for anything material, only the essentials, like food, water, wine and the truth in all things. He was busy thinking to himself in such an intense manner that his eyes looked like they were reaching out of his crown. They never did the formal greeting when meeting each morning because Socrates found it useless and a practical waste of time. Those precious breaths could be applied to exploring matters to their fullest. So going ignored upon entering was customary for Xenophon and he put the bread and wine he bought for his teacher on the table, and got down to it.

"Socrates, what is happening to Athens?"

Socrates neglected the current theory he was attempting to prove to himself and looked to Xenophon. "Democracy is happening."

"But Athens will never revive herself to her old glory with democracy," Xenophon said, exasperated.

"How so?" Socrates asked.

Xenophon took a breath to collect himself after his ruinous morning. "Men only think of what laws will help them now as individuals, not what will be beneficial to us all as a city in the future."

"I see."

He looked skeptical at his teacher. "You are going to compare democracy to a tyranny, but please let us remain focused."

"Please," Socrates said.

"When laws are put to a vote, an unseen child of corruption is born, but the people do not see it, and then they rejoice in satisfying their selfish whims."

"Sounds very childish," Socrates commented.

"Therefore, it is the people who are the child. When that child grows and has a problem, as all children do, they look for someone to blame and it is always the parents or in our case, the leader, our leader who gave the people a choice. At this time, we are usually at the precipice of war and our freedom is threatened. Our leader is then ostracized or put to death for his inability to guide us. But it is not his lack of leadership, it is the child's lack of forethought and responsibility to their city."

"Welcome to Athens, Xenophon. City of children."

Xenophon was still in no mood, especially not for Socrates's sarcasm. "I cannot stay here."

"Where will you go? What will you do?"

"Cyrus raises an army to take the throne from Artaxerxes. I will enlist."

"A mercenary with no soldiering experience? For what purpose? To what end? Adventure? Fortune? Fame? Death?"

"You are opposed to one of your students broadening his mind?"

"Is that what you call war? Better, let's call it *tourism*. I hear King Agis is deathly ill with fever after sacrificing in Olympia. Why don't you see if the Spartans will adopt you. Their government is incorruptible and your desires for death will come much sooner on *tour* with them. In either case, you will be branded as a traitor by your city."

"Spare me the lecture. You have taught me too well to treat me as a sophomoric schoolboy. *I have thought this through.*"

"What can you not find within yourself that is in Asia?"

"Honor, glory, fortune…Purpose! The things that are necessary to survive in our world. One cannot realistically go on in life with no material possessions and depend on others for food and—" Xenophon cut himself off.

Socrates's nerve was struck. "Some say that the truth hurts. I think they are right," he said.

"Forgive me. That was harsh."

"But true nonetheless. It is only Socrates who can live like Socrates."

Humored, Socrates and Xenophon shared a smile as they locked eyes.

"As a teacher to his pupil, tell me what I should do. I cannot stay here and watch Athens destroy herself again. And if you're not careful with your words, these democrats will also be your end."

"True enough. True enough. What do I think you should do was the original question," Socrates replied, as if it was obvious. "Go to Delphi and consult the Oracle. Ask if your Persian expedition will be a success."

Unlike Xenophon, Socrates was not at all exhausted by the elaborate conversation that seemed to be necessary to offer the most simple of counsel. He broke some bread off the loaf and dipped it in his bowl of wine. He then took a bite and was very pleased with his breakfast, while across from him, his student watched in wonder.

"You are an amazing man, Socrates."

"What is it that makes man amazing?"

Xenophon grinned while shaking his head in disbelief, not yet ready for another round of conversation.

# Lysander

The troops returned from Olympia, entering Sparta from her north and bypassing the village of Pitana. They were in marching formation with King Agis at the lead. He was gravely ill and being carried on a stretcher. His symptoms attacked him just after his sacrifice to Zeus and Nike. No one could explain, not even his doctors, how he suddenly fell ill, coughing up blood and suffering from frequent episodes of blindness, but he knew. Too many times he cursed Hades name in vain, secretly fearing his retirement from campaign. Agis lay still on the way to his house, speechless and motionless, glimpsing his last glimpse of the Shrine of Athena of the Bronze House. He knew his time had come. He was ready to sail down the River Styx and let Hades sort him out.

They crossed through the agora, where Spartan women, children, Equals, helots, and *perioeci*, the free dwellers of Laconia, took notice of the procession. They stopped doing whatever it was they were doing to show their respect. The news of Agis had already reached them the day before from one of their runners. The keenest eye on the king though was Lysander, son of Aristocleitus. He was a prominent and distinguished man with his long, silver hair and beard styled in the old fashion. He was a champion of the Athenian War, of Heraklid blood, but not of the royal family. He was sincerely saddened by the fate of his longtime friend and king, but it did not stop his mind from thinking about who would be next in line to the throne, as Agis passed by, meeting his eyes one last time.

Lysander went home immediately after, as dusk came on early. His house was modest and it lacked all luxury, just like any other home in Sparta. He was sitting at his oaken table, while he carved a secret message on a thin strip of leather that was wound around a staff. It was called a *skytale*. Only sparse words were written, and after, he unwound it from the staff. "Take this to Agesilaos at the garrison in Thebes," he ordered.

"Yes, master," Myron said. Then he pulled back the candle light he was holding for Lysander and accepted the skytale.

Lysander turned and stared at his helot dead in the eyes, wondering why he hadn't left. Myron's mind lapsed because his emaciated frame craved food and water. This was something he had not had since first light. Nevertheless, Myron snapped out of his daze, quickly, not requiring any further instruction and departed in all haste. Good thing for him. For if he had not and Lysander was forced to speak, Myron's forty-one-year-old body would be physically unable to make the trek to Thebes.

# Leotychidas

Queen Timaea, wife of Agis, gathered with a group of *Elders*, Spartan women, Equals, ephors and King Pausanias of the Agiad Dynasty in the corner of the king's bed chamber. The house was equally moderate to Lysander's home with the only difference being that the front doors were crafted and raised by Herakles himself. Those in the audience of the king though, were not there to console him for his sickly disposition, but to witness the claim of Timaea's thirteen-year-old son, Leotychidas.

"My king, I beg of you, please," the youth said, kneeling next to Agis.

But upon his deathbed, the king lay speechless, struggling for each feverish, blood gargled breath.

"I am the son of your wife and queen, Timaea."

Agis's heavy eyes rolled toward Timaea. "You wicked whore!" he thought, as she deliberately looked the other way and then down at the stone floor.

The others stared directly at him without any remorse. They knew all that he had done for Sparta, but Sparta does not serve one man or woman, rather all its citizens, helots, perioeci and allies live to serve her. So they hovered around their dying king, finding it necessary to conduct the stately affair, here and now, while they still could.

Agis's ill health did not diminish his mental capacity in the slightest. He glanced at all those attending and then back again to the timbered frame of his thatched roof. "Almost there," he thought, chuckling inside. "Almost there."

Leotychidas was now in despair, glancing to his mother for aid and then back again to his king, who still gave no reply. He decided to move in closer, hoping to warm the old man's failing heart. "You have never claimed to be my father, but before it is too late, please, tell me whose son I am."

For the first time in his life, Agis had the chance to do something for himself, so he chose to remain silent, comforted by imminent death.

# Agesilaos

Agesilaos, son of Archidamus, dug muddy soil alongside his fellow Equals. They were repairing an embankment at their Spartan garrison in Thebes, which the rains had washed away. Normally, this type of labor would be done by those subjected to Spartan authority because it was considered unbefitting an Equal, but when it came to military affairs, the Spartans wanted to make sure things were done right. So with his cart full of heavy, packed mud, he and another Equal hauled it toward the stone foundation of the garrison, while the downpour refused to end. Their crimson, soaked cloaks dragged across the sludge, while their feet battled for every step—slipping and sliding.

"Is this rain going to ever stop?" the Equal alongside Agesilaos asked, as they heaved.

Agesilaos looked at him, like he was a moron. "How the fuck should I know?" he thought.

Going ignored wasn't uncommon among Spartans. There was a valid point to it. So the Equal, being younger than Agesilaos, didn't let it get to him and he realized his own ignorance after the fact. The wooden wheels continued to slosh through the wet, and by about halfway to the garrison, it got stuck. A push was needed, first on the left and then on the right to walk it out. So Agesilaos and his peer leaned in and did what was required to free the load. However, the Equal persisted to talk.

"I'm sorry to hear of your brother's health," he said, straining with all his might.

Despite hearing his peer, Agesilaos didn't even bother glancing at him. He could care less for what he had to say, and at the same time, he was just too preoccupied with trying to keep his feet underneath him.

"He is an excellent king and served us well," the Equal continued to say, as the cart came free. "If he doesn't recover, you—"

Agesilaos looked across and gave him a stern glare, cutting his words short.

"What I mean is…you would make an excellent king, Agesilaos. You are one of us. All the Equals think so. You have gone through the *agoge*."

"Fast now," Agesilaos said, seeming to disregard him.

They picked up their pace, and when they reached the garrison's foundation, they rammed the cart while flipping it over on its front end to unload it, and then pulled it away. Agesilaos stopped at that moment and gave another cold stare into the eyes of this Equal, whom he barely knew, while around them were those that had known him nearly all his forty years. They had all overheard what their fellow said and waited for the half-brother of the king to respond. The Equal who prompted the conversation now felt unsure. He thought he was going to be scrutinized just for speaking, which was also quite common among Spartans.

"Ha!" Agesilaos said abruptly. "Look at me," he continued, as he emphasized his short height, standing a crown closer to the ground than the others. "My father was fined by the ephors for marrying too short a woman!"

The Equals, all save the one, began to laugh, while Agesilaos paced around with his congenital limp and exaggerated it to the fullest. "I am defected, man!" Agesilaos said with amusement. "I should have been tossed off Mount Taygetus at birth! By the twin gods, what happened?"

"But everyone knows Leotychidas is not the son of Agis," the Equal said.

"Only the twin gods know that. *And his mother!*"

The Equals laughed again. This time all of them, and when they settled down, Agesilaos turned serious. "I, like you, will be whatever Sparta needs me to be, but she must never have a crippled kingship."

Breathing heavy, Myron interrupted Agesilaos after running for the last two days from the Five Villages to Thebes. "Agesilaos, sir. My name is—"

"Myron, I remember. What news from Lysander?"

Myron extended his hand and delivered the skytale to Agesilaos as ordered. He caught his wind in front of him, until he received an intimidating glare.

"Forgive me, sir. I have been ordered to wait for your response, sir."

"Dismissed."

"Thank you, sir," Myron said, and he took his leave without delay to go search for food and water.

Agesilaos slid the skytale underneath his wool cap and returned to his labor as the rains intensified. While he hauled the cart away to retrieve another load, his peers realized they would not be hearing the message and they too resumed their monotonous digging.

∧

That night, after repairing the embankment, Agesilaos sought shelter by an oaken table in a torch lit area of the garrison. Grimy drops of water fell from the ends of his soaked hair and his muddy fingers smudged the leather, as he wound the skytale around his staff. It had to be done just so, so that its edges bordered seamlessly, covering it from end to end. This would only be possible because the staff was the same size as Lysander's. They shared an identical pair, just as the council shares their own identical pair with one of the kings, when he is abroad or on campaign. If two different sized staffs were used, then the message could not be read because the letters would not line up in a coherent manner. Finally, Agesilaos turned the covered staff on its side and read it aloud. "Are, you, ready, to, be, king?"

# Death of a King

Thousands gathered as the prayers commenced at the ancient funeral site, which was designated to fallen kings and mothers who passed in childbirth. Agis's doctors had done everything they could. The only remedy some pleaded for, was the sacred baths of Herakles in the pass at Thermopylae, but Timaea persuaded them not to take him there because of Agis's weakened condition. She claimed to fear that he would not make it so far away and that it was best to leave it in the hands of his god. The ephors sacrificed and the queen's motion was passed. The next night, Agis closed his eyes for the last time and he got his wish.

The late Eurypontid king lay still, adorned in a new crimson cloak and olive wreath, signifying the highest honors. The Agiad king and queen, as well as Queen Timea stood before him. They were flanked on both sides by the ephors and Elders. The Spartan citizens were positioned behind them and to their rear were the perioeci and helots. These latter two could have cared less about the death of their king as they fantasized about the impossible dream of their freedom.

Meanwhile, at the fore by Agis, the high priest offered a bull, the largest they could find for the sacrifice, and he gouged its sinewy neck with a blade. The beast gushed blood, like a fountain. It just stood there for a moment and spilled its life before buckling to the ground. The impact was thunderous, silencing the already mute throng. The priest then proceeded in the religious ritual by gutting the bull and removing its liver. The damn thing was so big, he had to cradle it, just to carry it over to the limestone slab they used for inspections. Even two of his fellows stepped forward, ready to aid him and then fell back in line after the priest gave a subtle shake of his head. As he set it down, the organ almost slithered off the rock, but the priest stopped it in a smooth almost undetectable fashion and then he inspected it in great detail. How was the color? Solidity? Shape? Smell? It only took a moment and then he nodded to all those attending. The liver was healthy, a truly favorable sign of Agis's passing to the Elysian Fields. The priest's fellows then stepped forward and they placed the organ on three vertical spits, which were grouped together. The loose blood and viscus solidified and blackened with a slight wrinkle almost instantly and then slowly cooked, no longer drooping down toward the flames. The smoke went up to Olympus, while Agis's polemarchs lowered him down in his grave and proceeded to top him off with soil. So while the polemarchs labored in that respect, the priest cut the bull up and offered the four legs to Zeus, Athena, Apollo and Artemis. The eyes went to the twin gods, may they both see at the same time. The testicles and penis went to Aphrodite, may she continue to give Sparta healthy sons. And finally, the main cavity was set horizontal over a large, low fire for the Spartan citizens to enjoy, as they would be celebrating their king's life. The polemarchs finished leveling off the earth and set the stone with Agis's name engraved on it. Then, everyone followed the priest by placing their left thumb on their brow.

"King Agis served Sparta well. He was a hero and the greatest king!" the priest announced rather abruptly, and then he poured a libation of wine on the ground.

Suddenly, Queen Timea began sobbing louder than all the rest, as if everyone else was holding back. "He was the greatest king!" she yelled, sounding ridiculous.

Then all those who attended began doing the same as they shouted deliberate and absurd praises for Agis. It carried on for some time, almost like a competition. However, when the helots and perioeci shouted theirs, it was forced, lacking all sincerity, but no one faulted them for it so long as they did what was required of them. Among the Equals, Agesilaos and Lysander stood next to one another, participating in the funeral rites until they concluded and the people dispersed to participate in the lavish festival.

Throughout the Five Villages, musicians played and citizens danced. One Equal in full war kit sang a song dedicated to their late king, bringing many to tears. Elsewhere, crowds were formed around the Youths, who were participating in wrestling and boxing competitions. Here, Lysander stood by Agesilaos as they cheered on Sparta's promising future.

"Did you know that the Persians bury their kings on the side of a mountain?" Lysander commented to garner Agesilaos's attention. "I tell you, all the places in this world I have seen, and we are the only ones who truly know how to honor a fallen king."

∧

Quick, short breaths and long, outrageous moans echoed outside the house of Agis for some distance, while everyone attended the festivities. Through the stone walls concealing his bed chamber, where he took his final night of sleep, the widowed queen coupled with an Equal, who was almost half her age. Her thirty-eight-year-old body was well sculpted, proving to be a fine specimen of her state's upbringing, as she was mounted on top of her lover, feeling free at last. Timaea had almost reached her zenith, tickling inside, when Leotychidas stormed in through the front door. He could hear her from forty paces away prior to entering the house and knew what she was up to. It made him fume. His mother's liberal ways had always displeased him. Timaea however, could have cared less, but she silenced herself anyway and placed a hand over her lover's mouth so that she could experience paradise before being interrupted by her son.

"Mother!" he cried from the main quarter of the house.

She concentrated hard on ignoring him as she slowed her motions, hitting her spot just so. She was almost there, when suddenly, she felt something missing. Timaea abruptly stopped and eyed her partner. "You lose your vigor, over a boy?" she asked scornfully, and rolled her eyes at the entire situation before getting out of bed.

"Where are you going?" the Equal inquired in a low voice.

"If you can't stick me like a real man, go! Take the window," she whispered in anger, and made her way to the front. "I swear, I am surrounded by children!"

Leotychidas turned and found his striking mother, unclothed in the doorway with her long, dark, flowing hair nearly touching her sex and partially covering her breasts. He could still remember sucking on them as an infant and wouldn't have passed up on a taste if one was offered, but that was not why he was here.

"By the gods, what?" she insisted.

"Who is my father? And speak the truth!" Leotychidas cried.

Calmly, she stepped toward her son, her body captivating him. This she knew. "If he could not rule the Spartans, then he wanted his son to."

Leotychidas took a moment to digest her words and became nauseous. "The rumors are true. My mother is a whore!" he thought, and then he reminded himself to maintain his composure. It didn't work. He immediately turned red in the face, as if he might burst into a Heraklean rage, while he glanced from his spear point back to his mother, vexed.

"Alcibiades. That is what I called you when you were young, but kill the queen?"

"Queen? Former, mother. Don't forget whore and traitor. Look at you! Are you not mourning your husband's death?" he exclaimed, and then he stormed out.

Timaea shrugged off the insult and returned to her bed chamber to find her lover halfway out the window. "Where are you going? Get back here at once and serve your queen!"

The Equal turned about and did what he was told.

Λ

Night fell across the border of the Five Villages, where the Equals stood guard at their various posts. They remained in complete darkness and silence, as torch fire and chatter were against the Laws of Lycurgus. By the eastern edge, at the River Eurotas, two Equals stood motionless with their eights tall, unfazed and alert, listening to horses approaching from the south. All Equals had been trained to be experts in stealth since their upbringing in the agoge, just a simple glance between the two, like wolves, was all that was needed to communicate. They slid their lids, which were resting on top of their crowns, over their faces and could distinguish between the different breeds of horses by the sounds of their thumping hooves. They knew Persians were approaching.

The Persians rode hard, as they did in their homeland, and relied on their mounts for vision in the night. Unexpectedly, their horses stopped without warning, frightened by iron tipped ash, which was threatening them. The Spartans seemed to appear from out of thin air, causing the mares to screech and buck wildly a kiss away from their bronze lids as their hind hooves slid to a stop. The riders too, were surprised, and despite being skilled cavalrymen, the lead emissary was thrown to the ground. The other two were fortunate. They were tossed around a bit on their saddles and brought their mounts back under control. The Persians had been warned prior to their departure by their master, not to ride too fast, or unseen men would appear from nowhere and take their lives. They did not take him seriously. After recovering from their embarrassing catastrophe, the lead emissary regained his ground and kept his distance, as he was wary of the two men of Laconia.

He cleared his throat and then he unclasped a small torch from his saddle. The fire illuminated from within a woven box of branches as he held it out in front of his face. "We are here to deliver a message to Lysander, on behalf of King Cyrus," the emissary said in perfect Greek.

The Spartans gave the Persians a contemptuous glare that they did not have the benefit of seeing. Then, without a word, one Equal left while the other remained. The emissary and his men kept an eye on the unwavering border guard without any reassurance that the Spartans would be of assistance to them. Soon after, the

Equal returned, appearing out of nowhere and said nothing as he returned to his post. The emissary was now even more bewildered. He eyed the Spartans for a moment longer, hoping to receive some sort of indication from them, but instead he received nothing, feeling completely in the dark.

The crescent moon had finally reached its zenith, when Lysander came strolling up in the pitch black. His silver hair was radiant in the moonlight. As he peered into the eyes of the emissary, he saw the nervous twitching of his pupils. This amused Lysander anytime he was outside at night speaking with foreigners because they were all accustomed to light. Hesitantly, the Persian extended his arm and offered Lysander a papyrus scroll, while hoping the Spartans nearby wouldn't leap forward and lop his arm off. Lysander accepted it and turned about in a comical sort of way, so as to be shoulder to shoulder with the emissary in order to borrow his light. The Persian felt even more uncomfortable at this moment, as Lysander read the lengthy message a kiss away from his face. "Why do they forever insist on using so many words?" he thought. "Two or three would suffice. Would it not?" He quickly got over it and then he finally finished reading the message before handing it back. Lysander's piercing eyes met the messenger's and an intentional moment of silence passed. This was mainly to amuse him due to the Persian's uneasiness, and then, he broke silence. "Tell Cyrus, that I will do all that I can from home, but I am no longer king of the Asiatic coast."

The emissary felt a great rush of relief, just to hear him speak. It didn't matter what he said. The silence and darkness was just too heart wrenching. "Cyrus has also instructed me to give you this," he said, as he reached inside his robes and offered Lysander a small silk purse.

Lysander accepted it, while behind, the two Equals gave each other a curious stare.

The emissary bowed his head and returned to his horse. He rode off into the night, thanking Ahuramazda for his life.

Lysander instantly realized new opportunity, while he watched their departure and pulled two coins from his purse. As he made for his leave, he tossed them to the guards. The Equals snatched the lustrous metal from flight, having never held gold before.

# The Messes

Agesilaos approached his house for the first time, since his yearlong absence in Thebes. His recall to Sparta was a timely coincidence to his half-brother's funeral, otherwise he would not have been permitted to attend. Sitting out front, enjoying the pleasures of the sun, some olives, red melon, goat cheese, honey water and the enjoyment of daily chatter, was his wife Kleora, his mother Eupolia and his sister Cynisca. "Mother," he said, announcing his arrival.

Despite their twenty year age differences, the three women were all *Helens*, a Laconic term for beautiful women. They spotted the one true man in all their lives and stood to greet him. "Agesilaos!" they replied as one.

Eupolia hugged him first and then he gave his attention to Kleora. She was attractive in an innocent, youthful sort of way with her dark hair, round eyes, wide hips and small bosom. However, Agesilaos didn't express any affection toward his wife, as that would be too embarrassing for a man of Sparta. In fact, it was more like a greeting of partners in trade. Kleora did take her husband's hand though and place it on her stomach. "We will have a son," she said.

Agesilaos became ecstatic, as he recalled their secret engagement in Corinth, when they snuck away from their duties to see each other. "Did you sacrifice?"

"To Artemis Orthia," Kleora replied.

Pleased, Agesilaos smiled. "We shall name him Archidamus," he said, as he caught his mother's eye.

She was honored that the name of her late husband would carry on. He then turned to his sister, who charged toward him and threw her arms and legs around him in a carefree, lively manner. At nearly the same age as Agesilaos, she was just like all the Equals, keeping physically sound.

Agesilaos held her up and spun around. "Cynisca!"

"Brother!" she said, as her feet touched back down.

"I see my sister maintains her youth."

Cynisca smiled. "We were just talking about you."

"I can only imagine. What scheme do you ladies have in mind today?"

Cynisca looked to the women and then back to Agesilaos. "Your kingship, of course."

"I live to serve Sparta, as we all do. I will not pursue anything more," he said firmly.

"My sentiments exactly," Lysander said, drawing near.

Agesilaos's family turned their attention to him. Lysander made brief eye contact with Cynisca as he stood next to Agesilaos. Her unspoken disdain for him led her back in the house. Agesilaos noticed, but ignored her blatant disregard, not caring either way what it was about.

"We must get to the mess," Lysander said to his friend.

Agesilaos eyed the women. "Ladies, please excuse me."

Kleora and Eupolia blew him a kiss as they departed, while behind them, Cynisca rejoined the women with a giggle to resume their gossip.

Agesilaos and Lysander headed down a dirt path, which cut through waist-high grass on one of Sparta's fertile plains.

"How many is that?" Lysander asked, breaking their silence. "How many have suggested it? Does this not convince you that the people want you as their king?"

"We are not a democracy, Lysander. It matters little what I think."

Lysander bit his tongue as the two proceeded to the messes.

∧

Dusk neared. The messes were set up in rows and columns, like men in the file, as countless Equals and Youths entered them. Inside Lysander's mess, Agesilaos sat across from him at the end of a long wooden table for their evening meal. The middle seated seven more Equals, including Demaratos and Theras, who were the same age and went through the agoge together. They were inseparable and now in their middle twenties. Both were blessed with rippling, sinuous muscles and they styled their beards in the new fashion. Meaning, short and pointed. At the far end, six Youths undergoing their upbringing dined with them. Demaratos and Theras were in command of them, as this was one of their duties until they reached thirty years of age. All kept quiet as Myron served them their traditional meal of Black Broth. It was a pig, stewed in its own blood and vinegar, and if they were fortunate, some herbs and barley were tossed in.

"Go heavy on the meat for the Youths, Myron. They need it more than we," Lysander said.

"Yes, master," he said, as he served him broth only, so he could dip his bread in it.

Once everyone was served, Myron exited the mess. He waited outside with more of his kind by the door, praying there would be some food leftover at the end of their meal.

Back inside, Lysander waited until Agesilaos picked up his spoon to eat. "I offer you my thanks, Agesilaos, for providing provisions to the mess," he announced, since he was unable to afford them, or at least, that was what he claimed to Agesilaos at the funeral.

Agesilaos was caught off guard as he lifted his head and looked at Lysander. "It's nothing. I take great pleasure in helping friends."

Lysander took his words literally, while everyone else raised their spoons to Agesilaos in gratitude.

Agesilaos looked across and noticed them honoring him. "Eat, I beg of you," he said, and the meager feast began.

The sounds of slurping, slopping and chomping filled the mess, while Lysander dipped his bread in the blood vinegar and took a bite. "Cyrus raises an army," he said, chewing.

"To clear his territory of Pisidians," Agesilaos responded.

Save for Ox, who was the eldest and largest of his age group, the Youths were too famished to pay attention. Demaratos was quick to notice and gave Red, a seventeen-year-old sunburnt Youth next to him, a firm elbow in his ribs. He then gestured for all the Youths to pay close attention. From one venomous glare, they stopped eating to listen to their seniors, despite the fact that their growling bellies were begging them to do otherwise.

"Others say to overthrow the kingship," Lysander said.

"He was not chosen as heir to the throne. His elder brother, Artaxerxes was. What say has he?" Agesilaos replied.

"Cyrus thinks differently. He believes his brother will cripple the Persian Empire by making war with us over past defeats, as well as banish all Asiatic Greeks from the coast."

"Is it true there is a Spartan among the Persians?" Cheese, a sixteen-year-old Youth asked, speaking out of turn.

At that precise moment, Ox backhanded him across the face for his lack of forethought. Lysander and Agesilaos stopped talking to observe the other end of the table, where they found Demaratos and Theras eyeing the Youths hard. In response, the Youths stared at their Black Broth and were reluctant to look anywhere else.

Agesilaos and Lysander then turned back to face each other. The half-brother of the late king stared at him questioningly and received a nod in regards to Cheese's question.

"Clearchus," Lysander followed up.

"These exiles steal our glory abroad, tarnish our name and values. It must end," Agesilaos said in distress.

"What will you do?" Lysander asked.

Agesilaos met Lysander's gaze with the utmost determination, remembering the old days with his friend and then sponsor, who brought him up to be the man he was now. "Mourning the king will soon pass. What Sparta needs me to do. What a boy cannot," he concluded.

Lysander gestured an imperceptible nod to Agesilaos, confirming that he understood his newfound desire for the throne. "Well, no doubt Clearchus is begging for a comb as we speak!" he said, changing the conversation with a joke.

The mess broke into laughter, when Agesilaos abruptly stopped participating in the mirth, which was a ploy to deceive the Youths.

He glared directly at Ox. The young ones actually thought they had evaded punishment for their unacceptable behavior. It was about to be a precious moment for the Equals, one that would bring back fond and horror filled memories of their own time in the agoge. "You there, what is your name?"

The laughter stopped, and warily, the Youth looked over. "Ox, sir."

"And you?" Agesilaos asked.

"Cheese, sir," he said, peering over Ox's shoulder.

"Why did you assault Cheese?"

"He spoke out of line, sir," Ox replied.

"Explain," Agesilaos ordered.

"Discipline and respect, sir."

"Tell us more."

"Discipline. He was only given permission to listen to you speak and eat his meal. Respect. For our elders, sir."

"Cheese, is Ox your elder?"

"Yes, sir. But I—" Cheese's desire to explain, earned him another steely glare from Demaratos and he quickly, yet reluctantly silenced himself.

Agesilaos was well aware of Cheese's faults and ignored them for the moment. "Nicely done, Ox. What are you, eighteen?"

"Yes, sir."

"Almost a full citizen, then. I look forward to it."

"Thank you, sir."

Agesilaos stared at Demaratos and Theras proudly, regarding their rearing of the Youths, and then he gave them a nod before returning to his meal. All the Equals continued to eat to make the young ones feel that that was the extent of their punishment. A moment later, Theras whispered an order to Red, who was dining opposite of Cheese.

"Why didn't you defend yourself against Ox? Are you a coward?" Red yelled.

Cheese was shocked by the surprise verbal attack.

"You'll let anyone hit you without fighting back? What kind of Equal will you become?" Red asked, lashing out at him.

All eyes fell on Cheese and a brief moment passed as they waited for his response. Cheese was at a critical juncture in his upbringing, proving himself worthy and unworthy, repeatedly. What he said now though was most important, and he knew he better choose his words carefully—not too long and well thought out. He surveyed all the eyes on him, then looked down at his stew, and then shifted his gaze back to Red. "A dead one," he replied, and then he eyed Demaratos and Theras for approval, who in turn looked to Agesilaos and Lysander in the same manner.

Lysander nodded to Agesilaos in an approving way since he was the eldest. Agesilaos in turn, faced his fellow Equals. "He can take a joke," he said, followed by a nod.

Demaratos and Theras said nothing to their troop of Youths, as the message was clear. Cheese proved himself worthy, but if only he could do it consistently. The Youths were then permitted a brief celebration with the hope that the lesson was learned for all. Cheese smiled as his fellow Youths congratulated him on his Laconic reply and then he glanced at Demaratos, who gave him a wink for a job well done.

# Courts of Counsel

Xenophon went to Delphi alone. He made the walk from Attica in two days, stopping halfway at his relative's house for an evening meal and some rest before he was on his way again. He wasn't much for conversation during his visit, as he was feeling desperate to get the answer he sought. "Socrates told me to ask if my Persian expedition will be a success," he said to himself, but his secret desire to see the world and erase Athens and democracy from his mind distorted his rationale. "Maybe there is a god, a specific one I should sacrifice to, to ensure a safe campaign? That would be the wiser question to ask, no? Best to just get right to it. Then I can get out of Athens for a while and see things." His thoughts carried on, changing like the tides. "To do something with my life rather than talk my way through it, that's living. Is it not?" He stumbled on a rock and stubbed his toe. "Shit on Styx!" he said, excited and nervous, and as he squared himself, Delphi had fallen in his sights. "Socrates said…to ask which god I should sacrifice to for a successful expedition. All right, here we go then. There's nothing to it."

He entered the Temple of Apollo and offered the priest some coins by placing them in an amphora. He then stepped forward as instructed and kneeled before the sage vessel that Apollo communicated through. He thought the Oracle was beautiful. She wasn't much younger than him and he thought she would make an excellent wife, and give him beautiful sons. This was another desire nagging at him that he had yet to fulfill. "Snap out of it, you fool, before I wring your neck!" Xenophon said to himself. He quickly erased his wishful thoughts as soon as he realized how delirious he was and how intoxicated the Oracle was on narcotics. This was his first time to Delphi to seek counsel and he really wasn't sure what he was doing. He glanced at the vast treasury to his one side that all of Greece paid tribute to and then to the priest who welcomed him inside. He nodded to Xenophon and the student philosopher began the only way he knew how.

"I am Xenophon of Athens…son, of Gryllus," he said for good measure. "I come to ask which god I should make sacrifice, to have a successful expedition in Persia."

The Oracle's dilated eyes went blank as she leaned back and discreetly inhaled some noxious gas seeping out of the stone floor. Right away, her body slipped and slid through a series of sporadic movements, as if Apollo was having his way with her. She seemed to be enjoying it too, while her loose chiton, which was made of fine linen, slipped this way and that way on her frail, yet pleasant body. Xenophon marveled over her apple-shaped breasts and bare sex as they uncovered and covered. This made him ponder his earlier thoughts for a moment. He then began to wonder what her visions were like, but only the gods knew what she really saw in such a state. Another moment passed, while Xenophon watched her wander the plains of oblivion, and then just like that, she returned.

The Oracle, with her black, dilated eyes, pushed herself off the floor where Apollo had left her wanting more. She then peered directly into Xenophon's eyes and penetrated his soul. "Zeus," she said.

His jaw dropped and his eyes went wide with devastation. "What was I thinking?" he asked himself. "Socrates told me to ask if my Persian expedition will be a success. Not to which…By the gods! How did I…Fuck me all the way down Styx!"

∧

"Moron!" Socrates said, chastising Xenophon. "You were supposed to ask if your journey would be successful! Not to what god you should make sacrifice! How could you be so—"

"So? So what?" Xenophon exclaimed, and he slammed his hand on the table. The bread, wine and olives that he brought for his teacher upon his arrival jumped. Then he rose to his feet. "Say it!" Xenophon said, begging for a fight, but his teacher was too wise for that. "I love you, Socrates! As I do my father, but you have lost your marbles, old man! We shall see who the moron is!" Xenophon shouted, and then he stormed toward the door without another word.

Socrates felt terrible. He loved Xenophon too, just as a father does to his son, but forethought told him that this was the best way for his favorite student to learn, so he refrained from calling him back.

As Xenophon threw the door open, he nearly hit another pupil and good friend coming to visit the old master. "Plato," Xenophon grumbled, and he brushed past him.

Plato was clueless to Xenophon's rage and entered, unsure what to expect.

# Λ

In Sparta, King Pausanias of the Agiad Dynasty sat on his throne in court. The skin under his eyes was dark and tired. His long, black hair had begun to age. While Pausanias styled his beard in the old fashion, his upper bare lip had been left untouched for many days. Next to him was an empty throne, as it was formerly used by Agis. He gazed forward with heavy eyes at the council sitting on their ascending stone seats, which filled half the circular court. Standing before them, he glimpsed Lysander and Agesilaos. Pausanias then let out a great yawn, and under his cloak, he began to twiddle his thumbs, as he returned his attention to the imperfections on the four Doric columns supporting the roof. Some whispered tales that he was cursed by one god or another, but the truth was that he was bored with all things Greek. He truly longed for the old days. He remembered them well. The days when all Sparta cared about was Sparta and the Peloponnese. Now they have to concern themselves with the whole of Greece, and Asia. There was also a time when the Agiad king dominated the Eurypontid king, even though it was a dual kingship. Agis however, shattered the Agiad's reputation with his victories in the Athenian War and dynasty roles had been reversed ever since. So now he felt on the outs, a mere figurehead to an age-old tradition going on now for five hundred years. He didn't care who ascended the Eurypontid throne. "What did it matter?" he thought. "What will be done, will be done." He did however, fulfill his duties to the minimum required, and here he sat, observing the most pressing hearing that Sparta faced.

"Ephors, Elders, Agesilaos stands before you today," Lysander said, as he stood next to his lifelong friend and presented their testimony to the council.

The council consisted of five ephors, twenty-eight Elders and the kings. Of the Elders, there was Pythagoras. He was more than eighty years of age. His mind was still intact, as sharp as the point on an eight. No one was certain of his exact birth though. Some say he was born on the eve of the first Persian invasion. Others say the second. All they knew was that he was as ancient as their laws. They afforded him a seat, front and center, not only for his hearing, but as an honor bestowed upon him for his undying devotion to Sparta.

Also facing the council, a few paces away from Agesilaos's side, was the defending party. Actually, it was just Leotychidas. At thirteen years old, he was a youth, but not like other Youths. He was expected to inherit Agis's kingship, and therefore, he was not permitted to enter the agoge. Now with his legitimacy being contested, he found he had very little influence as he stood all alone, defending his right to the throne. Least to say, this created much angst for the lad as Lysander carried on with his oration.

"Not for personal reasons, but for selfish ones. He, like all of us, lives to serve Sparta. Agesilaos is a true descendent of Herakles. He has undergone the rigors of the agoge in his youth, and to this day, he has exceeded all expectations as a true Equal."

Leotychidas objected. "But the rhetra states that the kingship goes to the son, not to the king's brother. He can only become king if there is no male heir," he said with confidence. Leotychidas had rehearsed that argument with Timaea since the night prior, as it was his only defense.

In response, Agesilaos stepped forward a few paces, revealing his limp. His long, dark, brown hair and beard styled in the old fashion was combed and had yet to turn old. His body was anointed with a blend of castor and olive oils. He possessed an unbelievable amount of scars on his body from countless days in service. The glisten from the oil forced everyone to take notice to his marks of sacrifice. The council admired him for it, and in contrast to Leotychidas's smooth unblemished skin, the lad was inadvertently assisting his opposition. Then there was Agesilaos's physique. He was at the age he was and still in his youth. Slim, trim and his muscles bulged from their limbs. And then he spoke, effortlessly, commanding attention. "Then it is I, who should be king."

"Uncle, explain yourself to all who witness, why we should break the Laws of Lycurgus."

Agesilaos looked to the boy and then to the council. "Agis had no son. How could I have a nephew?" he stated, and then he stepped back to his place.

Leotychidas knew that his origins would be put to question, but he was stunned nonetheless. He became red in the face, yet for a lad, he contained his anger quite well as the governing body let off a slew of murmurs and whispers.

Then Lysander stepped forward, and when he did, it was like two claps of thunder from Zeus. He carried such weight with the council, not only as a champion of the Great War, but as a former ephor who was still under sixty years of age. It was a unique honor bestowed on him. "Perhaps, the council should consult the Oracle on this matter," he said plainly.

The ephors and Elders looked to one another in agreement. Then Pythagoras cleared the mucus from his throat. "Adjourned, until further notice," he said, and stomped his staff on the stone ground of the court.

Lysander escorted Agesilaos out, passing Leotychidas's scornful glare which had no effect, save for making the boy feel worse and desperate. He then looked to King Pausanias who hadn't said a word or showed any signs of interest during the entire hearing. What he was too young to know was that years ago, after the Great War, Pausanias defeated the Athenians in a battle and rather than staying in Attica to enforce their strict laws upon them, he returned home. Charges of grave misconduct were brought against him for his ill decision and it was he who stood before the council with his life on the line. In the end, he was narrowly acquitted. So while Pausanias met the boy's gaze, he saw himself at the mercy of the council and did not offer Leotychidas the sympathy he was seeking, just an empty, dull stare.

# A Brother's Quarrel

The sun reached its zenith in Cunaxa, beating down hard on both brothers and their armies. Parysatis had convinced Artaxerxes to release Cyrus from chains and reappoint him as satrap of his former territories. It was during this time that Cyrus conspired behind the king's back and raised his army. This was a remarkable feat in itself because anyone who caught wind of something beneficial to the Great King would be sure to tell him in hopes of a reward, as well as to be in his good graces. Of Cyrus's supporters, there were many who called themselves loyal to his brother at the time of his ascension. In fact, all the lands in the Persian Empire including the Greeks on the Asiatic coast preferred Cyrus the Younger. They say he was the fairest ruler during his father's reign, when he was the satrap for all of Lydia, Phrygia and Cappadocia. In those people's minds, he was their king, a trusted leader and severe punisher of those who broke their oaths, or worse, the Great King's laws. He reminded them of his legendary forefather Cyrus the Great. Live and breathe under any god you deem necessary, so long as you pay your annual tribute. Support me and I will support you, so long as you pay your annual tribute. Muster your arms and support me on the field of battle and I will do the same for you, even when you are too poor to pay your tribute. Word of Cyrus's loyalty and justness had spread long before, and all were secretly disappointed when Artaxerxes succeeded the throne.

Artaxerxes had retreated and evaded him for fourteen days, which kept the spirit of Cyrus's army high. Cyrus could feel his victory and kingship. His mother prayed for it, as the two brothers finally mustered on the field of battle along the Euphrates River. The plain was hard, dusty and dry with vast patches of wild grasses here and there that never grew above the ankle. Prior to this day, Artaxerxes ordered his men to dig a ditch, allowing only a narrow pass by the Euphrates. The ditch was three men deep, five men in breadth and extended inland all the way to the Median Wall. So as soon as his brother's men funneled through the narrow pass, they would be boxed in with nowhere to retreat.

Cyrus's mercenary army consisted of approximately the following:

10,400 Greek hoplites
2,500 Greek peltasts
100,000 Persian soldiers
20 scythed chariots
600 Persian cavalrymen honored as Cyrus's personal guard

Across the field, the Great King's army consisted of approximately the following:

1,200,000 Persian soldiers
200 scythed chariots
6,000 Persian cavalrymen honored as the king's personal guard

The Persians have always feared fighting Greeks, despite outnumbering them a hundred to one, and for good reason, they have never beaten them. Meanwhile, back across the field, Cyrus rode at a trot from wing to wing before his Greek contingent, he and his mount, wearing their armor in front of the men of bronze and iron, dazzling in the bright sun. "We Greeks and Persians have intimate history. We began as enemies, and through great peril and bloodshed we are now the best of friends," Cyrus announced.

Xenophon was among the middle ranks of the Greeks and rolled his eyes at Cyrus's words. He and the men could care less for what he had to say. They were all miserable in the insufferable heat, and besides, they were only there for one reason: Gold.

Cyrus continued. "When Sparta needed coin to win the Athenian War, we gladly gave them the resources they needed."

Xenophon broke silence. "This fucking heat readies me to kill, not this *skata* he speaks," he said to his new Athenian friend Ariston.

Ariston was three years his senior, but he looked no older with his short, wavy, brown hair hanging over his brow. He and the other Athenian hoplites within earshot offered a grin in agreement to Xenophon. They too were offended by Cyrus's words.

"Because of my father, Sparta controls the entire Greek world and the coastal cities of Asia. Now it is I, Cyrus the Younger, son of the Great King Darius, who must win a war against his own brother to save his people! And to save our friendship with the Greeks! And it is you, men from all over Greece who represent your country in miniature, united, for one common cause." Cyrus allowed the Greek army a few breaths to digest his words. "Are you with me?"

The army banged spear against shield in a cacophonous melody and shouted their enthusiasm in response. Xenophon participated in the clamor, but he wasn't at all ready to believe in Persian propaganda. A moment later, Cyrus's translators repeated his oration down the line of his Persian contingents. They let out a delayed cheer, and when it dissipated, a horn bellowed, several of them in succession from the center to each wing, and the army began to march in battle formation. Xenophon was now getting what he asked for, a bit of tourism to broaden his mind. He felt calm, yet giddy for his first engagement. He was positioned with all the other Greeks on the right wing and led by a Spartan exile, a monstrous and savage mercenary named Clearchus.

"See you on the other side," Ariston said to Xenophon.

"I think the chances are favorable," he replied sarcastically.

Ariston bulged his eyes with concern, this being his first engagement too.

Across the pitch, Artaxerxes's million advanced without so much as a word of praise from their king. Swirls of dust polluted the scorched air and eventually blinded the armies.

"I can't see a thing. How many are there?" Ariston asked, followed by a cough.

"Don't know," Xenophon said naively. But as he watched their general intently, he came to the philosophical conclusion that fear must be striking the Persians. "But I don't think they'll fight us."

"How do you know?"

"Because of him," Xenophon replied, while motioning toward the fore at the Spartan exile.

Ariston and Xenophon watched Clearchus lead their contingent through clouds of grit whipping every which way, undeterred. Clearly, he was the roughest, toughest, most fearless, war hungry hoplite in the army, save for a few other Spartan exiles in their regiment. Beneath his battered lid, which was polished to a gleam, they could see his dark, gray-brown, wavy hair and his silver streaked locks, four on each side, two to the front, two to the back, draping over his shoulders. His beard was short and pointed with white streaks, honoring his thirty year career as a mercenary who longed for home, yet was banished for life. He still wore his crimson and maintained a lambda on his twenty, never forgetting where he came from.

The thundering gap narrowed to a *stade*. At that moment, the Greeks began singing the *paean*. At a hundred paces, the Persians began to lose heart at the sight emerging from the dense haze. The Greeks were garishly colorful with their bronze armor that was accompanied with reds, blues, yellows and whites tailing them. Some hoplites were so poor they wore no cloak at all. The uninterrupted Greek march that the rest of Cyrus's army followed suit to, sent a rift through the enemy's cohesion. Simply put, many of them regretted their loyalty to the Great King.

Cyrus began front and center along the front line and he was now behind his army, waiting with his six hundred cavalrymen for the engagement to begin. He was filled with excitement and noticed the enemy falling out of order. "Can you see it Artapatas? They fear the Greeks."

Artapatas was his most trusted and loyal servant, as well as one of Cyrus's six hundred. "You are already king, Cyrus," he replied.

Cyrus smiled triumphantly, as his right wing of Greeks found themselves lined up with the enemy's center due to the vast front of Artaxerxes's million. Cyrus was able to decipher this through the debris by glimpsing two opposing sets of panoply and recalled a discussion he had with Clearchus just days ago. "Take out the center and you'll find my brother. Kill him, and you kill them all." It wasn't an easy thing for Cyrus to say because of the implications of Persian loyalty. Clearchus told him that he would do what he could, meaning not a chance in Hades's realm could he guarantee that. He knew full well how many he would be up against and only his Greek Fates could execute that strategy. Cyrus was now quite pleased with Clearchus for satisfying his wishes, unaware that they were unintentional. He thought him to be an honorable man of his word, as the two fronts met in the crush.

Artaxerxes also waited in the rear of his army with his entourage. He was beside himself as the Greek mercenaries butchered his front twelve lines in the blink of an eye.

"I absolutely hate the Greeks," Artaxerxes said, as he glanced to his side. "No offense, Ctesias."

Ctesias was Artaxerxes's Greek friend and doctor, who tended to the entire royal family. "No offense taken, Great King."

As Clearchus and the Greeks pushed forward, a gap opened up in the center of the Persians' line due to a frantic retreat on each of their wings. Cyrus's army now outflanked his brother's and they became overwhelmed on all fronts. It was at this critical moment, that the dust cleared from the center of the pitch and Cyrus's god, Ahuramazda, showed him his path. He spotted his brother's location from a distance of two furlongs away, through the split cloud of debris, which was illuminated by the sun.

"What is he waiting for? Where did his men go?" Cyrus asked, unable to see.

"He may have sent a contingent to come up behind the Greeks, my king," Artapatas said.

"They would certainly like that!" Cyrus joked and he shared a laugh with his good friend and servant. "But not today. Attack!"

Cyrus and his six hundred advanced on horseback at breakneck speed. They charged through the fray, passing the Greeks, and into the broken lines of the Persian troops, but in the mess of things, his personal guard lost their unity.

"Cyrus!" Artapatas shouted. He was trying to stop him because he was the only one left riding with him. He looked over his shoulder again and confirmed that the six hundred were held up in a skirmish of their own. "Cyrus!" he yelled again to no avail. The tumultuous clamor was just too loud, nothing could be heard.

Cyrus weaved through the enemy. His horse was fearless, as was he. Artaxerxes's six thousand personal guards were so preoccupied with the Greeks at their center and Cyrus's Persians flanking his wings, that he only had a hundred or so defending him, and by some miracle, Cyrus made it through, unscathed. He raised his sword high in the air, screaming his war cry, and struck his brother across the shoulder. The blow penetrated his armor and knocked him off his horse. Half of his one hundred shielded him with their bodies as Ctesias immediately dragged him to safety behind the masses.

Cyrus wheeled his mount around to finish him off. He felt unstoppable. "This is how a king is made!" he told himself, and as he did, a Persian javelin struck him just below his eye. It extended halfway out the back of his crown. He would never be king now, only a claimant. He would no longer be regarded as Cyrus the Younger, but Cyrus the Pretender.

Artapatas watched his master fall to the dirt. "Cyrus!" he yelled, worried, leaping off his horse. He slammed to the ground in a tumble, blooding himself up on loose stones and dove on top of his master, while the other half of the one hundred cleaved and punctured them both with blades of every kind. Cyrus, died twice.

The Greeks continued their charge, mutilating every single soul in their path, unaware of the fate of Cyrus. Clearchus displayed his Spartan prowess with efficient and tireless killing maneuvers. The mercenaries trampled and crushed the fallen, wounded and alive, while fatigue hit Xenophon and Ariston hard. They only received limited training upon their arrival and their muscles were taxed by the repetitive thrusting of their spears, and bearing of their shields and lids.

"I thought you said they weren't going to fight?" Ariston asked. He was completely winded as he wielded his spear.

"You call this a fight? They're throwing themselves into our spears! I'm going to drop of exhaustion!" Xenophon replied, when up ahead of them, the remaining Persians sounded their retreat and dispersed in all haste.

Clearchus signaled his men to stop by raising his ash, while the other four generals down the broken and crooked line of the Greeks did the same.

Xenophon's legs shook. He fought to stand. "Thank the gods for Spartans," he said to himself, as he figured they were the reason he was still alive.

Suddenly, Clearchus turned about, raised his twenty and eight, crossed them overhead, and all the Greeks shouted in victory. "Nike!"

Ariston looked to Xenophon and they both pulled their lids off, allowing them to rest on top of their crowns, while they shouted with the men. Their faces and hair were caked in a red mud from the sweat and filthy labor at hand.

"We did it, we beat the Persian king!" Ariston exclaimed.

The hoplites around them grew rowdier and thirsty for wine, while Xenophon stared forward at Clearchus, who looked as if he was searching for someone. "Look," Xenophon said.

Ariston observed Clearchus at the front. He was approached by their neighboring general, Menon from Thessaly.

"Where is Cyrus?" Clearchus asked him.

"I will keep looking," Menon said.

Clearchus then took notice to the confused expressions, which began to riddle his men's faces. He didn't like it. Everyone was expecting Cyrus to triumphantly prance down the line in celebration of his kingship, but it hadn't happened. Order was needed. "Line up! Get in battle formation!" he yelled to the men, as he singled some of them out. "You there, square yourself! Get in order! You two, on the line! Now!"

The commands were passed to the rear and the army snapped in line. Down the mercenary front, the other four generals did the same, and slowly and suddenly, the dust cleared and it became eerily quiet. All the men found were themselves, standing under the sun and blue sky in a vast, desolate world with hundreds of thousands of dead Persians strewn across the land.

Ten thousand four hundred Greek hoplites and twenty-five hundred Greek *peltasts* were nearly thirty-three days' march inside the Persian Empire, alone. There was only one fatality on their side, save for Cyrus and Artapatas, and it was a Persian on the far left wing, who got hit by a missile. The rest of Cyrus's one hundred thousand troops and six hundred cavalrymen had vanished, disappearing without a trace in the endless hills and sands. Those closest to the wings, including Xenophon, were now only realizing their dire predicament.

"Shit on Styx!" Xenophon exclaimed.

"What do you speak of now, philosopher?" Ariston replied.

"Our leader is dead and ten thousand Greeks are stranded in barbarian lands, you idiot! Look around you! We are fucked, proper!" Xenophon rubbed his temples and stared at dead eyes buried in the sand, which were staring back at him. His current plight frustrated him more than his conversations with his former teacher. "Better luck on tour with the Spartans," he thought, and then he glanced up, spotting Clearchus shaking his head. At that moment, he could have sworn he read the Spartan's lips. It looked as if he said, "Persian loyalty," in disgust. No doubt, a Laconic comment, confirming he was correct about their situation.

"How do you know? How do you know Cyrus is dead?" Ariston asked in a panic, while the others turned to listen.

"Who else would he celebrate his victory with, his brother?"

∧

Every Greek including the other four generals looked to Clearchus for leadership. He ordered the dead to be cleared away and the men to return to camp, which was back by the ditch near the field of battle. This took until night. They left the enemy corpses stacked up like a mountain on the far side of the plain. Let them rot, they figured. Fires were placed around the border of their camp, as were guards, who were posted in groups of three. The rest of the Greeks either ate what they could scrounge up, tended to their wounds which were mainly minor scrapes on their feet and arms, or they made repairs to their armor, anything to keep occupied. Nerves were rattled. Wine was drunk until there wasn't any. The men were thinking the worst since no one recovered Cyrus's body, nor his prized mare. The only good sign was the Euphrates, which offered them an abundant source of fresh water. Libations were poured all around as an offering to those they worshiped. The Greeks thanked the gods for sparing them, while at the same time, they prayed for a sign to show them the way.

On the northeastern edge of camp, a posting of guards heard horses galloping louder and louder in the darkness.

"Riders approaching," one guard said to the others.

All went quiet. They looked around, unable to make out who it was. They gripped their javelins, ready to throw or thrust at the most insignificant sound, when suddenly, a boxed torch appeared around three Persian riders.

"Barbarians! Stand fast!" the Greek ordered.

The Persians stopped a good measure away, while one of them dismounted and the other two kept their bows drawn from their seated vantage. The one on foot now walked with the light straight toward the Greeks and stopped at the halfway point between them.

The Greek turned to his men. "If I drop, kill them all," he said fearfully and approached the stranger with caution.

They stared at one another, comparing their similarities and differences, until the Persian raised his arm, which in turn, made the Greek squeeze the shaft of his spear.

"This message is for the Spartan," the Persian said in Greek, as he offered him a papyrus scroll.

The Greek felt a tremendous sense of relief. He accepted the message and the Persian turned his back to him, crossed over to his ride, and all three wheeled their mounts around and vanished, returning to wherever they came from. The Greek stood there, making sure he was safe, staring into the black abyss, and then he returned to his men, slowly coming to terms with how vulnerable and exposed they were.

# ∧

Clearchus despised the indoors, preferring to be outside at all times, but Cyrus insisted as part of his employ. This was more for Cyrus's reputation than for the Spartan's well-being. So here, in his hempen tent, built upon a wooden foundation with three steps leading up to the entrance, he met with the other generals of the Greek army. They were Menon, Proxenos, Agias of Arcadia and Socrates the Achaean.

"At least, we were victorious," Socrates said.

"How by Nike's blessed cunt can you call this a victory?" Agias complained. "We are cursed!"

"Don't speak ill of the god!" Socrates countered.

Menon interjected over their bickering. "I say we disband the army and go our own ways."

"We will be that many times weaker," Proxenos said. "Besides Menon, you'll walk out of here with fewer riches, if you have fewer men to plunder with. Isn't that why you're here?"

Clearchus rolled his eyes in a huff. "We remain one army."

The generals looked at him questioningly.

"General Clearchus, sir," a voice interrupted from outside.

Clearchus excused himself and made his way to the front, where the guard delivered the message to him.

"From the Persians. Messengers in the night, sir."

"Dismissed," Clearchus said, and he returned inside to read the letter. After a lengthy study, he looked to the generals with a smile. "Tissaphernes requests a truce. He invites us to stay as his guest."

∧

The next morning, Xenophon, Ariston and the rest of the army watched the five generals depart camp and ride off with their Persian escorts. A feeling of doom and gloom clouded over them at once. They didn't trust this Tissaphernes fellow at all. Cyrus's tale of his betrayal had already spread through the ranks some time ago and they all agreed that he should have defended Cyrus when he was arrested.

"To trust him is ludicrous," Xenophon muttered. "What was I thinking, coming here?" He dashed in front of the men toward his childhood friend. "Proxenos! Don't go!"

Proxenos looked back, spotting the philosopher running toward him. "Don't worry Xenophon! I'll be back in no time! Remember, we're the mighty Ten Thousand!"

Worried, Xenophon stopped his pursuit. He was winded, dusted and sunburnt all over as the gap increased. His body still ached from yesterday's labor and he couldn't push himself any farther. He bent over, hands on knees, and caught his breath, when Proxenos glanced back again, giving him a sliver of hope.

"Aren't you glad you came? You would have missed one hell of a party!" Proxenos yelled to him.

Xenophon was forced to squint from the sun breaking over the horizon. His spirit was crushed by his friend's lightheartedness and he returned to mope with the men.

# Λ

The sun was at its zenith by the time the five generals entered the Persian camp. It was more like a city on the move, where any whim for any occasion could be satisfied. The generals dismounted and their rides were led to water as they crossed over to Tissaphernes's tent. While they were impressed thus far with the respect shown to them, the generals, save for the Spartan, scanned cautiously in all directions before entering. Clearchus gave a low chuckle. He was amused by their fear as they stepped inside.

Tissaphernes's tent was luxuriously decorated. Suffering was obviously not in his lexis as the generals found the most dignified and powerful Persian satrap of the times, lounging on a silk covered bed with servants ready to attend to his every need. When Tissaphernes saw them, he stood up with excitement and spread his arms in a very soulful and joyous manner. "Friends! Please, come in. Allow me to introduce myself. I am Tissaphernes, satrap of Lydia and servant to the Great King," he said in Greek.

"Doesn't look like the home of a slave," Clearchus mumbled.

Tissaphernes overheard and gave a laugh. "You. You are the Spartan, Clearchus?"

Clearchus nodded.

"Laconic humor! Very good. Please, sit," Tissaphernes said.

The men hesitated.

"*Sit* and let us introduce one another. Then we will share a meal and I will tell you the king's terms."

The generals were impressed with his Greek and his manners, and sat together on a wool covered floor, together, side by side opposite their host. Slaves brought in a roasted ostrich on a golden platter behind them. It was dazzled with oil and herbs, and stuffed with a pig, which was stuffed with a pheasant, which was stuffed with a hen, which was stuffed with a mullet, and there was more oil and herbs throughout. The foreign meal and unusual aroma intrigued the generals. They glanced back at it and then resumed their focus on their host, desperate to hear the king's terms.

"Where is Cyrus? Does he live?" Menon inquired inquisitively.

Tissaphernes glanced at the tent wall ten paces behind them. They were made of extravagant linens and silk, which prevented sand and debris from penetrating, while allowing the breeze to enter. From within this swaying facade, five Persian Immortals, the most skilled fighters in the empire, appeared with their swords drawn, and silently, they crept past the slaves carving the feast. Tissaphernes returned his gaze to Menon. "Cyrus? Cyrus turned mad and lost his head. No one has seen him since," he replied, and then he turned his attention to the Spartan. "Clearchus, you are an exiled Spartan who still loves war. I could use a man of your caliber, but the king, he has different plans," he said, cheekily laughing.

They became skeptical at once, and in the midst of their brief confusion, the Immortals, renowned for their methods of assassination, struck the Greeks hard and fast without a whisper. Not even Clearchus had time to react before they were all beheaded. All, save Menon.

Menon trembled at the gruesome finish his generals met, while his head remained clutched in the arms of an Immortal, who had a blade pressed firmly to his throat.

Tissaphernes continued with the king's terms. "Menon, your father is a good friend of the Great King. That is why you live. That is the only reason."

# A Crippled Kingship

The council reconvened in court a great deal of time later, which was after the celebration of the Karneia, when the moon had finally waned. One of Sparta's eldest seers stood front and center, facing the governing body, while Agesilaos, Lysander and Leotychidas gazed at the back of his thinning, white crown.

"Upon asking the Oracle if Agesilaos should ascend the throne of Sparta…She stated…Boasting Sparta, be careful not to sprout a crippled kingship. You are surefooted and unexpected troubles will overtake you. The storms of war will be the destroyer of mankind," the seer said, losing his breath.

The Elders and ephors gravely looked to one another and quietly discussed the prophecy, which would decide the fate of Sparta. Agesilaos didn't express any concern, but he truly felt that he had suffered a defeat. Across from him, Leotychidas was smirking in premature victory, thinking the kingship will surely stay with him. Pausanias was present at the hearing to say the least, while Lysander didn't like what he was seeing. After a few idle moments, he could no longer tolerate the blathering of old men.

"My king, councilmen, please," he said.

Pausanias's eyes perked up, looking to Lysander, as did the governing body. His ability to garner their attention with such ease made Leotychidas cringe.

"You trusted me with the navy to win the Great War. Now trust me when I tell you that the Oracle does not refer to Agesilaos's deformity from birth as a crippled kingship. She refers to the son of Alcibiades, the traitorous Athenian as our king."

The ephors and Elders remained silent and respectful to Lysander by refraining from further hearsay.

"It was Agis himself who fled from his wife's bed and never returned after Poseidon shook his house. The gods and the truest form of all, namely time, deem it so. Ten moons later," Lysander said, pointing at Leotychidas. "He was born. The bastard son of Alcibiades we Spartans were graceful enough to rear. And now he contests the throne? A half-blood? An Athenian?"

Silence deafened the assembly. Leotychidas was devastated and at a loss for a rebuttal. Agesilaos was now feeling quite optimistic. He also mused, if it was during any other affair, such a long speech would have seen Lysander fined by the ephors, as all citizens of Sparta were required to be short with their words, and if they couldn't be, they shouldn't speak at all. Nonetheless, it was a necessary risk. They were putting their names and lives on the line for the throne. If they lost, they joked prior to the proceedings, they could end up at best like Clearchus in Persia, begging for a comb. Pythagoras inevitably stomped his staff and court was adjourned without another word.

∧

Leotychidas took a long, sullen walk home with his head down, entered his house, and pouted in misery on the bench by an oaken table.

"There's a true Spartan for you," Timaea said sarcastically, while stepping from the bed chamber, where her lover had just been.

Leotychidas glanced up. She was naked all the time it seemed to him and he let his crown hang to the floor once more.

"While you feel sorry for yourself Leotychidas, I've taken action to defend your throne."

Tears shed across his rosy cheeks. "Do you not realize the severity of this crisis?" he asked, peering back at her. "We stand to lose everything, even our citizenship!"

Motherly, Timaea stepped over to him, sat behind her son, and consoled him by wrapping her arms around him. Leotychidas could smell the almond oil she had anointed herself with and he could feel his mother's sensuous curves, as well as something moist in her loins, which pressed against his rear. It aroused the young lad, whose body was changing quite rapidly in the most humiliating of ways.

Over his shoulder, Timaea noticed his cloak pitched upward and clutched his sex. "Not bad, my son," she said seductively, and then she ran her hand up his torso, placing her palm under his chin, and gently forced him to turn about and face her.

The young boy's emotions were being pulled in every direction. He became confused about his entire life, his origins, morality and all, as he peered into his mother's hazel eyes.

"Everything has been arranged," she said confidently, while her hand ventured back south and moved his cloak aside.

He looked down at the ash his mother grasped. "What do you speak of...mother?" he questioned, falling under her spell.

"You have many supporters among the Equals. Even your foe, Lysander is by your side."

At that, he gazed straight back into her eyes as she continued to caress him.

"Regardless what the council decides, you will be king."

"But the council…sacrifices…as we speak…to make the right decision."

She kissed her son on the lips, silencing him. "Let them sacrifice a young girl if it suits them. If Agesilaos is crowned, he will not last long because we will kill him. If you are crowned, then you will banish him from Sparta for attempting to corrupt a centuries old tradition." She leaned in for another kiss and this time fed him her tongue.

He wasn't sure what to do with it, but he was enjoying it. She then lowered down and placed her mouth on the tip of his ash to ensure his vigor was all that it could be, and then looked him square in the eye. "Now," Timaea said, as she held his sex upright and rose on top of him. "Stick me like a real man."

Leotychidas lost his breath as Timaea sat upon him. He never felt so afraid and so in love in all his life as he returned to her womb. His back dug into the edge of the table, which he was using to support himself, while she rose up and down on him, thinking about his father.

"Oh! Alcibiades!"

∧

Within the Five Villages, the Spartan gymnasium was the most elaborate. It consisted of several grounds. There was the *athlitika*, an area with various machines, which were built from rope, wood and stone, and used to strengthen every part of the body. Nearby, were the *sands*, where sixty beds of sand, all of various sizes, were used for their wrestling, boxing and *pankration* training. Bordering the sands and athlitika, was the *pitch*, which was a wide stretch of cut grass and used for dashing and javelin throwing. At the far end, was the entrance to the *trek*, a trail used for long distance running. It encompassed all Five Villages and southern Laconia, offering every type of terrain the Peloponnese had to offer.

Spartans of all ages trained daily, utilizing the entire gymnasium. They were oiled down and nude. Many worked on leg strength. Others did back, arm, chest and neck movements. On the pitch, a group of Youths were dashing, while trying to outrun a javelin throw. Older Equals throughout, watched their younger betters with enjoyment on the sands, complimenting and criticizing their martial abilities. Some would even step in, to tutor them on the proper way to perform a particular technique. Lysander and Agesilaos had just finished pushing themselves off the ground one thousand times, performing ten rounds of one hundred with their twenties on their backs. Tomorrow, they would pull themselves up that many times. As they made their way from the athlitika to the sands, they marveled at the Youths' diligence. Red and Cheese were among them, squaring off to fight.

Red punched Cheese directly in the jaw and dropped him, like an old sack. The blow was monstrous. Blood leaked from his mouth. He didn't move. His peers thought he was out and they cheered Red on, while he bragged as he stood next to him.

Meanwhile, Demaratos and Theras were on the neighboring sand bed. Theras came in fast and hard with two punches, left and right.

"Hold!" Demaratos said, smiling and slapping the blows away. "Take a look."

Theras dropped his guard and turned to look over at Red and Cheese.

Red continued his celebration, unaware that Cheese had opened his eyes. He gave a grin and grabbed Red just above the ankle, while driving his shoulder into the back of his leg. Red fell to his one knee and tried to turn about, landing in a twisted fashion on his back. The Equals and Youths became engrossed. Everyone at the sands, hundreds of them, began crowding around the match, cheering on their favorite or just hoping for a good fight.

Cheese managed to get on top of Red and he punched him in the face with alternating blows, pulverizing him. Red kept a level head though, and he finally grabbed Cheese's left arm as he struck. Then Red began to muscle him, and with a bit of leverage, he was able to throw Cheese. He tumbled hard to his side and ate sand, while Red straddled his back to ensure that he couldn't get up. Red took his left arm again and bent it at the middle joint so that Cheese's fist was in the center of his back. He then moved Cheese's arm up toward the shoulder. It didn't take much, just a bit, giving it some torque, and he held it there. Cheese drove his body deeper into the sands to release the agonizing tension, but no matter what he did, his shoulder felt like it was on the verge of breaking. The Equals and Youths yelled for Cheese to yield, but he refused to do so. Red continued holding his arm just within the maximum range of motion one has, and surveyed the crowd. There, he found Demaratos and Theras behind him and eyed them for a command.

They both gave Red a short nod.

Red finished the crippling technique, ripping the ligaments in Cheese's shoulder.

*POP!*

*POP!*

*POP!*

Cheese bellowed out in pain and the match was over. The Equals and Youths cheered for Red and insulted Cheese for his ignorance.

Demaratos eyed Theras. "You're it," they both said, but Theras got the words out quicker on this occasion and Demaratos was up.

"It never ends," he said under his breath, and confronted Cheese.

The mass of Equals and Youths became quiet as Demaratos loomed over Cheese, who was still down favoring his injury. As the Youth opened his eyes, he became aware that the entire gymnasium was watching.

"On your feet," Demaratos commanded.

Cheese fought to rise and did.

"What point did you prove by not yielding?"

"That I won't give up, sir. To show my courage," he said, wincing.

"You call that courage? I call it an act of insubordination!" Demaratos shouted.

Cheese didn't understand the difference.

"Since when do you not listen to your elders command? Did they all not tell you to yield?"

"I could not hear, sir."

"How will you hear commands in the crush? How will you be useful in war, if you show no discipline or awareness in times of chaos? Your selfishness has made you useless! How are you to hold a twenty? You will be flogged!"

Cheese looked up at Demaratos with sincerity and regret.

"Say nothing," Demaratos said, and he put his arm around Cheese's good shoulder to present him to the mob of Youths, who were backed by the Equals. "Equals never give up. That is true. But we fight and die for one another, not for personal glory. Is that understood?"

The men and boys shouted their war cry.

"Back to your training, everyone," Demaratos said.

Everyone dispersed and resumed their gymnastics, while Demaratos remained with Cheese. "You have it in you to be the finest Equal. Is that what you want?"

"Yes, sir," Cheese said weakly.

"Then I will sponsor you, until you are of age."

Cheese smiled, while still grimacing in pain. "Yes, sir. It would be my honor."

"It will be my honor as well. Go see my helot, Theodoros. He is an expert at pain relief."

"Thank you, sir," Cheese said, and as he looked over, he realized the entire gymnasium was eavesdropping on them. Then he turned and walked away, feeling a mix of embarrassment and joy, while favoring his busted shoulder.

"That's a fine choice, Demaratos," Agesilaos announced, as he approached with Lysander.

"Thank you, sir. He reminds me of myself, when I was his age," Demaratos said, and then he glanced behind them. "Sir, behind you. Look!"

Agesilaos turned around and watched Pythagoras carry a garland as he led the ephors, Elders and King Pausanias toward him in a ceremonial procession. He looked over to Lysander and then at Demaratos and Theras. They had all dropped to one knee and bowed their heads. Agesilaos was in awe and faced forward.

He was completely taken unaware, as he was confronted by the council. He then held back a smile forming on his lips and dropped to his own knee. Pythagoras stepped forward while Agesilaos lowered his head and he crowned him with the olive wreath. The king rose and found everyone bowing in respect.

"All hail, King Agesilaos!" Pythagoras announced, as the king's eyes came to a water.

Hundreds of Equals had flocked into the sands behind the procession and they all shouted their war cry three times in succession.

After the crowning of the Eurypontid king, Agesilaos led the procession through the Five Villages with Lysander by his side. The council, the Equals and Youths from the gymnasium, and more followed along. Citizens, perioeci, and helots bowed in respect as the king approached and then they shouted their praise when he had passed. Many of them however, had never heard of Agesilaos before and didn't know who he was, since he spent most of his days away on campaign or at foreign garrisons. Others thought it strange to have a cripple as a king. His limp cast doubt with them. Agesilaos could sense this and he was determined to make the most of his new labor. He told himself that he had proved himself virtuous during the agoge and he would do the same as king. He looked forward, waving at the people. "Is there anything you need, Lysander?" he asked, as they ventured south to Amyclae.

"All I need is my twenty, my king," Lysander said deliberately.

Agesilaos realized this and restated. "Is there anything I can do for you as a friend, to show my gratitude for your assistance with the council?"

"That would be unconstitutional, my king."

"The laws don't state helping a friend to be a crime."

"In that case, send me to Persia, to place Cyrus on the throne."

"I will speak with the council."

"Thank you, my king."

"It's nothing. I take great pleasure in helping friends."

∧

Xenophon was heading home. He just returned from hunting and had dead rabbits dangling by the ears in his grasp. Some distance ahead, his worried father Gryllus stood on the balcony at his country estate in Athens. "Run Xenophon, before it's too late!"

Being so far away, Xenophon couldn't make out what his father said, so he smiled while he raised the hares up to boast the fresh kills. In that instant, a lightning bolt struck the thatched roof on the house, setting it ablaze. Xenophon was thrown back as he blocked his eyes from the flash and awe. The flames quickly grew, engulfing the entire estate and his father as he ran toward him, but he was too late. His father could not be saved.

∧

Ariston was sitting by Xenophon's side as he woke up in a sweaty panic. "What god torments you, Xenophon?"

"Father Zeus!" he exclaimed, and then he rose to his feet, determined. "Where are the generals?"

"There has been no word."

"It has been twenty days! What are we still doing here?" he questioned in a state of despair, and marched off.

Xenophon stormed the Rhodians' quarter, pointing a finger. "You there, tell your captain to meet me at the general's tent."

Next, he fell upon the Thebans. They were miserably sitting around with nothing to do, just like everyone else. "Your highest ranking to the general's tent," Xenophon ordered, and he carried on without stopping.

"Who does that fool think he is?" one of the Thebans asked his men.

Xenophon pushed through camp and passed some Thessalians on the right. "Your commander is to be at the general's quarters, now!"

Ahead, was another contingent from way up north in Arethusa. "Your highest ranking to the general's quarters."

On and on he went, getting the word out, making his way through the Ten Thousand, and finally, to Clearchus's tent.

At the entranceway, Xenophon met with all the Greek captains. "The only reason they have come is because they have nothing better to do," he thought. "I'd better make this good."

"What's this all about then?" the Theban asked.

"Please, come inside. I must tell you of my dream."

The captains congregated inside the tent. One of them was Chirisophos, a forty-year-old exiled Spartan. He was just like any other man from Laconia, callous and war driven. Once Xenophon saw him, he was thankful to the gods that he had been banished from his homeland and decided to live his life out here, rather than in Sicily. Xenophon was beginning to take a strong liking toward the Spartans. He didn't quite understand it yet, but they made him feel more confident when they were around. Without further deliberation, the philosopher told them of his dream and of his sacrifice to Zeus before he left to go on tour.

"If Zeus sent you this dream, then we must respond in his favor," the Theban said.

Chatter grew in the tent and the feeling was unanimous. Sacrifice to Zeus? Yes. But which direction does one go when they are lost and surrounded in enemy territory?

"Enough!" the Rhodian said, and the assembly fell silent. "Xenophon, you are a student of the wisest man in the world. You tell us…What should we do?"

All eyes fell on him.

"Be quick about it, Athenian," Chirisophos said.

Xenophon eyed him and then the other captains as he gathered his wits. For a brief moment, he envisioned he was back in Socrates's house, frustrated about the return of democracy that morning he first ran into Proxenos. "We must assume our generals are dead," he began. "However, we have a powerful army that has defeated Artaxerxes in battle. Whatever we do, let us not be afraid of our enemies, nor let us be reckless. For we need all of our men to escape this place. Our scouts say that Tissaphernes's army blocks our passage west to the coast and the king's army prevents us from travelling north. No doubt they have both sent for reinforcements during our wait. We should continue east, as far as necessary, until we can circle back around to Greece."

Chirisophos gave Xenophon a nod, while the men talked their ears off. Xenophon felt he just received Spartan approval, but he couldn't be sure from such a straight face. What he was sure of, was that they both tired of the men discussing matters so ineffectively. In fact, Xenophon felt the need to impress the Spartan, some secret desire that was burning away at him. "If anyone has a better idea," he shouted. "Now is the time! Otherwise, all those in favor, raise your hand!"

A silent moment passed and everyone raised their hand. Xenophon was exasperated by the sequence of events, but pleasantly surprised by the outcome of a vote. "Right then," he muttered, looking at all the eyes on him, which now assumed his leadership and caused his belly to drop to his loins. "Democracy it is."

# Book II
## Burden of Command

Nine moons she labored for her love. Then she cut their tie and washed the blood away. It would be up to the gods now, she thought, as she bathed her newborn infant son in straight wine to test his strength. The boy did not wince. He embraced the drink of men and opened his mouth wide. Proud, she smiled and wrapped him in a cloth to gently pat him dry. It was at that moment, that she discovered a congenital mark on his back. It was pinkish in hue and it distinctly resembled the alpha, the logos of their rival city, Athens. She concealed her grief when she handed her son away for inspection, praying he would be permitted to live.

This duty was performed by the old seer, who was still nimble, as he ascended the peak of Mount Taygetus. He stood atop its southern point. It was as close as he could get to the sun, to see the infant in his truest form. The boy remained calm so high and so far away from his mother's bosom. The seer regarded that feat, said a prayer, and began his examination.

He inspected the boy in all sorts of ways. He held the boy in one hand and pushed on him from toe to crown, studying his reactions. He waved a single finger across the boy's eyes and watched him follow it. He whispered sweet words in the boy's ears and then yelled at him as if he was mad. The boy showed no fear, only joy and promise. He pulled a sprig of rosemary and mint from his person and brushed it along the boy's nose. He did not flinch. The seer took all the infant's responses into consideration.

He had been called to this duty for the last sixteen years since his retirement. He loved to loathe this burden placed on him. So far, he was quite pleased and then he began to scan the surface of the boy. He gazed at every contour the boy possessed. The bottoms of his feet, his scrotum and breasts were all sound. He then turned the boy about, peering at his anus and finally up his spine, and that was when he saw the birthmark, glowing red like fire in the sun. The seer's first thought was Athens, when a dark cloud covered the peak and blocked the sun. It was a grave sign that dismissed the infant's chance to *live. The seer was deeply saddened by his duty, and the inevitable, because Sparta needed sons.*

*At the base of the mountain, hidden in tall brush, the mother watched in secret. She was forbidden to be there. Her newborn was no longer hers the moment it came out of her womb. The infant was the property of Sparta, as were all her citizens. As she looked up, she could make out the seer as a figure only, and then suddenly, a small black entity was cast out. It plunged to the earth, causing her breath to stop. She scratched her body all over, dashing through the brush toward the edge of the ravine, where unfit infants were discarded. She saw her love among the rotting mass of undeveloped bones, which were centuries old. He no longer breathed life. Her insides seized her as she gazed upon those seeds of death. She wanted to take the boy back, place him back in her womb, and start again, but mothers were forbidden to retrieve their child or even bury their loves, since they were not deemed fit for the state. She looked skyward as the sun revealed itself once more, cursing inside, wishing the seer and Sparta dead, and then she made her way back to her village. She passed by many citizens, who were already informed of the outcome. They greeted her as if it never happened, like any other day, and she responded in kind.*

# On Leadership

Agesilaos grew tired of his kingly duties and craved war. Since he took the throne, he had become miserable from the most mundane tasks. He was a hoplite who turned king and did not have the patience yet to deal with such petty ordeals. He had already told himself that he would do his best, so he pushed through. As time passed, he began to see the advantages and disadvantages as a leader, and learned quickly. However, the agonizing duties of his kingship did seem to be endless. The most recent one was his inheritance from Agis. He was left with his house and a large share of farmland just outside the Five Villages. Since his mother was well situated, he gave these to Kleora's parents because they had little means. Secretly, he knew this would please his wife, but if that was the sole reason of his decision, favoritism of that sort would be deemed illegal and charges would be brought against him. The last of Agis's property were his horses, many of them, all trophies from his campaigns abroad. He didn't know what to do with them. Agesilaos, like any other Equal, preferred to use his feet and saw no use for them. So he gave them to Cynisca in an effort to prevent any jealousy from arising between her and his in-laws.

His sister was baffled when she received them. She could have cared less for riches or new property, and she knew her brother knew this. As a little girl, she used to ride as a passenger on chariots from Amyclae to the northern villages. Other than that, she might as well have been an Equal, and she certainly knew nothing for the care of horses.

"What am I to do with them?" she asked him.

Agesilaos glanced from the horses in the pen on his in-law's new land back to his sister and shrugged his shoulders before walking away. He thought she could figure that out for herself. As for him, he was just glad to be done with such a trifling affair.

So of course, when that issue was dealt with, another arose. An informant approached Agesilaos and Pythagoras about a conspiracy led by a man named Cinadon. Cinadon lost his citizenship some time ago. He was no longer an Equal, yet he was still expected to serve the state as if he still was one. The humiliation of his demotion angered him greatly and he vowed to overthrow the constitution by way of declassifying all citizens, so that those who could not afford their tribute to the state would still keep their citizenship. Meaning, he wanted to make Equals, equal.

Agesilaos and Pythagoras knew this could have ill effect on the state and they responded appropriately. Cinadon was arrested, beaten, flogged and impaled. During his torture, the truth came out, as not many could withstand Spartan punishment. He claimed that he was not the leader of the conspiracy, but a follower of Timaea and Leotychidas. Whether it was true or not, it was good enough for the state. Upon Cinadon's admission, Agesilaos acted so swiftly that while Cinadon's lifeless body was being dragged by a horse through the Five Villages to ward off future conspiracies, he placed thirty knights around Timaea's house so that none could escape justice.

Timaea was on her reed stuffed bed at this time. She had sticks pushed inside of her from both ends. It was the position known as the *hound*, where her lover was to her fore and her son flanked her rear. Agesilaos had crept inside quietly with two knights and caught them off guard. The king was appalled. He thought she looked like a lamb on a spit. Timaea's mouth remained occupied as she looked over and found Agesilaos standing in the doorway. Not only did she break the Laws of Lycurgus for being a conspirator, but also for her conduct with Leotychidas. Sparta needed sons, not monsters.

"How patriotic of you," Agesilaos said sarcastically.

All three knew they were finished and they willingly marched out of the house, half aroused, only to face Pythagoras and a mob of citizens angered by the former queen's conduct.

"You are hereby banished from Sparta," Pythagoras announced. "Go now or feel the point of an ash!" he yelled, utterly repulsed.

The knights cleared to one side to allow the citizens through. They cursed and denounced the three, and pelted them with squash, apples, melons and rocks, as they made a hasty naked retreat by foot out of the Five Villages.

This earned Agesilaos great favor with those who were secretly in doubt of his leadership. Today, he was also supposed to meet with the council regarding issues with their Peloponnesian neighbors. It was routine to burn their crops every now and then to remind them who was in charge. When he arrived, there was endless discussion about whose crops they should devastate. It drove him mad. So he left early to hit the athlitika. He was dying to break a sweat, even bleed a little in a boxing match if there was time, anything to separate himself from the old men of the council.

# ∧

The Ten Thousand began marching east when dawn broke. In their wake, was a great fire. They burned everything in excess, from wagons to tents, to anything that wasn't an instrument of war, or needed for food and water. By nearly midday, when they lost sight of the battlefield at Cunaxa and the Median Wall, each and every one of them trekked past Cyrus's head on a stake. His one eye stared at them, apologizing for the predicament he left them in, as flies, maggots and ravenous birds fed off his royal crown. The effect was great. The army thought about it long and hard. If the king would do this to his own brother, what would he do to them? It broke the men, and soon after, they got their answer. Just prior to crossing a narrow watercourse, they passed Proxenos, Socrates, Agias and Clearchus. Their heads were also mounted on stakes. The Spartan gazed straight forward, fearless. The rest looked like they had been spun around, as they rested crooked with their eyes wide, almost alive. These barbarous trophies signified Persian loyalty and sent despondency hurling through the ranks. They crossed the river and that was when the army was stopped and an assembly was called.

The Ten Thousand had chosen five new generals the day before. Xenophon was among them. He replaced his friend Proxenos, and once again, he felt compelled to address the men. Between his growing affinity for all things Spartan and the teachings of Socrates, Xenophon thought of every solution to every foreseeable problem the men would encounter during their brief morning march. It was no easy task and it caused tremendous pain across his brow. He, just like his men, wanted to get home. He knew it was possible, but to try and convince them would be a formidable challenge. Most pressing, beyond their safety or their next meal was the men's morale. They had many fears. So he reminded them that it was *they* who beat the Great King's army in battle, and that the Great King and Tissaphernes fear *them* because it was *they* who did not hold to the truce, when *they* took the lives of their generals. This went over well with the men. As for being severely outnumbered, his speech continued as follows:

"Persia has always outnumbered Greece. The number of men they have is staggering. But I say, when has any Persian army every beaten the Greeks?" Xenophon asked them, and then he began counting with his fingers. "At Marathon? No. Thermopylae? No. Plataea? No. *Cunaxa*? No. When? Never!"

The men were impressed with his brilliant mind, which caused their fears to subside. Mild laughter and jokes began to erupt here and there about the so-called mighty Persian Empire, so Xenophon decided to pour honey on top.

"And remember…Those Persians who fought against the Great King with us have all fled, probably to the other side to fight alongside our enemy. Those natives are cowards and you are brave. Artaxerxes now has a million cowards coming after us. They could be here at any moment!" he said, and then he looked at one of the troopers standing before him. "You there, how many cowards can you kill?"

The man hesitated, thinking hard, while the army waited eagerly for his response. "The whole lot!" he said suddenly.

The army screamed and shouted praises to each other. They were beginning to feel unstoppable.

Xenophon was relieved and he deliberated further out of necessity, while realizing they desperately needed to get moving again. "If you want to get back home and see your loved ones, show the gods what brave men are. Death is inevitable, so make your life count! It is victors who do the killing, and it is the defeated that die!"

The army cheered for Xenophon, including Chirisophos.

Finally, he addressed the precautions the army should take to ensure the safety of the men. Everyone listened, as Xenophon proposed a hollow square marching formation. It seemed logical. This would allow them to place all their precious valuables, the supplies, baggage animals, slaves and followers, inside for protection against potential enemy harassment. When he put forth the motion, a man unexpectedly sneezed. The army perceived it as the sign they sought earlier to show them the way. They dropped to their knees, bowing in reverence to Zeus, Xenophon's savior and now theirs. When they rose to their feet, the motion was put to a vote. All hands were raised in unanimous favor of Xenophon's proposal. Then the army formed up in the hollow square and they began marching toward the unknown, when Mithridates, a Persian, and thirty of his riders approached.

∧

Myron returned from the southern coast of the Peloponnese at Taenarum and delivered a message to his master. He had met with a Persian emissary, who was still loyal to Cyrus in secret. Lysander set the stone down, which he was using to sharpen his sword, and learned that Cyrus was dead despite his victory, ten thousand Greeks were stranded in Persia, and the Council of Ten that he instated to rule in each of the Asiatic Greek cities during the end of the Great War were being killed by order of the Great King. This meant Persians were now enslaving Greeks. This angered Lysander because his life achievements during the Great War were being erased from history. Now all he would have left were the trophies he dedicated to himself at Delphi. He sensed this was going to happen and he desperately desired to relive his glory days by correcting things in Asia, and in so doing, making his achievements everlasting. He had become increasingly restless in Sparta, and like Agesilaos, he needed to get back on campaign. As he continued reading, he also learned that there was a Persian naval fleet, expanding by the day at the southernmost point of the Asiatic coast in Phoenicia. He had no doubt that they were preparing to invade Greece. So he wrote a concise reply, appealing for them to continue writing to him, but to also request aid from King Agesilaos. He handed it to Myron and sent him back down to Taenarum.

Lysander resumed sharpening his sword as he obsessed over his return to Asia Minor, when someone knocked on his door. "Enter," he said thoughtlessly.

Cynisca entered as iron scraped wet stone. Lysander wasn't expecting to see her, but he acted as if it was no great surprise. She stood several paces away, brooding. They were former lovers. Cynisca still cared deeply for him, but during the Great War when he was appointed Sparta's Naval Admiral, he left for many years, and when he returned, he brought gold with him and showed his citizens what the rest of the world desired. This was against the law, as was anything else foreign in Sparta. She despised him for it because many of her close friends became corrupted by outside influences, longing for things of no consequence. Lysander however, was incorruptible to riches of any kind. He returned as he had left. He exploited the idea of riches though, out of his secret desire to become king, which he knew would never happen unless the constitution was changed. This would be difficult, he thought, but not impossible. So instead of being punished by way of fines, torture, death or exile, he was honored. Lysander was offered a position with the ephors. It was a one year term, but no one under sixty had ever been so fortunate. His newly appointed position on the council was under the condition that he would remove all riches and corruption that he plagued the citizens with. He agreed and things returned to normal in Sparta, at least from the council's perspective.

Lysander observed Cynisca's consternation, as her anger slowly dissolved. It had been four years since they had spoken. "Can I be of service, my lady?" he inquired.

"Forget the past," she said.

"Done," he replied.

His willingness made her hesitate for a moment. "I worry for my brother. So tell me, do you love him as you once did?"

"I have always loved you both."

Cynisca felt relieved and surprised as she crossed over and stood before him. In response, Lysander set his blade and stone on the table and stood to meet her. They were a kiss apart.

"Then protect him from his enemies."

Lysander gazed into her eyes with heartfelt concern. "Done, my lady."

She met his gaze and then embraced him, as she glanced at his sword and then the scar beneath the white hairs, which ran across his muscled chest and told of the last time they spoke.

# ∧

Ox, Red and the rest of their troop were there as Demaratos brought the whip down across Cheese's back. His shoulder was thrice its normal size. The injury had been dressed by Theodoros, first with castor oil to aid in reducing the enlarged joint. Next, he placed a wad of myrrh and leaves from the willow to bind to the oil. These were for calming the pain and to prevent possible infection. He then protected the entire injury with a cast made from bark of the same genus. To keep the dressing in place, he wound some linen tightly around the joint and his body. Three times a day, he fed Cheese a swallow of the willow's nectar to assist with his discomfort and boost his strength. This treatment helped greatly with his shoulder, but had little effect with the lash that was tearing across his flesh.

The Youths watched in silence next to Theras, while Demaratos brought the ox tail whip down for the twentieth time. They had all been in Cheese's place before. No one in any of their histories had made it beyond thirty lashes. Cheese stood strong with his good hand pressed against the flogging post. To avoid crying out, he thought about how many before him placed their hand on the ancient timber that was stained with the blood of his ancestors. It kept him strong, while his back was being flayed. He winced this time and his legs were beginning to fail him. That made twenty-five. His peers prayed that he would survive because not everyone did. They loved him, despite his learning disabilities.

Demaratos pulled the whip back for twenty-six. He could tell Cheese might be able to handle one more after this. It was up to him to administer the punishment and see it through, and it was up to Cheese to yield before his sponsor gave him his final lash. All he would have to do to yield was drop his hand from the post. Those were the rules. The boy had to learn his place and what was expected of him. The problem was, that so many of their prodigies never knew when to quit or when to yield, or the difference between the two. Quitting, is cowardly and gets those next to you on the line in battle killed. Yielding, tells you when to back off and hold the line in order to keep your men alive. It was the Youths most difficult lesson. Demaratos remembered how he struggled with this very concept during his time in the agoge as he brought the whip back down.

Rib began to protrude. Cheese's hand slid down the post and his knees began to buckle. He should yield now, Demaratos thought, but he did not. Cheese knew if he fell without yielding, he may never rise again, and if he yielded to soon, he would be called a girl, or worse, a trembler.

The Youths, with Theras's permission, called out to Cheese. "Yield!" they pleaded.

Cheese glanced at them with a painful smile. They could see his eyes were elsewhere though, as he faced back forward. He figured yielding wasn't an option or his shoulder injury at the sands would prove vain, but if he kept going, he will have taught everyone else a lesson. The problem was, that he was still not grasping the concept being taught to him.

Twenty-seven.

His knees hit the bloodied mud, but his hand remained defiantly on the post.

"Give up," Demaratos said under his breath.

Cheese refused.

Twenty-eight.

"Yield, Cheese," Theras murmured.

Twenty-nine struck near the exposed rib, which grew and shrank with every breath. Cheese's hand stayed, while his head crashed into his injured shoulder. The bruising pain in his joint brought him back around though, and gave him the strength to endure.

At thirty, Demaratos was determined for this to end. Thirty-one, thirty-two and thirty-three came in fast and hard like lightning. Cheese fell. He was out. There was no acting this time, like at the sands. His peers figured him dead, while Theras stepped behind the troop and put an arm around Red and Ox to comfort them. They were all saddened by his stubbornness. Demaratos wanted to rush over and get the boy some treatment, but it was forbidden. Cheese would have to stand on his own, if he was going to stand at all.

"To sleep," Demaratos ordered.

The boys obeyed without hesitation. They knew they would talk of it later at the barracks, when it was safe.

# On Education

Ox and Red were in their barrack with the other Youths. The troop would sleep next to one another in three columns directly on the ground with only their cloaks for warmth. Insects of every kind would visit them in the night, sampling their flesh or crossing their bodies as if they were great mountains. The Youths were accustomed to it. Come winter, they would be permitted to sleep on a linen sack filled with reeds from the River Eurotas. They would look forward to this small luxury afforded to them as a way of distracting them from their constant hunger. The Equals intentionally kept their meals short of filling them, so they would be forced to steal, even though theft was against the law. This was another critical lesson in their upbringing.

One Youth during the reigns of the early kings was so hungry he stole a fox, but in order to hide his crime, so as to avoid being caught and punished, he kept her hidden under his cloak. The vixen desperately wanted to be freed and she eventually sank her teeth into the boy's belly to escape. His innards were being torn out in a gruesome manner, but he maintained his grip on her and stood without the slightest grimace. He would have rather died than expose his crime to his betters. And so he did. The boy was gutted and bled dry. When he fell, his sponsor was nearby and he decided to investigate the matter. As he approached, he saw the fox escape from underneath his crimson, leaving the cloak draped by the Youth's side. The sponsor saw his wound and understood exactly what had happened. He was proud of his prodigy for making the right decision. Hence, it was better to die than be caught.

Red and Ox were mystified by the legends and lore the Equals passed down to them, this one in particular. They kept that tale in the back of their minds every night, when they would sneak out after Demaratos or Theras performed their evening inspection. They would go and steal a spot of bread or cheese, whatever they could get their hands on, but they were far from hungry this night. As they lay, they thought about him tirelessly. Every time they tried to think of something else, it would somehow relate back to the vision of their peer face down in the mud. Sneaking out was no different. Cheese was the stealthiest thief among them. It was how he got his name. He had never been caught and always saved some for Red and Ox. In fact, Cheese was the only one out of the three who made it through the gauntlet unscathed, when they were required to steal the cheese from the Shrine of Artemis Orthia.

"Do you think he's dead?" Red asked in a low, somber voice.

Ox was extremely upset. "Of course he is!" he whispered. "He should have yielded like we told him to. He never listened."

Red thought long and hard about dying as he tried to make out the dark timbers running across the underside of the thatched roof. Death terrified him and then he looked back at Ox. "But he broke the record? Thirty-three lashes! He should be honored, shouldn't he?"

"I don't want to talk about it. Go to sleep," Ox said.

They both rolled on to their backs from their sides and stared into the darkness.

"Maybe he's not dead," Red went on to say, angering Ox.

"You saw him. He's gone."

The oaken double doors of the barrack unexpectedly creaked open at that moment. Red and Ox shifted their gaze to catch a glimpse. It was Demaratos. He walked through the rows of boys in the dark, inspecting them with the scant moonlight that shined through the windows. He felt terrible about Cheese as he took a count to ensure each Youth was in the barrack as expected. Each face was a constant reminder though. When he got to Red and Ox, he stood over them for a moment. The boys had shut their eyes before he approached and then they opened them just slightly. Demaratos met their gaze, like animals in the night. He lowered down to a knee between them and placed his hands on their thighs. He gripped them hard, making the boys feel like they should cry.

"Have you seen him? Did he stand, sir?" Red asked softly.

Demaratos shook his head in despair. "He remains down. His breath has given out. Cheese, will not stand," he whispered. "But we shall honor him for his courage and for the lesson he taught us."

"Lesson, sir?" Red asked.

"To love," he said. "Do you understand?"

The boys did not.

"What Cheese did, took all the bravery one has because he loved us all. He did not give up at the sands and he lost the use of his arm. If he was of age, this would have made him useless in war until he could heal. So I punished him for making an ill decision. Then again, he would not yield to my whip. Now he is gone forever and he will never be useful in war. He did not decide this for himself. His god chose for him. I am sure of it, as your god guides you. His purpose in life was to teach us to remember the difference between quitting and yielding."

The boys looked to one another and then back to Demaratos. They were completely engrossed, as their commander continued taking his time to speak with them personally.

"Love commands these two in war. If he did not love you, he would have quit and perhaps, many Equals would have fallen. But he did love you and that is why he would not yield either, to make sure you remember to live for the Equal by your side. That does not mean throw your life away needlessly. Yield when you are commanded to and never quit loving one another."

Water filled their young eyes. Bumps ran down their limbs. They wanted to sniffle, but instead they let the mucus drip from their noses, so as to not seem girlish. Their upbringing this night felt nearly complete as they understood his words, entirely.

Demaratos could sense this. "Shed no tears. We shall honor him together for the rest of our lives and remember what he gave to us."

Red and Ox nodded their heads.

"Sleep then," Demaratos commanded, when the doors barged open. Alarmed, he glanced over as did Red and Ox.

In staggered a crooked, bloodied soul. He looked half dead. Or perhaps he did die and his god sent him back. He stood swaying at the entrance, ready to topple over as all the Youths began to wake up and shout his name.

"Cheese!"

Demaratos sprang off his feet and caught him as he fell, just like he wanted to do earlier this day. He thanked the gods for bringing him back as he carried him in his arms toward his place of rest.

Cheese lifted his head and slurred. "Equals never quit, sir. I will never yield."

Demaratos almost responded, but he decided not to as he met Cheese's disorientated gaze.

"Never quit, never yield," Cheese chanted, and then he let his head hang back over his sponsor's arm.

Demaratos lowered him down and gently rolled him on to his front in between Red and Ox. "I know where your heart lies, Cheese. Rest now and get well. That's an order," he whispered in his ear, and then he rose back up to a knee. "Ox, retrieve Theodoros. If he sleeps, beat him awake."

"Yes, sir!" Ox said, and he dashed out of the barrack.

Red looked to his peer in the dark. "I knew you were alive, Cheese. I knew it."

"Never quit, never yield," he repeated.

Some of the boys couldn't help, but tear up. It was a beautiful phrase that soothed their hearts, making them feel like men after all the hardship they had been trained to overcome.

Red looked to Demaratos. He was amazed. "He has one powerful god, sir."

"That he does."

They both looked back to Cheese, who shut his eyes. He was out, again.

When Theodoros arrived, the entire troop surrounded Cheese with enough torch fire so that he could mend him properly. He used water and linen to clean the dried blood and dirt away. For all of his wounds, he dressed them as he did Cheese's shoulder, save for where the bone came through. For his rib, Theodoros showed some ingenuity. He pulled the skin above the rib down and the skin below up, so as to cover the opening, and then he asked Demaratos to hold it in place. He did. Next, Theodoros pulled a thin piece of iron from his person. It had a miniature ring fastened to its end. The instrument was no thicker than a few bundled hairs and no longer than one's finger. Then, he tore a piece of linen into a thin, long strip. He threaded the strip through the ring on the end of the instrument, and tied Cheese's flesh together by weaving the tool under and above the skin, all the way across, until it sealed. The Youths as well as Demaratos marveled over Theodoros's skill.

Theras arrived at the conclusion of the procedure. He and Demaratos surveyed all the Youths with pride and then they met each other's eyes. The troop's bond of brotherhood left them feeling nostalgic. They felt they had trained the Youths as well as any other, and with little time left in the agoge, they couldn't wait to campaign with them. They regarded it with a nod, but then, after another glance at the boys, they noticed Red was missing.

∧

Red hadn't just been sneaking out of the barracks for food every night, he had been visiting Daphne. An underage affair was against the Laws of Lycurgus. He had also been drinking with her to the point where one goes mad. This was also forbidden. They would meet in the forest under the cover of darkness, having their way with one another. Red would pull away from her every time, just prior to his seed being released and she would rub it into her belly like an ointment. She told him when the time came for them to have a child that it would ensure the infant would be strong. Daphne was a Helen, proper, and nor was Red her first like she was for him.

This night, Red was compelled to see her. What happened to Cheese affected him greatly. He told her the whole story, but being the same age and a girl, ensured that she was only a good listener. It didn't bother him. It just felt good to express himself in ways that were not permitted around the boys. It led to a lot of wine, laughing and loud coupling. During their fourth round, they heard another group of Youths moving through the woods, like hounds on the hunt. Red knew their tactics and knew they had already been spotted. The only thing that mattered to him was Daphne's reputation. He picked her up in a stumble and hid her in an abandoned wolf den, where he and the boys would stash food from time to time. When these rival troops met, it would always lead to an all-out brawl. It was expected of them. Murder and harm of any kind to women and girls however, was forbidden. The skill being taught was never to be seen or cross the enemy's path, but that was inevitable in the Five Villages and that was the whole point, just another lesson in stealth. He crept away from the den and stood up to reveal himself. As soon as he did, the troop pounced on him and disappeared just as fast. His face was bloodied and lumped up from countless heels stomping on his crown at once.

When she felt safe, Daphne crept out from the dark hole and frantically searched for her love. She found him and knew he needed help, but not from any of his peers. She blamed herself for what happened and truly loved him for protecting her. Because her reputation and family's name were on the line, she turned to the only person she could trust, her mother.

"Do you love him?" she asked Daphne, as she smelled the wine on her breath.

Daphne swayed in her stance. "How could I not?"

"Very well."

Her mother sent her helots with orders to deliver him to the perioeci. They lived not too far away and they were isolated from the Five Villages and others of their status. There, she brought Red around by throwing a bucket of cold water on his face. It cleansed his wounds well enough, revealing a gashed lump on his brow and another below his eye. He needed no further treatment. She had seen much worse and she knew injuries could be deceiving in appearance until the blood had been washed away. As Red gazed around, he had no idea where he was. There was an entire family of strangers tending to themselves to his one side, and to his other, Daphne peered from behind a beautiful woman, who hovered over him.

"Do you love my daughter?" she asked.

Red regained clarity at that moment and realized who she was. "Yes, my lady," he said and snapped up to a sit.

"Then be on your way and speak not a word of this."

Red understood the implications of an underage affair, but he also sensed a mother's desire to please her daughter. He stood up feeling dizzy, gathered himself, and walked out of the house, offering Daphne a parting glance. She in turn, gazed back into his eyes and then to her mother's. Not a word was spoken. Once Red was gone, her mother looked at the perioeci most threateningly. The free dwellers of Sparta got the message to remain silent, or else.

Red crept back into the Five Villages, dodged a few of the Elders and Equals by remaining in the shadows, and returned to his barrack without getting caught. Once inside, he woke Ox up.

"What happened to you?"

"I can't tell you," Red said. "But you must do something for me."

"Done."

Red punched Ox in the face three times below the eye.

"What was that for?" he whispered in anger.

"We ran into the other boys. And now I owe you one."

Ox didn't say another word, and somehow, he fell back asleep with ease. As Red rested his head on the dirt, he glanced at Cheese who still managed to maintain his breath. He thought it would be no less than three moons before he was up again. It didn't matter. He was just glad he lived.

During the next day, Theras and Demaratos gave harsh, questioning glares to Red, but they never confronted him. They knew what had happened because no secret was a secret, unless the Five Villages knew about it. So while Lysander now dined with the kings, that night at his mess, Demaratos had Theras bring a helot in with an amphora of unmixed wine. The ceramic jar was full, and when the slave held it up, it spanned the length of his torso. All the Youths, save Red and Ox, stared at him, wondering why he was present.

"This is what happens to you when you drink," Theras said to the Youths, and then he looked to the helot. "Drink."

Red swallowed his dry throat hard, as the helot grasped the amphora with both hands and took a swallow. He then looked back to Theras for further orders.

"Did I say stop?" Theras asked rhetorically.

The helot took many swallows, one after another. By a quarter way through, he began to sway, burp and wince from the burn his insides felt. By halfway through the straight wine, he could barely stand. The man was deathly thin and he hadn't eaten since the day before. Another sip and he spewed all he had drunk on the earthen floor.

"By Zeus!" Theras exclaimed. "Keep it together."

"I cannot, sir," the helot slurred.

"Did I say speak? Drink!"

His eyes were nearing the back of his head, while the boys continued to watch him funnel down the wine. Suddenly, he dropped down on both knees, sitting on his heels and shaking his head. "No more, please," he begged and looked to Theras for pity, but he received none.

The helot continued drinking. He struggled to place the amphora to his mouth at a quarter full. The boys observed this man in awe, as he rapidly fell into ruin.

"Drink!" Theras yelled again.

He did, until the jar was empty. His insides felt like they were failing him and then he vomited blood all over himself, and finally, he collapsed on the dirt.

"Do you see that?" Theras expelled, while staring directly at Red. "Study this man! This is what happens if you drink in excess!"

The boys did, vowing never to end up that way. Red was hit especially hard and he glanced back up at his mentors. They were both grilling him. The message was clear. Red knew they knew about Daphne and nothing more needed to be said. He also knew he wouldn't be seeing her again for quite some time.

Theodoros eventually entered with their bread and Black Broth and served his masters. After, he checked the status of his peer. "Demaratos, sir," he said.

They all curiously glanced over.

"He is dead, sir."

# ∧

Socrates sat on the lower stone steps to one of the entrances in the agora, immersed in conversation. He was surrounded by many of his followers, young and old. Passersby would also stop to listen for their personal amusement of the lively man, who was renowned for his logic. Some would even travel from far and wide to engage him in a battle of wits. He always won the debate, but he never became arrogant as a result. In fact, it was quite the opposite. Socrates, by the will of his god, was determined to spread moral goodness and piety among the people. The only consequence was that he publicly humiliated many political figures by exploiting their faults, sometimes without provocation on their part, and therefore, he had accumulated a growing number of enemies. He meant no harm in an evil sense, it was just his way, deemed necessary by his god.

As for his pupils, they were also his closest friends. They loved and cherished the old philosopher. He was the best of company, quick to share a laugh and helped them sort out their troubles by way of his spirited conversation. Nor did he charge a fee as a teacher, like so many other so-called wise men would do, because he considered himself the student and his friends the teachers.

Today, he was debating love in regards to democratic leadership with an Athenian councilman by the name of Hilarion. At one point, Socrates spoke for a great length of time and then he just stopped. His mind continued though for a good while. His audience could see it on his expression, as he experienced one of his many daily revelations. His wide, bulging eyes seemed to pop farther from his crown, and when he returned his attention to his pupils, they would slowly retract back in place, and a warm, rosy cheeked smile would form around his snub nose.

"Hilarion, you stated as a man of the people that you love the people, regardless if they vote against a motion you put forth. You also said that you believe love is unselfish loyalty, and that through this love, your political aspirations are intended to spread moral goodness, and thereby, benefit the people."

"That is correct," Hilarion said.

"And I said that could only work in reverse. A councilman must act and make decisions with moral goodness from the start, and it is only then, that love will reveal herself. Meaning, love will never blossom unless your intentions are pure. If your intentions are not pure, your role as a councilman in our democracy will never benefit the people."

"That is what you said," Hilarion replied.

"Well, what if no one voted for your proposals? Would you love the people still?" Socrates asked.

"If no one voted for a law or a new order I proposed that would benefit the people, I would imagine that I would need a new trade, Socrates."

The mob laughed, but this was the answer Socrates expected, the one that played out in his vast mind.

"If the people wanted you to resign and take a new trade would you love them despite it?" Socrates inquired.

"As long as my resignation was of benefit to the people." Hilarion emphasized, while deliberately meeting the eyes of all those attending.

"Do you please everyone you love, Hilarion?"

"That is a part of love, is it not?"

"Do you love a woman upon first sight or after you have gotten to know her?" Socrates asked.

"That depends upon the woman," Hilarion said with a clever smile, while garnering more laughter.

"I am beginning to understand what you call love," Socrates said, and then he paused. "I must ask you another question."

"By all means, my wise friend."

"What if your father committed manslaughter and the people wanted him punished? Would you charge your own father for the crime and put him to death if he was found guilty? Or, would you disappoint the people?" Socrates asked.

"My father would have my head if I did that," Hilarion joked again. "But with love, comes heartache. Does it not?"

"It does, it surely does. But do you love your father?"

"Yes, of course. My mother too."

"Then since your father is among the people and you would disappoint him, it is rather you, who wants to be loved by the majority, so that you can retain your occupation."

"I am to make a living," Hilarion said.

"That is not love, Hilarion. Do you not see? That is the seed of corruption you planted in your mind to always think how you can remain in power. Love moves in two directions simultaneously, to and fro. If you did not let that seed grow and strived for moral goodness from the beginning, it is only then, that you can experience true love with the people. And only then, could you have heartache and fall in love at first sight."

The audience was in awe and on the edge of their toes as they waited for a rebuttal.

"Well, I suppose I…I never thought of it that way," Hilarion said painfully, and then he went mute.

The throng broke out in laughter as they watched him, including Socrates, who gave Hilarion a hug and then raised his hand like he was the victor to show he had no ill regard toward the man. This garnered cheers from everyone, while Hilarion leaned in toward the philosopher's ear. "I believe you've tarnished my reputation."

"Nonsense," Socrates said. "Love is truth. It will set you free."

Hilarion knew how sensitive the people were and he expected he would need a new occupation by day's end.

Meanwhile, Plato was among those spectating. He had escorted his teacher to the agora this morning and he would have enjoyed the debate more if he had not felt compelled to keep a keen eye on the throng. He knew his teacher's enemies were out there somewhere. He continued to glance around during the excitement, and through the mass of swaying tunics, he spotted Meletus spying on Socrates with his political cohorts, Anytus and Lycon.

Meletus was a former poet turned young man of the Council. He had a sickly look to him with his long, straight, black hair, hooked nose and beaked face. He represented the city's poets, artists and actors, just like other councilmen represented craftsmen, tradesmen, fishermen or farmers. He stood, peering from behind a Doric column, fuming and plotting the demise of the old man. Just ten days ago, Meletus was in the same humiliating situation as Hilarion. He thought he could outwit the master. In the end, he was defeated. His ego had met its match and his closest friends had lost respect for him. Even worse, they became followers of Socrates. Meletus's grudge consumed him. He was unwilling to let it go and he quickly began mingling with those who despised the old philosopher as well. Namely, Men of the Council and Assembly, who introduced new laws, held extreme power and influence, and wanted to reform Athens to their liking. Suffice to say, Meletus's first objective was to kill Socrates, legally, for corrupting the youth. He could have hired an assassin and been done with it, but he wanted to humiliate the man in public first.

Plato faced forward and crossed over to his teacher. Then he took him by the arm and gracefully escorted him away in the opposite direction of Meletus, and out of the agora.

"Socrates, you must stop these public debates and leave Athens at once," Plato said with concern.

"Or what?" Socrates asked.

"Or they will kill you. I am sure of it."

"You know as well as I that only guilty men run."

"But if you continue in this way—"

"I love my city, Plato. Nor am I guilty of anything, save following the will of my god, and there is no crime in that."

Plato lowered his gaze in a defeated manner. He remained quiet the rest of the way to his teacher's house. When Socrates opened his door to enter, Plato stopped him by placing a hand on his shoulder.

Socrates turned around and saw his jaw clenching. "Well by all means, don't restrain yourself on my account."

"At least, stay inside for a few days until tempers wear."

Socrates looked at him plainly. "Any word of Xenophon?"

Plato sighed. "Cyrus was killed in battle. If he lives then he is stranded, but with a large army."

"I see," Socrates said. "And what do you think?"

Plato couldn't refrain from grinning. It humored him that Socrates never yielded from further discussion, no matter how it made others feel. "I think with all odds against Xenophon, he will flourish."

"Ha! His tenacity and brilliance would make him a fine leader," Socrates said with a smile.

"Yes it would," Plato said, still concerned.

"Same time tomorrow?"

Plato wished he could make him see reason, but he refrained from another attempt. "Yes, Socrates. Same time tomorrow."

The next morning, Plato returned with their breakfast and sat at the old, busted table that Xenophon used to share with his teacher, when Meletus and twelve armed hoplites stormed through the door. They jerked Socrates to a stand and tethered him in irons.

"You are under arrest for heresy and corruption of the youth," Meletus said with a smirk.

"He's done no such thing!" Plato exclaimed.

"Worry not Plato, but please inform my wife and children that I do not believe I will be home for dinner, perhaps...not ever."

Socrates's mild manner made Meletus vexed. "Take him away!"

∧

Mithridates came in peace, claiming to be a friend of Cyrus, but he soon proved otherwise. He expressed his concern for the Greeks' plight, telling the generals that there was no route that would lead them to safety and that the wisest course would be to come to terms with the Great King. The Greeks knew what the king's terms were, so Xenophon volunteered himself to speak on behalf of the generals. He politely thanked Mithridates for his counsel and told him that it was best that such a small force not stand in their way. Mithridates smiled and bowed cunningly in response, and then he departed at once.

Persian loyalty had now exasperated the philosopher so much so, that he denounced and despised all natives openly. Least to say, he was fitting in well with the mercenaries. When the army resumed their march, Mithridates returned, approaching their rear line with a force of six hundred light armored troops and cavalry. Xenophon and his men suffered hard losses from native archers, slingers and cavalry, who would pick one of the Greeks out of their line, charge, and stick them with their blades before riding off. The rear of the hollow square quickly learned how vulnerable their new formation was while the rest of the army remained clear of danger. During the attack, Xenophon ordered his men to chase them down on foot, but the Persians refused to fight straight up and retreated, only to return and be chased off again. By the end of the marching day, Mithridates's force disappeared. Their harassment tactics had exhausted Xenophon and his rear contingent, but they did make it to the next village, took the supplies they needed to move on, and also learned of their location from one of the villagers, who they took as a hostage.

The next day, the Ten Thousand departed well before dawn. By midmorning, they found themselves standing on the sandy bank of the Great Zab River. The generals sacrificed to the river god and Zeus Savior. The signs were favorable and the army prepared to ford the watercourse at her shallowest point. It was half a stade in breadth. Without any appearances from Mithridates, the fore of the army trudged across, carrying their weapons overhead. Once they made it, the rear followed them up, escorting the baggage, animals, slaves and followers to the other side. It took until the sun was beyond its zenith and that was when Mithridates showed his face. This time he brought with him a large number of Tissaphernes's men, reinforcements from the king and many of those who fought with Cyrus.

Xenophon defiantly stared at the Persian horde from across the Great Zab. Despite being greatly outnumbered, he had had enough. "You claimed to be our friend, Mithridates!"

"Of course I did, my friend!" Mithridates shouted back. "But if I capture you, you shall no longer be my friend!"

"Pursue us, and all of your men shall die today!" Xenophon said threateningly.

"I have no fear of Greeks, for you are easy to kill!"

Xenophon hesitated in anger. "We shall see about that!"

"Yes, my friend! We shall!"

Xenophon was now under extreme pressure. He was the only one among the Ten Thousand who had been educated. So not only did everyone rely on him for leadership, but they had suffered casualties, were being chased, and his men would be in desperate need of provisions sooner, rather than later. He thought it all through as the army distanced themselves from the Persians and found there was no easy solution, save for overcoming one obstacle at a time. He had already told the men what to do in preparation of another rear attack and then it came.

The Ten Thousand were marching north along the Tigris River with the Great Zab in their wake. However, this time they placed their baggage train unguarded at the fore and positioned their hoplites in the center of the hollow square. It was a risky maneuver. Volleys of arrows and stones descended upon them, but they all fell short or wide. In response, Xenophon signaled the trumpets and they sounded off. The signal commanded the army without a word needed. The rear of the hollow square split down the middle and shifted toward their closest wing. The heavy armored troops then poured out and charged at an all-out run toward the natives. It was the last response Mithridates expected after the damage his men inflicted on them yesterday. So the Persians continued with their volleys, as they were ordered to do. The missiles and stones flew directly over the charge, and again, missed the main body of the Ten Thousand.

Xenophon learned the hard way that they couldn't survive another day of harassment. So he held an assembly with the generals the night prior to prepare for another inevitable attack. During which, a mercenary from Rhodes stepped forward and proposed that his people craft hundreds of slings, ones that could shoot twice as far as a Persian model. They were known for such inventions and the motion was put to a vote and passed. The Rhodians hadn't slept a wink and they were now formed up in a line in front of the main body, which was now facing back toward the Great Zab as the hoplites charged. The Rhodians pelted the Persians relentlessly until the countercharge was met, so as to not kill their own men. When the Greeks engaged them, the Persians retreated to the Great Zab, losing many along the way. This was a part of Xenophon's plan, to create chaos. He knew the Persians feared Greeks and he knew they would retreat as they had before, like the day prior and at Cunaxa, but the river would slow them to a stop. He was right. There were so many of them waiting to cross, they began trampling over one another. It was chaos. When the hoplites arrived, they put the Persian horde to slaughter. Mithridates made it out alive with only half his army and rode off in haste. To ensure the Persians wouldn't attack them again, the hoplites butchered the dying and dead, and left their mutilated corpses on the bank of the Great Zab, as a warning to the Great King to beware of Greeks.

When the Ten Thousand reunited, they shouted their victory cry and hailed Xenophon as their hero and champion. To them, he wasn't just as good a hoplite as the next, he was a wise general. Xenophon however, knew the truth. He realized from the first day of his campaign that war was nothing more than risk, where depending on the situation, one must measure how many deaths they are willing to risk to be victorious. So he chose to remain pious. He claimed that Zeus was the one they should thank for their victory, and in return, they should send the god an offering. The sacrifice was made and the Ten Thousand continued their journey north, passing many abandoned wonders of the ancient world.

In this respect, Xenophon's tour definitely had its rewards as he gazed in awe at exterior palace walls, dating back to the days of the Assyrians. They were so massive that they rose over one hundred men tall and spanned endless ground. Even the old gods of worship were still clearly depicted along their stone mosaics. It made him wonder how long man had been in existence and who would be next to rule this foreign land.

Finally, after many days without contest, the Persians came into view. They were across a pass, along the neighboring mountain path, from which the Greeks ventured. Mithridates had reunited with Tissaphernes. They had thus far remained out of sight the entire time and were hoping for an ambush, but the terrain gave them away. Meanwhile, the Greeks were ascending the first of what looked like endless clay mountains into Carduchi. This was hard country. Far to the north, they could see that the mountains were blanketed with snow and clouds skirted their peaks. To make matters worse for the Greeks, it was the wet season. Hard rain fell.

Xenophon was positioned in the rear of their marching column. He was the first to spot the Persians, when Chirisophos had ordered him and his peltasts to the fore. Xenophon didn't think that was a wise decision as he looked to the captain of his light armored troops. "Unless I signal for you, remain here and guard the rear," he said, and then he rode his horse toward the front of the column, snaking his way uphill between the line of troops and the cliff's edge as the rains spattered his face.

He eventually made it to the fore and approached Chirisophos on top of a lower peak. They were both miserably soaked. "What is it?" Xenophon grumbled.

"Look," Chirisophos said, as he was always short with his words.

Xenophon placed a hand across his brow to block the rain. When he looked forward, he saw their next ascent was occupied by armed Carduchians. He scowled in frustration. "Well, what now? Persians are across the pass to our south."

"It changes nothing," Chirisophos said. "We must take that height."

"Yes, but how?"

"Send a *sortie*."

"A sortie?"

"Me and your peltasts will charge up there and sort them out."

"I'll go. You stay. I'm swifter of foot."

Chirisophos skeptically eyed him. "I didn't think you had it in you, Athenian."

Xenophon didn't think he did either and ordered the trumpets to sound off. The peltasts received the signal to maneuver to the fore. The army had to shift to their inside to allow them by on the narrow ledge. They were pushed into the craggy mountainside as muddy water sluiced down the ascent. The peltasts trudged through it, taking extra precaution with every step to prevent falling off the edge. By the time they reached Xenophon, the rest of the army had caught up to them. They were packed tight in a double column, as they waited on the peak and watched the sortie depart.

The plan was to run as fast as they could down the path of the mountain and up the next without getting killed by Carduchian archers and slingers. However, there was a problem. The Persians had already dispatched a contingent by way of a longer route to come up on the northern side of the Carduchians. It was now a race, and they were all enemies of the other.

The peltasts went first in a mad, suicidal dash down the slippery slope. Xenophon followed them up on horseback as he held his shield out in front to block the volleys of arrows and stones descending on them.

"Run! Give it all you have!" he commanded, as the peltasts made it down the narrow path and began their vertical climb. At this point, Xenophon came upon the last man in the line of runners who was lagging behind. "Push yourself, man! Do this for your country! For your wife and children!"

The man unexpectedly stopped and hugged the mountain wall along the slope to shield himself from death. "We are not on level ground, general!"

"No, we are not," Xenophon said, referring to the terrain.

"I mean, you have a horse and we do not!"

Xenophon's jaw dropped in the middle of the chaos. Native archers and slingers were adjusting their aim with deadly accuracy. The rain was preventing them from looking up at their destination and the bloody Persians were attempting to take the vantage from the other side. Nobody knew how close they were. Without a moment more to lose, Xenophon leaped from his horse, took the man's javelin, quiver and bow, and dashed toward the peak. He screamed and grunted, passing many of them. "It can be done!" he yelled. "It can be done!"

When the peltasts saw their general defy the vertical path, they found a new fire within them and pushed their bodies beyond their limitations. The sortie charged uphill, like lions possessed and neared the natives on the peak. It was so steep. Their legs burned and trembled. A few vomited in motion. Chirisophos and the main body cheered them on, while across the way, the Persians shouted their men to victory as they made it across the lower pass and began their ascent. The Greeks finally engaged the Carduchians and sorted them out with thrusting points, but most of them escaped over impassable terrain, which only they were accustomed to. They finished off the remaining few with their javelins and then tossed them off the drop.

The men gasped for air and looked to one another. They were unsure of what just happened. Xenophon was one of them, but he quickly snapped out of his fatigue induced daze. "To the other side!" he ordered.

There was no time to lose and they moved to the north side of the peak. Halfway down, they saw the Persians running up the vertical path. The exhausted sortie reached in their quivers and loosed their missiles at them, wildly. They had no aim from their heaving chests and trembling limbs. So they just let off as many rounds as they had and somehow annihilated the enemy without leaving a soul left alive. Surprised, they turned to their men across the gap and raised their arms in victory. "Nike!"

The army cheered for them and then they shouted insults and taunted the Persians from across the pass. Tissaphernes's horde felt the agony of defeat and they silently retreated back into the mountain.

Weary, Xenophon eyed his peltasts as he labored for air. Most of them had already crashed to the ground from their exhausting efforts. "We must ensure the army makes it safely across. On your feet," he commanded, despite his own desire to collapse and then he heaved a few more breaths. "On your feet! It can be done!"

# The Krypteia

Agesilaos departed his house under the cover of darkness. He did not explain to Kleora where he was going because his task was of the sensitive kind. Earlier this day, he received word about the Council of Ten's plight in Asia Minor, as well as a third Persian invasion. This brought a small measure of joy to his tedious duties. The fact that Asiatic Greeks and Persians loyal to Cyrus had requested aid, and his fellow citizens had been expressing how pleased they were with how swiftly and effortlessly he dissolved the conspiracy, Agesilaos was finally beginning to feel like a king. Even Pausanias climbed out of his hole.

Lysander was by Agesilaos's side when it was necessary, and together, they convinced the council to make war with Persia Sparta's most pressing concern. Agesilaos then took it further. He appealed to the council to give him an army for an invasion and he guaranteed to put the cost of the war on Persia. Meaning, he would plague them with so much trouble on their own land that they wouldn't be able to set sail for Greece. Pythagoras and the council were pleased with his notion because if a third invasion did occur, it was unclear what the outcome would be.

Before Sparta defeated Athens in the Great War, they used the notion of freedom as propaganda to gain allies to assist them with their victory over their rival. Now that the war was over and Sparta reigned supreme, Greece's unity was fragile because instead of liberating their allies from the Athenian yoke, Sparta enforced her strict laws upon them. The other critical factor was their helots. They outnumbered the Spartans by more than three to one. The helots had revolted in the past after Sparta suffered devastating losses from a great quake, and they could not afford another such occurrence at this time. So in response, the council pressed Agesilaos with concerns of their own. They handed him the names of thirty helots, who they felt were a threat to the safety of the Five Villages.

"Done," Agesilaos said, and they sacrificed to Pythian Apollo. The liver was healthy. So with the signs favorable, Agesilaos would dispatch the helots, and in return, he would get his war.

The *Krypteia* handled these affairs. Agesilaos met them in the forest outside of the Five Villages this night to inform them of their duty. Thirty Youths were handpicked to assassinate the thirty helots. This was what the Krypteia was, a council of Equals, who ordered a group of Youths to take care of Sparta's dirty dealings. For the Youths, it was another lesson in stealth and murder, and to become accustomed to both. Ox and Red were among them, while Cheese remained on the mend. They went out this night, but only twenty-nine returned. Ox, the biggest, strongest, most promising Youth of them all had been slain. It was a devastating blow, which struck the Equals and Youths hard. They now sought revenge on all helots, but it was forbidden. The Krypteia was a secret order. Most citizens thought it only rumor. They thought real men, men of Sparta, would never behave so dishonorably. They were right. That's why the Equals sent the Youths.

After Ox's death, Agesilaos was forced to meet with the Krypteia again. He stressed that they must find the one who killed him, otherwise there would be no campaign against the Great King. The Spartans or any Greek for that matter, always referred to the Persian king as if they were Persians themselves, but they said it in a mocking fashion, as in, *the Great King*. Oh, they loved to loathe.

The Krypteia did their utmost. Their passion for war with Persia has always been a dream, so it only intensified their eagerness to fulfill their king's order. They found the culprit hiding in Tegea, which was just north of Laconia. He was dwelling in sanctuary and they dared not kill him outright on sacred ground, so the Youths surrounded him for many days and nights until starvation brought him out, and then they dispatched him.

With the helot problem remedied, Pythagoras and the council felt reassured that their precious Equals were safe from another rebellion. In return, they granted Agesilaos his desired force to invade Persia. The Five Villages were exhilarated when the report reached their ears, as all Equals hoped they would be included in the expedition. Lysander was certainly looking forward to his Asiatic return, but Agesilaos seemed intoxicated during his evening gymnastics at the athlitika. He proclaimed himself the second Agamemnon for the second Trojan War!

# Book III
## Achilles' Heel

*Three brothers once fled from battle. When they reached Sparta, they found their mother and told her what they had done.*

*"What is it you want from me?" she asked.*

*The eldest brother stepped forward. "To tell you that your sons live, mother."*

*"I did not bring you up to be vile cowards!" she said.*

*"But, mother," the eldest son said.*

*"But nothing!" the mother exclaimed. She pulled her tunic up and flaunted her sex. "What do you propose now, to crawl back up in here where you came from?"*

# Kings and Knights

Agesilaos picked thirty Equals for his Persian campaign, including Theras and Demaratos. Those Equals who weren't chosen were envious during their departure because they were going to be missing the fight of their lives, a fight that could leave Persia in ruins. Everyone wanted to be a part of it. Agesilaos also freed two thousand helots and drafted them into his army. By doing so, the tension between the helots and the Equals increased over Ox's death. Along with them, were six thousand allied troops, or rather, mercenaries. For thirty days, the army trained together, sometimes going through the night and into the next day. The helots proved their worth, displaying the utmost obedience and readiness alongside the troops, which greatly surprised the Equals. Their animosity slowly wore by the time they reached the shores of Asia Minor, as they would now rely on each other as brothers in war.

Prior to their departure from Sparta, Agesilaos gave his men the day off before they would march to Thebes, and then from there, sail to Asia Minor. During that time, Theras had voiced his concern to Demaratos about finding a suitable wife prior to them reaching thirty years of age. If they didn't, their status as an Equal could be revoked. The reason behind this, was that Sparta has always needed sons, but never more so than now. The number of Equals had been halved by the time the Great War was won and this was why mercenaries and freed helots now served alongside them. Since they would be off to Persia and weren't sure how many years they would be gone, they strolled through the agora that morning and searched for any women that looked the part. It didn't take long before they were approached. One was a Helen. She approached Theras. The other not so, but her appearance was still quite pleasing to Demaratos. For the women, it wasn't often that handsome, young men, draped in crimson would walk by since they were always at war or training for it.

"You are Eirene and she, Aspasia, my lady?" Theras asked curiously.

"We are," Eirene said.

"Will you marry us?" Theras proposed outright, as he had always been more carefree than Demaratos in unfamiliar situations.

"I only desire one husband," she replied, causing both her and Aspasia to laugh at their awkwardness.

Demaratos was experiencing some sort of wretched knot in his stomach, as was Theras, while the two women whispered to one another. They could handle any amount of danger and did not fear death, but a woman? The boys had no idea what kind of fight they were in.

"Forgive me, you take my meaning another way," Theras said, interrupting their chatter.

Eirene turned her head and looked at them square in the eyes. "Enough," she said, commanding their attention and they snapped to. "Meet us at Pitana Grove."

"Yes, of course, my lady," they both said.

They parted in opposite directions and took different routes to get there, so the men would not be humiliated by their peers.

When they arrived at Pitana Grove, they saw the women in a clearing, which was surrounded by long, amber grass that was near a stream. They slipped their tunics off and stood there, presenting themselves to be taken. The women were tanned and oiled. Eirene had much smaller breasts than Aspasia, but both their bodies were in fine form. Demaratos and Theras nervously glanced at one another, as if they were heading into war against three hundred Argives. Then, they courageously crossed over toward their adversary and were now face to face.

The women grabbed the men and brought them in closer. Theras and Demaratos felt like boys. They were completely apprehensive, as female lips engaged theirs. They weren't sure exactly what to do with their mouths, save pucker their lips. The women found it hilarious, but the boys kept giving each other the eye, telling the other to stand strong and hold the line. The women of Sparta also trained in wrestling and boxing, and went about it just as diligently as the men. So they had no trouble taking Theras and Demaratos to the ground. Eirene and Aspasia brushed their cloaks aside, ensured they had their vigor, and then they mounted them. The boys were now undergoing a different type of agoge. Penetrating the women, made them feel as if they had died and passed on to the next world.

"Something is happening," Demaratos said in a panic.

"Yes, to me as well," Theras said, as they reached out to grab the other's hand.

The women laughed hard. They found such pleasure invoking fear into their men.

"Stay strong, brother!" Theras said. "Not much longer now!"

"Indeed! Get off!" Demaratos exclaimed to Aspasia.

"Off!" Theras shouted.

The women glanced at each other with a giggle and then they slowly dismounted, unafraid if the seed was planted. But it wasn't fast enough for the boys and they forced their women off of them. They landed with a gentle thud to their inside, their backs touching, just as the boys released their volley. This was something they had done to themselves with their hands many times before, but to have it done by a woman was a whole different matter. The missiles hit them and their women in the faces. The girls broke out in uncontrollable laughter, as the boys were mortified. Eirene and Aspasia wiped their men clean and then they rubbed the ointment into their bellies. Demaratos and Theras slowly began to realize the humor in their inexperience and they offered an awkward chuckle.

Once the laughter subsided, Theras looked directly in Eirene's eyes. He was in love. "Can we do it again, my lady?"

She gave another laugh, treasuring his innocence. "Until you've mastered the skill, my love."

Demaratos turned from his friend to Aspasia. "Uh, I as well?"

"Yes, Demaratos. You as well."

∧

That evening during their day off, Agesilaos ate at the kings' mess with Pausanias, Pythagoras and Lysander. Since Lycurgus established the laws, the kings have always been served two portions of dinner. One for them and the other they would give to someone they felt, who was deserving of an honorable mention. Pausanias sat directly across from Pythagoras and Agesilaos, and Lysander was by his side. They were discussing the various duties they would have, while Agesilaos was away. They had resolved matters regarding their Greek neighbors, but they were in a disagreement about the possibility of a lingering threat of conspiracy, which involved Timaea and Leotychidas.

"We should ask her to return home, and then dispatch her and the Athenian," Pausanias suggested.

"Let them rot in Argos. The wench is a whore, the boy a monster," Pythagoras grumbled.

"Leaving them be, could influence many, if they haven't already," Pausanias continued.

"So send some of your knights to sort her out, while I am away," Agesilaos suggested, as if that would end the discussion.

"I will not risk the lives of my knights to satisfy your fears."

"Fear?" Agesilaos countered in anger.

"My kings, please," Pythagoras intervened.

Agesilaos glanced at Lysander, who remained unusually focused on his meal. He was looking for support, but he didn't receive any. He then glanced back across at the king. "You are correct, Pausanias," he said in a frustrated manner. "I wouldn't want you to overexert yourself. I'll sort it out when I return home." Blatantly, Agesilaos slid his second meal over to Pythagoras while he glared at the Agiad king with cold, steely eyes.

Pausanias was equally vexed as he stared back at Agesilaos and gave his second meal to Lysander. Lysander unassumingly picked his head up as he noticed it and resumed eating his first portion, still without uttering a word.

# Λ

The next day, the Spartan army marched to Thebes. Their arrival was unwelcomed, as they could tell from the endless glares of resentment. The Thebans never liked them. In fact, they despised them because of their ill history together, and with a Spartan garrison in their agora, they were reminded of it daily.

Fortune blessed the Thebans though. Agesilaos planned to sail immediately, but first, he wanted to sacrifice in the same spot that Agamemnon had done when his army had sailed to Troy. The liver was healthy and he set it over the fire. However, when he returned after inspecting their ships to ensure the organ had burned, some Theban youths came through prior, one by the name of Epaminondas, and they kicked the offering to the ground. Agesilaos was outraged by the sacrilege. He demanded for the culprits to come forth and face justice, but no one did because the Thebans were pleased by the vandals' actions. Agesilaos was further infuriated because the winds were favorable, so he could not delay any longer. As the fleet of ships departed, Agesilaos stared back on the top deck, threatening them all. "I curse you! I will come back here, and devastate you! I, will be your downfall!"

# The Mountains

The army rendezvoused with Xenophon and his sortie by day's end, but Carduchi proved treacherous. The Ten Thousand pushed on despite it. They continued north, mounting peak after peak, opposed by the natives from the full moon till it waned. The rains had yet to end. Provisions remained at a constant minimum. Fatigue plagued them all. They were on edge, wet, and quick to lose themselves to the uncertainty ahead. They managed by living village to village, taking what food there was without wasting valuable energy on further plunder. The men survived on one meal a day, sometimes none at all. To fill the void of hunger, fear of injury and illness, and the desire to return home, they turned to their baggage. There were many slaves among them, including men, women and children. The Rhodians shared one girl who was barely fifteen years of age. They would do what they wanted to her at every stopping point. Sometimes two Rhodians would stick her at once. The anguish was horrifying for her. Some slaves died as a result. It was like this throughout, no matter where they came from, whether Argos or Leuctra. The Thebans liked boys, so they had their way with a select few. The Spartan exiles could go without satisfying their desires, as they were content with misery. The Cretans took what was left, the ugliest of the bunch, men, women, goats, it didn't matter to them.

There was one slave however, who stood out among the rest. The Athenians claimed her before anyone else could. She was nearly Xenophon's age, and by Spartan standards, a Helen. The Athenians assumed, because of her beauty, that she was from a royal Persian line of some sort. They prided themselves on penetrating her every night, one after the other. They would literally line up and wait their turn. At first, she embraced it as a means for survival. She figured if she pretended to enjoy it, they would be gentler. She was wrong. It only roused their aggression toward her because of their prejudice toward Persians. Eventually, she could no longer pretend because her insides could no longer withstand the trauma. Fresh blood stained her loins and robes daily. Men saw what was happening and did nothing. The fighting in the mountains had gotten to them—changed them. They could no longer envision home. This was their life now. Some days she would be unable to walk and she was forced to lay prostrate on a wagon filled with supplies, and still, the Athenians did not yield.

Xenophon participated in this once, and the next day when he met her eyes, he found himself lowering his gaze. He vowed that he would never partake in such depravity again. He felt terrible and purified himself in the next river they came across, but he couldn't stop the army from what they were doing or mutiny could arise. Ariston was one of them. He was not the moral man Xenophon thought him to be and they had become quite distant during their journey. The entire affair upset him greatly. He would get over losing his friend in time, but she was the only exception to his Persian prejudice. He had come to genuinely feel for her, prior to her spoiling. He thought if it weren't for the rest of his countrymen ravaging her, she could have made a good wife and given him the children he had been longing for all this time. It was not meant to be. One morning before dawn, she gathered her strength and threw herself off the mountain.

All things considered, the Ten Thousand were doing well as they braved the dangerous terrain, until they reached a pass where a river cut through it crosswise. They would all be vulnerable to attack if they entered, but the men had to get across the watercourse in order to reach the only scalable face of the mountain. This way, they could reach higher ground. Through the course of their journey, they found taking the heights to be essential. Not only did it keep the men safe, but the vantage also provided them with a general sense of their position. However, the Carduchians were always scattered along the varying peaks in their path. As usual, Xenophon ordered volunteers to go forward and capture the mountain, so the baggage train could safely pass through. He estimated two thousand men should be enough to do the job. As the volunteers went forward, the natives allowed them to cross the river and begin their climb. The Greeks ascended pathways formed by the Carduchians or made their own way as they went, and that's when dreadful sounds erupted. The mountain trembled beneath their boots and loud claps of thunder echoed, relentlessly. The men felt the earth shake as grit danced over their toes. Shadows grew overhead, and when they looked up, they found giant boulders descending upon them. Most were the size of wagons. Others were smaller.

"Retreat!" a volunteer yelled. "Retreat!" he yelled again, and then he hugged the mountain wall as one of the boulders narrowly missed him.

The men, who had yet to find a foothold, ran, while the men on the pathways took their chances and searched for other routes up the mountainside. They had all grown accustomed to taking foolish risks. They struggled till dark, attempting to summit the peak as the Carduchian onslaught continued, but it was pointless.

When the volunteers returned to the army and reported their findings, they learned another contingent had been sent out. They took their only captured guide with them, who reluctantly offered to show them another way. He was middle aged and a bit feeble. They had another guide who was younger and more able, but he was killed by way of torture because he refused to cooperate with them. They learned from their surviving guide after the fact, that he had a daughter he was trying to protect from their savagery. What the Carduchians refused to recognize, was that the Greeks would have preferred to pass through their territory in peace.

These natives were fiercely independent and the only free people in the Persian Empire. They had never allowed themselves to be subjugated by the Great King. It was more due to their impassable country that made this possible though. So when they saw the Greeks, they attacked them, like they attacked the Persian horde long ago when they tried to take their freedom.

The alternate course forced the troops to backtrack and head around the other side of the eastern mountain, which bordered the pass. It was a longer route, but it proved much easier going. They stealthily weaved back around the mountain and made it to the first peak the volunteers had tried to reach. This brought them to their first engagement of the day. The Greeks slit all twelve of their throats before the Carduchians knew they were upon them.

By the time the first height was taken, it was very late and the Greek contingent realized that more of the enemy was still directly overhead on the highest peak. The Carduchians however, were unaware of what had transpired. They thought their own men were still down below. The Greeks figured this, since their onslaught came to an end. So they took advantage and remained at their fortified position throughout the night in total silence. Come dawn, the air was clouded with a thick, milky mist and fine rain. The Greeks ascended the mountainside and came to within a spear's reach of the enemy without being noticed. At that moment, the trumpet sounded off. It took the natives by surprise, while the Greeks appeared from out of the clouded air. They attacked and took the final height.

The army, along with the baggage train, reunited with the contingent by way of the alternate route and they descended the eastern mountain. It was no sooner that they saw a three headed peak directly ahead, like steps, but this time, there was no other route. So again, they would have to take the height.

The sun had yet to reach its zenith, so there was still time to accomplish this before day's end. The peltasts were ordered to the fore and they charged up the first slope. Volleys of arrows and stones rained down on them. One trooper had his leg crushed by a rock the size of a melon. His brothers left him in pain and continued their charge. Once they reached the peak, they killed a few Carduchians, while the rest predictably fled. They shouted across the gap for the main body to proceed and then took the final two peaks in the same manner.

The army continued down the other side of the three headed mountain and came upon the tribe's village, while some of the peltasts were posted across the peaks to ensure the baggage train's safe passage. The army found it abandoned for the most part just like the others, but this village was the largest they had come across. It was no wonder the Carduchians became so hostile. It proved to be a true treasure. There was enough wine for every man to drink himself mad twice. They did, singing songs of praise for

Xenophon's leadership. The philosopher had one swallow with the men, but he just wasn't in the mood for any companionship. He was genuinely tired and still angry about the men's depravity. So before he lost his temper, he crept away into one of the homes, which still had a fire burning inside, and he went to sleep.

Ariston was on the wine, when he found him. "Xenophon, you must wake up!" He didn't, so Ariston placed a hand on his shoulder. "Xenophon," he called again and nudged him.

Xenophon was sleeping on his side, when his groggy eyes finally opened. His body was so stiff, he felt like he was embalmed in wax. "Ariston," he said with alarm. "How long have I slept?"

"Barely a wink. There is a problem with the baggage train," he said urgently.

"What? What happened?" Xenophon asked, as he wiped his eyes clean.

"Our guards fell asleep and were slaughtered by the natives. The baggage train has been halved."

"An ambush?"

"Yes, Xenophon."

The general sat up, reluctant to rush outside. "Back away," he ordered coldly.

Ariston stepped back and sat on the ground across from him, realizing how close they had once been. "I know I let you down."

"What is this you speak of now?"

"The slave girl," Ariston said.

Xenophon met Ariston's eyes and then he looked down.

"I have not been myself, neither have the men. When she took her life, it…it awakened us."

"How so?" Xenophon asked with a Socratic tone.

Ariston looked at him. His eyes watered. He was unable to utter any words and wanted to cry, like a young boy.

Xenophon saw it, while he too swallowed the lump in his throat. "We all joined up for glory and plunder, Ariston. But if we don't behave morally, like true men of Greece, we will have no glory, no treasures, no tales of bravery to share with our families. Those are the truest riches."

Ariston's stony skin from the campaign crumbled in that instant. Tears shed. He didn't care. Xenophon was right. "Do you remember, when we met on the voyage and I taught you how to row?"

Xenophon smiled briefly and then he hesitated for a moment. "Are we still friends, Ariston?"

"Of course we are, the closest."

The young philosopher was now a hardened hoplite, and as he smiled at Ariston, he finally understood what Socrates was trying to tell him. "I'm such a pigheaded fool," he thought, and then he went to lay his head back down. "Wake me when the sun goes down, will you?"

"What of the baggage train? The other generals are looking for you."

"Shit on Styx! Must I do everything?" Xenophon exclaimed. Then he forced himself to his feet and marched outside with his friend.

∧

They sorted the remainder of their baggage, halving it again by leaving unhealthy animals and unfit slaves behind before continuing their northern pursuit. The Ten Thousand remained relentless as they battled the hostile Carduchians and their unforgiving land, while Tissaphernes still had yet to make another appearance. Every hill and mountain was a war against the natives. This was their day, every day, and they remained victors. There was loss of life, but it had been minimal. It was usually the result of injury and then infection. Many of the men had cut themselves wide open on the jagged rock during their skirmishes. Sometimes there wouldn't be any water for two or three days at a time and the wounds were left unclean. Then, fever would set in and seal their fate.

After two moons they pushed farther north into the unknown. They reached snow covered mountains and fought for every step, taking hostages whenever they could to use as guides. Carduchi seemed endless. Its tribes were infinite. The Ten Thousand crossed frozen rivers, wide and deep. They had been where no Greek had gone before.

Another moon passed and the land flattened. The Carduchians vanished. Tissaphernes had been forgotten. They didn't know if they were even in Persia anymore. The snow remained and the cold was unlike anything they were accustomed to. However, the Ten Thousand went unopposed and they were able to cover thrice their usual ground in a day's march. The men were overcome with joy by this. They passed through villages with ample food and supplies. They took what they needed and marched on. Despite the cold, things were going very well and they truly thought they had made it through the worst of it. They crossed more rivers and covered more land. The endless white was so serene and eerie, some thought the army had died and passed on to the next world.

By the sixth sun, the man who appeared to be the ruler of this strange realm approached the army with a cavalry escort. Their horses were smaller than a Persian's, so the Greeks weren't sure if this was the Great King's land or not. They stopped just within shouting distance on the army's right flank. The generals moved to within earshot and waited for their leader to speak, but he did not. The man next to him did.

"Welcome Greeks, to western Armenia! I speak for the Persian satrap, Tiribazus!" the interpreter shouted.

Xenophon looked to the Spartan general. "They know who we are. They have heard of us, Chirisophos."

Chirisophos grumbled, as if it was of no importance.

"We would like to reach peaceful terms with you!" the interpreter yelled.

Xenophon kept his eyes fixed on the Armenians, while he continued to speak to the Spartan. "How large do you suppose Persia is?"

"Large," Chirisophos said.

The interpreter continued. "Take any supplies or women you need, and leave our land unburned! In return, we will escort you on your passage west!"

"I'll wager two days before they make their attack."

"Three," Chirisophos said.

"Agreed!" Xenophon shouted to the Armenians.

Suddenly, Tiribazus's army formed up behind him and faced west. Their dress was all white and they seemed to appear from out of nowhere. The Greek generals fell back into file and the two armies marched together with only a short gap between them. Angst swept through the Greek ranks. Everyone was waiting for Persian loyalty to show herself. It carried on like this for three days.

On the third night, a tremendous amount of snow fell. During which, the men were digging trenches to sleep in at their camp, when two scouts brought back an Armenian foot soldier they had captured. Xenophon and the generals tortured this man and got the information they needed. He and Chirisophos were both wrong. Tiribazus's attack would take place on the fourth day as they left the satrap's domain through a narrow pass.

Xenophon personally executed the hostage by sticking his sword through his sternum and then he ordered the army to form up in silence. They left their campfires burning as a decoy and moved out in two columns. The strongest were placed in the fore to cut a path through the snow in order to make it easier going for the weaker men. They eventually came upon the Armenians' camp, which had moved into a forest to shelter them from the storm. The snow took down many trees. One fell in the distance, as they surprised the enemy. The engagement was fierce, yet brief, as many Armenians felt the iron points of the Greeks, while Tiribazus and only a few of his fortunate men were able to flee.

They camped there on the spot, stealing the satrap's personal property. When the Ten Thousand woke the next morning, their bodies were entombed in snow and ice. Most of the men dug themselves out and fought to a stand, only to find that so much snow had fallen in the night that it reached their waists. The freezing cold burned them. Many others refused to get up, claiming they couldn't. So Xenophon dropped his dress and started chopping wood for their fires. "It can be done!" he said.

Those who were cowering became inspired and rose to the occasion, while those who were genuinely frozen, remained down, forever. Xenophon checked on them to learn of their condition. Their fingers, toes and noses had turned black. A few had succumbed so rapidly to the elements that their extremities had fractured. There was no saving them. So regrettably, the men ended their suffering.

The Ten Thousand weren't able to offer their brothers a proper burial either. They left them in their icy tombs, and with sorrow filled hearts, they pushed west into another snowstorm. The men were getting battered. Many in the rear of their double column lost their will to fight. They wanted to die. They just couldn't take the suffering any longer. When this was reported to Xenophon, he dropped out of file and approached his discouraged troops. They were scattered along the trail, leaning against one another as vicious winds whipped the snow every which way.

"On your feet!" he screamed over the howling wind.

The men remained huddling together on the ground and said nothing.

"Don't you want to see your families again?" Xenophon yelled.

"I can't do it anymore!" one man said. "Leave me be!"

"You will die if I let you be. I did not give you the order to die. Your generals and army need you. Get on your feet, now! That's an order!"

They still refused, and Xenophon knew he couldn't linger much longer, or he too would perish. He felt they had come too far to give up, and he wasn't going to leave them behind like the others. In desperation, he grabbed the closest one with his bare hands and jerked him to a stand. Xenophon held him in place and punched him square in the jaw. His hand hurt like hell. "You will address me as general, sir!" he thundered, and punched him again. "If I give you an order, you will obey!" he shouted in rage, and then he shoved him in the direction of the army. "Get moving!"

The man obeyed.

Xenophon turned to the others, who looked warily at him. "What are you waiting for? Or should I put a beating on you too?"

"I'm sorry, general," one of them said, as they fought to a stand and rejoined the column.

Xenophon trekked farther back, finding more and more who had lost heart. He demanded obedience from them all, until he came upon those, who he could not save. It devastated him, but there was no time to dwell on it. He ran back to the rear of the column to ensure the troops remained in file and continued west.

Then came the sun. When it hit the snow covered plains, it scorched the men's eyes. Many went blind before dusk neared, and in an act of desperation, they took their own lives. The Ten Thousand were in dismay by the time they reached the next village. They didn't know how they would be expected to carry on. But here, the Rhodians showed their ingenuity again. One of them had spent time in Egypt and he learned how to keep the sun out of his eyes. There was an oily substance, unlike olive oil, that they discovered the natives using on their bodies. It was made of lard, almond oil, sesame oil and the nectar of the pine. The natives used it to protect themselves from the bitter wind and cold, but when the Rhodians saw it, they mixed it with earth, so as to darken it to a black. The Rhodians told Xenophon to spread it across the skin just underneath the eyes, and in turn, the general ordered the army to do the same. When they proceeded the next day, they discovered that the invention actually worked, preventing further loss of sight.

Finally, they reached warmer lands, but they were without a guide and had been marching for so many days without knowing their location, the men began to speak ill of Xenophon's leadership. Xenophon immediately ordered the army to stop and he held an assembly with the other generals and captains. It was an informal gathering with all of them standing in a circle around him. Xenophon already heard their gripes on the march and responded as follows:

"Save for those who gave their lives so we could live and those who lost their will in Armenia, have I not brought us this far, free of harm?"

Chirisophos scoffed. He thought the assembly was an absolute waste of time. The other generals had no quarrel with Xenophon either, but some of the captains and their men felt otherwise.

Xenophon continued. "So tell me captains, how could I have done better? We held a vote for every decision the army needed to make. All votes had been unanimous," he said, staring at them vehemently. "I did not declare myself a general. You all voted for me as your leader, and now you turn on me and blame me for our misfortunes? Yes, we ventured far and wide, so as to avoid an all-out war with a million men on open ground. Yes, I guided you through mountains with endless fighting. Yes, we braved the fiercest cold any of us have ever felt. And here we are, one march closer to home. So why now? Why do you wait until now to speak ill of me, to tell me that others could have done better? Why did they not speak up when given the chance? Help me to understand, please."

One of the captains took a step forward. "My men don't understand how you know which direction is west to Greece and which isn't. They fear that things will only get worse."

Another captain addressed Xenophon. "My men feel the same, sir."

Then a third captain stepped forward. "My men are upset by the abuse they suffered from you in Armenia, sir."

"Your men wouldn't be alive today, if I hadn't put them to beating. They should be thanking me, not slandering me. As for our direction, I can only rely on what our guides told us in the past and what my god tells me. I have never been here. This is not where I come in the summer, nor do I go to Carduchi to relax in the winter."

The assembly laughed.

"I am doing the best I can. Now if you have anything else to say or know the shortest route home, speak now and we'll put it to a vote."

No one uttered a word.

"If you still want me to serve as your general, raise your hand."

All hands were raised at once. Chirisophos scoffed again. Xenophon was exasperated and his hatred toward democracy returned instantly. During that idle moment while he rubbed his brow to collect himself, the captains assumed the assembly had been adjourned and they began to walk back toward their men.

"Captains!"

They turned about and faced their general.

"I did not dismiss you," Xenophon said, scolding them. "Now try to keep your men alive and in line. And from this point on, use your own logic to explain what it is I do and why I do it."

"Yes, sir," the captains said obediently, while remaining at attention.

A silent, uncomfortable moment passed as Xenophon glared at them. "Dismissed."

The captains obeyed and they immediately spoke to their men, using their own logic in the best way they could to make them see reason. It worked. The troops felt terrible and they became conflicted about their unity. As the Ten Thousand proceeded west, every now and again, a trooper would break from the file and drop to the rear of the line to express their sincerest apology to Xenophon. The general was still fuming, but he found it was easier to just forgive them all, so they could keep pushing for home. However, they kept coming in. Xenophon couldn't take much more of it, mounted a horse which he retrieved from the baggage train, and reached the Spartan at the fore. "See that lake, Chirisophos?"

The Spartan nodded.

"One more stop," Xenophon said.

Chirisophos eyed him. "Be quick about it, Athenian."

When they reached the shore, Xenophon ordered the entire army to drop their dress and square the line. The trumpets sounded off and they marched directly into the lake until the rear lines were waist deep.

Xenophon was at the fore and he turned to face the men. He despised every one of them at that very moment. He thought he was better than all of them, but at the same time he needed them as much as they needed him. "I swear an oath to Zeus Savior," he said.

The men repeated. "I swear an oath to Zeus Savior."

"I will remain loyal and united to one another until we reach home."

"I will remain loyal and united to one another until we reach home."

"I will not question the leadership of the army, as I have a say in it."

"I will not question the leadership of the army, as I have a say in it."

"When I go under this water and rise, I shall be born anew."

"When I go under this water and rise, I shall be born anew."

They went under and the purification ritual unified the men. Oh, the joys of war.

# Agamemnon's Return

Agesilaos's voyage took thrice as long as it should have. As soon as the fleet sailed through the Euripus Channel and entered the Aegean, the winds died for three days. When the winds returned, they blew south and to the west, and with them came a fierce storm that threw them off course. The fleet reunited somewhere just north of Crete. The ships and their crew survived, but they were forced to row against a relentless current for the remainder of their voyage. Agesilaos blamed the Thebans the entire way.

Eventually, the army arrived in Asia Minor in the city of Ephesus, which was just east of the island of Samos. Upon their arrival, Agesilaos was still pouting over his sacrifice and his disastrous voyage, when the Asiatic Greeks flocked around Lysander instead of him. They praised Lysander for his return and prayed that he could restore order in their city. Agesilaos was by his side during this time and he went ignored by them all. The Ephesians had no idea that he was the king. Mainly, because all Spartans had such a plain dress that they all looked alike to foreigners. The other reason was due to Lysander. As the Ephesians kept coming in to greet their savior from the Great War, Agesilaos wasn't even introduced to them. He realized then, his longtime friend's true motives for returning. "Lysander wants to steal my glory!" Agesilaos thought. "He wants to feel like a king!"

Agesilaos was angered by this and felt envious by the love Lysander received, but he did keep it concealed.

Demaratos, Theras and the other knights weren't pleased with Lysander either upon landing, when he ordered them to unload the ships as he set off with the king. He was an Equal just like them. Who was he to give orders?

Agesilaos's first priority was to free the Asiatic Greek cities, but his animosity toward Lysander eventually got the better of him. Once the army's camp was set up outside Ephesus, the king held an assembly. During which, Agesilaos blatantly rejected several strategies suggested by Lysander to accomplish his aim. Lysander was quick to realize that the king was displeased with him and he knew of only one way to correct matters.

The next morning, Agesilaos paraded through the city with his knights. Their skin was oiled down and their muscles were swollen from their earlier gymnastics. They also wore garlands to present themselves as champions to the Ephesians. It had great effect. Simultaneously, Demaratos and Theras were in shock. They had never seen such a place filled with all kinds of strange looking Greeks and Persians, who lived together and had such unfamiliar accents. Lysander was close by as well. He was just down the road and chose not to join them because he was meeting with a potential candidate to replace one of the Council of Ten's members. This man was the son of one of the original ten who represented Ephesus. After speaking with him, he advised the candidate to introduce himself to Agesilaos and request the position of governor.

The candidate immediately approached the king in front of his entourage. He was a head taller than Agesilaos and bent at the knees slightly, so as to not tower over him. "King Agesilaos," he said.

The Spartans halted their parade and turned about to face him, while the king was secretly pleased that someone finally acknowledged him.

"Lysander has sent me. He said it would be advisable to request from you the position of governor that my late father once held. That is, when you kill the Great King and reappoint a new Council of Ten, kind sir."

Agesilaos eyed him scornfully. "Lysander," he thought, and then he addressed the Ephesian. "There will be no council."

"But, sir? Lysander sai—"

Agesilaos tilted his head, silencing him, as he wondered why he thought Lysander's word was law. The Equals backed their king up by glaring at him, hard. The candidate noted their powerful bodies, which were chiseled to perfection, before he met their cold, piercing eyes. He remained silent for a brief moment and then he fearfully fled back to Lysander.

When Lysander heard what happened, he caught up to the king and walked by his side.

"Good of you to join us, Lysander," Agesilaos said sarcastically.

"My king," Lysander responded condescendingly.

They didn't speak another word, and as they continued their parade in an effort to spread the idea of freedom from Persian rule, a stranger, on his own accord, approached Agesilaos.

"King Agesilaos," the stranger said humbly.

The king stopped and faced him.

"My name is Antipatros, son of Nikandros. I wondered if I may be considered for the role of governor, when you kill Artaxerxes, my king?"

"Yes, you may be considered," Agesilaos said without questioning his experience.

Antipatros smiled. "Thank you, my king," he said, and bowed before running off to tell his peers.

Then Agesilaos shifted his gaze to catch a glimpse of Lysander's reaction as they resumed walking. Lysander looked straight ahead, clenching his jaw, while attempting to contain his anger. The king grinned as his eyes returned forward, but as they made their way through the city, great herds of Ephesians continued to flock around Lysander.

By dusk, they returned to camp to have their evening meal at the mess and Agesilaos was now at his wit's end with Lysander. He thought it out carefully prior to their return and decided how best to humble the great man. The king gave his helot the evening off and appointed Lysander to be his meat carver. This deeply humiliated Lysander in front of the other Equals, but he did his best to take it in stride.

"Good evening, sirs," Lysander said comically to Demaratos and Theras, as they approached him at the carving table to get their servings of dinner. "I am Cyrus, pretender to the throne and I will be serving you a delectable lamb this night."

Demaratos and Theras wanted to laugh in his face, but they held it in, took their food, and chuckled under their breath as they sat at the king's table.

Agesilaos had always insisted that everyone else be served before him, and when it was his turn, Lysander could no longer pretend. It was just too demeaning and he lost his temper with the king. He tossed the slab down, half on the table, half on Agesilaos's dish. The Equals watched it happen and they became angry at the blatant disrespect to royalty.

"Problem, Lysander?" Agesilaos asked.

Lysander met his eyes. "I see you know how to make your friends look smaller than you."

"Yes, when they try to look greater than I," Agesilaos said.

The Equals were in awe. This had never happened in any of their histories at the messes, save for the Youths, who were learning the ways of men.

Agesilaos continued. "But if a friend contributed to *our* greatness, then I would be ashamed if I did not honor *this man*."

The king's knights remained silent, waiting for Lysander to respond. He was nearing the age of retirement, and therefore, he was at a critical juncture in his career. With the wrong response, he could easily have his citizenship stripped from him with one skytale reporting his insolence to the ephors.

"True enough," Lysander said. "Then please, send me to a post, where I may be of service to *you*, my king."

"Done."

# The Trial of Socrates

A crimson canopy shaded the agora to offer relief from the stifling heat. Underneath, the trial was underway for the Men of the Assembly and the citizens to witness. The men of the court were made up of five hundred councilmen, a herald, and five hundred one jurors who all sat in their designated seats on wooden benches. The jurymen were mainly farmers and getting paid three obols for their time. It was a day off for them. Despite the foul stench of sweat, hundreds of citizens attended. Most were there for revenge or amusement, and the rest were loyal to Socrates. Namely, Plato, Crito and Phaedo. They were deeply concerned for their friend's fate. It was the biggest court hearing since Alcibiades was ostracized from Athens. There was hardly enough room for the people to breathe, but still, they crammed into every possible hole and corner they could squeeze into. Across from the men of the court, Socrates sat all alone. He watched as the water clock began pouring from a spout on the bottom of one amphora and fed into the mouth of a second one, which was offset directly below. He had until the water stopped. The herald had already cross examined Socrates and Meletus at the start of the trial. Then, Meletus, the accuser was given his turn to speak. The sun was now at its zenith and it was time for the old philosopher to defend himself.

"I will not try to prove or disprove my innocence or guilt, but I will speak the truth so that you can understand for yourself if I am guilty or innocent of the charges brought against me," Socrates said, as he began. "But I shall warn you my jurymen, councilmen and my fellow Athenians, I have been told that I can make the weaker argument defeat the stronger. That I am wiser than you. That I speak to gods Athens does not recognize. And that I have corrupted the minds of our youth. I shall attempt to dispel all of these notions. Please be patient and do not interrupt, as I must try to undo many years of slander against me in the short amount of time that I have been given."

Socrates looked at the men of the court and all the spectators. He glimpsed Plato, Crito and Phaedo sitting together. His ancient eyes continued to search and he noticed many more who used to be his friend. They scowled at him or looked away from him when he met their eyes. Then he glanced at the water clock steadily trickling and knew that he still had time.

"Allow me to start from the beginning and explain how I believe I got my reputation for being *the wisest man*. I shall call to witness the most sacred authority and that is the god at Delphi. On that day, when we all heard that the Oracle said that there were none wiser than myself, I did not understand what Apollo meant. What did the god mean by this? I have never claimed such a thing. I have only had an interest in spreading moral goodness and discovering the truth in all matters. So I went around, as if Herakles was performing his twelve labors if you will. And I went and spoke to a man. He was a sophist, like I, but he claimed to have incredible wisdom. I am supposed to be the wisest of men, but here is a man who claims to be wiser than I am. How could this be? What was the god telling me? This sophist is also a member of the Assembly with many more pupils than I, and he sits with you now. But I will refrain from mentioning his name because he knows who he is."

A member of the Assembly attending the trial discreetly lowered his gaze.

"After speaking to him, I discovered through my assertion of reason and logic that he was not very wise at all. I attempted to show him that he only thought he was wise, when he really was not. This man did not like this, I assure you. He and most of you here today resent me for the very same thing. In fact, after speaking to his pupils, I came to the conclusion that *they* were really the wiser. I did not finish my labor there though. I found more so-called *wise men*, which resulted in the same conclusion. Now, they too resent me. So I went and spoke to many others of different trades. I found that poets and seers are really the same," Socrates said, meeting Meletus's eyes. "Their words come from a divine inspiration, but they know not what they speak or what it means. Ask them for yourself to explain what they have just said in a poem or prophecy and they cannot. Now, they too resent me." Socrates turned back to the jury. "Lastly, I approached several craftsmen with different skills and found they knew many more things than I. So I thought about this with reason and logic, and I said to myself, if I were the wisest of men, how could I not know how to craft a chair from wood or know what kind of tree is best suited to be crafted into the chair?"

Socrates's supporters and the citizens laughed, as the Men of the Council and the Men of the Assembly grew wave like scowls across their brows. They were in no mood for jokes. These men wanted Socrates gone, legally, no matter how painful the day might prove to be.

Socrates continued. "So after puzzling through these conversations and it did take some time, mind you. I came to the conclusion that the god has claimed that I am the wisest because I have realized, in respect to wisdom, that we are all ignoramuses!"

More laughter erupted, but the men of the court were becoming increasingly annoyed. They sneered and whispered to one another. The scorching heat and smell of the agora weren't helping either.

"To prove this point further, gentlemen," Socrates said, as he waited for the court to settle down. "As with any question put to the Oracle, when has the god ever spoken directly? In all of our histories, the god has always spoken in riddles, has he not? So only now because it suits your cause to punish me to the fullest extent of the law, so I imagine, do you take Apollo's words in vain and accuse me of heresy!"

Plato hung his head in his hands.

The Council's frustration peaked because Socrates wasn't going to bend to their ways like all those before, who have stood where he stands now. Socrates was going to fight.

"Do not mock the court, Socrates," the herald commanded, after many of the councilmen complained.

"I assure you I am taking this with the utmost seriousness. However, do not expect me to tear and grovel like so many of the accused before me. I will not. I am here to speak the truth. Now, I would like to proceed to the crimes that Meletus has brought against me before my time runs out."

"Very well," the herald said.

"So after going around and speaking to everyone to see who was wiser, they or myself, I realized their hatred of me was the cause of my unpopularity and this is why I sit here today. However, it would have been heresy if I ignored what the god had said and not asserted myself to find the truth in Apollo's words. Then, you who were once my friends might still be my friends. As well, Meletus would not have charged me with the crimes he says I am guilty of, and all of you would actually be guilty of heresy for not upholding the law because I ignored the god's word."

The men of the court became outraged and appalled, but most of all, they were speechless. His blunt arguments had never been dared before in court.

Plato hung his head a second time. "He's going to get himself killed," he said, while Crito put a comforting arm around him and another around Phaedo.

The councilmen, including Meletus and all the others who wanted to get rid of the old man, needed to see the proceedings through with all the proper formalities. It was imperative, so they would appear just in the eyes of the people, but their plan was hardly following its predetermined course because Socrates, well, was Socrates.

The philosopher observed the trickling water and then he continued. "I see by the expressions on your faces, that I speak the truth because I have not offered you high praise. Only guilty men do that and then you let them go free, despite them being accused of serious crimes, such as murder." Socrates turned to the jury. "Jurymen, look at Meletus. He is the angriest of all. He says I have corrupted the minds of the youth. But I say Meletus is guilty of treating serious matters lightly and insignificant matters harshly. I shall prove it. Meletus brings people to trial on frivolous grounds for the inconsequential, which he has never claimed in the past to have a deep interest in, such as myself. Simultaneously, he does not bother with important matters of the state that he speaks so passionately about in front of the people." Socrates turned from the jurymen to his accuser. "Meletus, you would regard it as a very pressing matter to expose our young people to the best possible influence, would you not?"

Meletus wasn't expecting to be singled out, but he should have been. He stood from his seat and waited as all eyes focused on him. He told himself that he couldn't lose this time to Socrates in a debate, and answered, "Of course I do."

"Well, who are they? Who should fathers send their sons to for a proper education?"

Meletus opened his aquiline mouth to speak, but nothing came out.

"You see. His tongue is tied. He does not know who would best teach our young because he has no interest in such a pressing matter, which affects the state."

"The law!" Meletus slipped in.

"The law is not a *person*, Meletus. Tell me what *person* is qualified to teach our young Athenians, so they may benefit from this man. Since you care so greatly, you should know of them."

Meletus hesitated. He felt like he was the one being accused of a crime.

"Allow me to assist you," Socrates said. "Would the jury be worthy of educating our young?"

"Yes," Meletus said quickly.

"Just certain jurymen or all of them?"

"All of them."

"What about the citizens who join us today?"

"Yes, they too."

"And the Men of the Assembly?"

"Most certainly."

"So all the members of the Council as well?" Socrates asked.

"Yes, that is correct," Meletus said.

"Then all of Athens, save for myself, is worthy of educating the young?"

"Yes," Meletus said emphatically.

"Well, how fortunate we all are to have so many outstanding teachers for our young. Athens is in no short supply then," Socrates joked. "But if that is true, let us take the example of horses. If you owned a horse, would you want it to be the swiftest, strongest, most obedient horse it could be?"

"Yes, I would," Meletus said.

"So who would train that horse? Yourself? The jurymen? The Council? What about your wife or daughter?"

Only the spectators laughed at that last question.

"Neither, I would send the horse to the finest horse trainer I could afford," Meletus said.

"Precisely!" Socrates said. "So what is the difference between educating a horse or our young? Don't they both require someone knowledgeable, someone who has experience and proven themselves in the past to be worthy of such a skill?"

Meletus didn't answer.

"I'll answer for you, Meletus, even though the law requires that you do answer my question. Of course they both require a particular set of skills, which not everyone in Athens possesses. Now, I am sure you can all gather by now that I am innocent and that Meletus has a personal grievance with me. In such a case—"

"I object! This is an outrage!" Meletus shouted, interrupting Socrates.

"I object to you and this whole tribunal, and demand order! It is my turn by law to speak!" Socrates shouted back, and then he glanced at the water which still flowed. Then he observed the citizens, Men of the Assembly, jurymen and Council. His enemies were vexed and they began to scoff at the whole affair. The citizens seemed to be enjoying every bit of the proceedings and passed on what had just transpired to those behind them, who couldn't hear or see the trial. Meanwhile, Plato could hardly sit still, while Meletus was rubbing his brow to relieve the pain emanating within his crown. Socrates's mind however was still spinning, and after a brief moment, he finished thinking through his final comment. If only the water holds, he thought, and then he resumed. "I will continue to prove my innocence for Meletus's sake. He is either slow to learn or his arrogance won't allow him to dismiss these flippant charges. In either case, I will also continue not only for him, but for all of you because I am sure there is nothing more dangerous than this old man that sits before you." Socrates looked at Meletus. "Meletus, is it true that evil men are a bad influence on their associates and good men are a good influence on theirs?"

Meletus was so angry he refused to participate.

"Come now, wise sir. It isn't a difficult question," Socrates said.

"Yes, it is true, Socrates," Meletus grumbled.

"Would anyone, save the mad, prefer to be abused rather than benefited?"

Meletus went mute again. He couldn't believe the trial was going so horribly wrong. It was turning out to be a real debacle. Aristophanes, the playwright, couldn't have thought of this one, he thought.

"The law commands you to answer," Socrates said.

"No," Meletus replied.

"Then what are you saying? Are you saying that all of my pupils, the hundreds of men and young men who have at one time or another associated themselves with me, have done so because they enjoyed being abused?"

Meletus didn't respond.

"Well, tell me this. Do you believe I corrupt the young intentionally or unintentionally, Meletus?"

"Intentionally," he groaned.

"How, can you be so much wiser than I, when I have lived twice as long as you? You have already stated that everyone would prefer to be benefited by those they associate themselves with rather than abused. You also stated that I intentionally corrupt the young. So what you are really saying is that people don't like to be abused so they choose for themselves to follow me so that I can abuse them. That is a contradiction, Meletus."

Meletus went red in the face. "You have twisted my words, as you always do! Speak sensibly!"

"It only appears that I have twisted your words because I have exposed you as a liar. It seems possible though, and it is only theory, that some of the young boys might run off after listening to me speak and then try to model themselves after me, and in so doing, offend another person. As a result, that person then blames me for the offense, which adds to my list of enemies. So Meletus, it sounds like what you believe to be corruption of the youth is an *unintentional* act on my part. And since it is *unintentional*, and all I have done is to follow the will of my god, Apollo, who is yours and every other citizens of this city, I am not guilty of heresy or corrupting our young. But perhaps, since my conversations have *unintentionally* influenced some of the young to go get them in trouble with others, is the court any place to settle such a grievance? Could you not have pulled me aside and explained what has happened to make me aware of the situation? My eyes are wide open. They don't bulge so far from my crown for no reason."

The spectators laughed and cheered. The men of the court had already made up their minds, even though the proceedings had yet to finish, while Meletus turned away, refusing to cooperate anymore.

None of it stopped Socrates from continuing though. "The answer is yes. You could have spoken to me in the agora or in private to correct matters. So it seems that this entire day of court has been about you. You are still upset about that day when we debated in the agora, Meletus. But I assure you I meant nothing wicked toward you, as you do to me. It was as you have stated my actions to be, *unintentional*."

Socrates glanced over at the water clock. It dripped to a stop. The herald was quick to notice and he stomped his staff without hesitation to adjourn the hearing. The citizens stood and applauded the old philosopher for his profound testimony. Everyone knew he was innocent, enemies included. However, Plato and the rest of Socrates's friends were deeply concerned that the jury's vote could be swayed. Bribery plagued the court, which was why the jury was more than five hundred men strong.

∧

An amphora was passed through the jury so they could cast their vote. White stones were for innocent and black stones were for guilty. Once this was done, several of the jurymen counted them out and reported the outcome to the herald. The jurymen then took their seats and the herald stood to address the court. "Two hundred twenty-one, against. Two hundred eighty, for. Socrates has been found guilty for heresy and corruption of the youth."

Plato sunk deep into his seat. He was devastated. He knew this was going to happen. Crito looked to the heavens and said a prayer, while Phaedo wept. The Athenian citizens shouted and screamed insults at the jurymen, accusing them of being bought off for an extra obol. They challenged the Council too, demanding another vote. Then the citizens began pelting them all with volleys of olives and all order was lost.

The herald shouted, commanding order, and finally, after much time had passed, when everyone came to a relative calm, he continued. "Meletus," he said, exasperated. "What punishment do you propose for the guilty?"

Meletus stood up enthusiastically, even though he had been sitting so long he couldn't feel his rear. "I propose the punishment of death," he said with conviction.

The citizens gave more boos and threats to the men of the court.

"And Socrates, what do you propose your punishment to be?" the herald asked.

The court went silent as everyone leaned forward, unsure of what he could possibly say at such a critical juncture.

Socrates took his time before responding by taking three swallows of water to cool his throat. "You know, I have never cared for the things that most people have cared about, like riches or titles. I mean, look at me. I do not bathe. My robes smell putrid and they are no longer their true color. Dirt covers my skin and nails. My beard is unkempt and is as old as the wind. What I am saying, is that I have been reduced to poverty by serving my god. So if I could pay a small fine and be done with it, so as to get back to my labor, I would. However, I do not have the means. Having said that, I do believe the punishment must fit the crime, and please keep in mind jurymen, that my accusers give you the impression that they are devout and wise through their dress and oaths, while I speak the truth and give you reality. They are well fed and I am not. Take a look at them and then at me, and you will see that I speak the truth. So as for my punishment, I would suggest…"

The entire court looked on in anticipation.

"Free dinners for the rest of my life."

Phaedo fainted, as the citizens around him applauded louder and bolder than they had all day. Crito clutched his chest, which was squeezing him, while Plato took his turn to say a prayer. The councilmen, herald, Men of the Assembly and jurors were left with their mouths agape. The entire court was in disbelief.

∧

After the jury had voted again, a juryman whispered the outcome of the vote to the herald and he returned to his seat. Then, the herald signaled for the court's attention with his hands to conclude the brief recess. "Gentlemen, your attention please!" he announced. "As for the punishment of Socrates…Three hundred sixty in favor of Meletus. One hundred forty-one in favor of Socrates."

The crowd roared and thundered against the outcome. They wondered how the guilty verdict could have been so close and this vote was so extreme.

The herald continued as he shouted above the din. "Socrates, you are hereby condemned to death! However, in light that this day is the second day of the Mission to Delos, we shall delay the execution until the ceremony concludes! Guards, escort the prisoner back to his confines, where he will remain, until his execution!"

The screaming of insults and threats to Meletus and the jury reached new heights. During which, Socrates stood. He was feeling detached from his beloved city as he glanced across the court. The councilmen and Men of the Assembly smiled and joked as they were relieved it was finally over. He also noticed many hands reaching out to shake Meletus's hand. To Socrates's other side, Plato, Crito and Phaedo stood together, silently meeting his eyes. The old philosopher winked at them to try and ease their aching hearts as two armed hoplites approached to take him away. "Hello, gentlemen. How does it feel to condemn a man to death on such a blessed day? Fear not, I am not claiming you are heretics," he said sarcastically.

The hoplites stared at each other. They were unsure if they were being insulted and then they placed him in irons. Each guard then held Socrates by one of his arms and they made for their leave.

On his way out, the philosopher looked across the court at his accuser. "Off I go, Meletus! You to live and I to die! Who knows which is the better, *but our gods*!"

# Cynisca

The green hills of Olympia hosted all of Greece during this year's Olympics. Thanks to Agis, Sparta was competing and they were expected to be victorious over all. During this religious festival, which was dedicated to Zeus and a time when all of Greece swears an oath of peace, the Eleans maintained their animosity toward the Spartans, but they were not as discontent as those competing in the four horse chariot race. While women were forbidden to compete in any event, this year, for the first time in Olympic history, there was a woman managing Sparta's chariot team.

It took Cynisca little time to figure out her purpose in life. Most Spartan women were concerned with raising the finest sons for war and the healthiest daughters, who would in turn provide future sons. However, Cynisca had no daughters, her two sons died in the agoge just three years past, and her husband fell during the Great War. She was also at the age where it was suicide to try and bear another child. It had been done, but most women and their newborns did not survive the birth. Agesilaos foresaw this gap in her life and she loved him for it. When she spoke with her brother last, she told him about her plans for the Olympics. He dared her to do so, claiming it was not a matter of manly skill for such an event, but a matter of means. She disagreed, stating it took wit and talent, and vowed to win. And so, the friendly wager was on.

Cynisca manipulated the finest craftsman in Laconia. He was perioeci. The perioeci dwelled throughout the southern Peloponnese. They were free, so long as they served in war and followed Spartan law. This man was to handle the cost of providing and building a worthy chariot, and in return, because she wanted a competitive rider, she allowed him to provide his son.

Cynisca knew nothing of chariot racing, but she was strong-minded, unwavering and pushed herself to learn as she went. When they first began their training, the rider couldn't tolerate her ignorance of the sport or her relentless training methods. Nor could he do anything about it. They went day and night. She demanded obedience from him and forced him to be as strong as any Equal. The craftsman's son was sent to the athlitika. He didn't see the relation, if all he had to do was stand in the car and crack his whip. But Cynisca was certain it could only help, she just didn't know why, not yet. Cynisca required obedience from her horses too. They were taught one word commands, which were reinforced with a whip and she ran them into exhaustion nearly every day.

It seemed at first that she was the only one who was going to survive the grueling regiment she demanded. As time went on though, she understood the concept of the sport entirely. She knew where and how the rider must be positioned on the car to gain speed, slow or turn. She learned that the wheels on her chariot would snap, if the rider was not balanced correctly on a turn when going at an all-out pace. He was thrown to the ground many times until she understood that concept. There were many other aspects of the sport like this that she taught herself. She also gained an in depth knowledge of horses, as she had run several of them into the ground. They never stood again. It was almost as if the horses taught her the correct and incorrect ways of racing because the sport revolved around their natural abilities. She ended up studying them at all times of the day, whether training or not, and she decided what they really needed was a Spartan's edge. Cynisca forced them to run individually, while pulling a sled twice the weight of the chariot and rider. The craftsman's son too, finally saw her logic behind the gymnastics regime he was ordered to follow. The lighter and more stable the load, the faster the horses could go. Simply put, after all their training together, Cynisca and her rider finally respected one another, despite it being a tyrant-slave relationship. As well, her horses knew who their master was. Cynisca was the only one they allowed to stroke their manes or feed them by hand without getting bit.

With their training complete and the games about to commence, they ventured to Olympia with the other Spartan competitors. All odds were against them, but she did qualify for the championship round of the four horse chariot race.

The course consisted of four turns with a furlong between them, which the riders had to go around twice. The men, spectating and competing, all taunted and insulted Cynisca for being a woman during the entire three days leading up to the final event. Least to say, Cynisca handled herself with Spartan grace. It was a good thing too that everyone attending swore an oath of peace or the Spartans would have dispatched those who had disrespected their king's sister. The men had acted like pigs and called her a thigh flasher because her customary Spartan tunic revealed her upper legs. Sometimes so much so, that depending on her movements, one could catch glimpses of her sex. One of them even made an indecent advance by grabbing her rear and she backhanded him across the face. The man buckled to the ground, more out of surprise than from pain though. The crowd laughed, finding it all amusing, but he was the last one to try that foolishness again. Others say she wanted to be a man instead of a woman due to her desire to compete. She ignored their words because she came from the Five Villages. She was spawned from kings and champions, and those who spoke Laconically. "By the gods, who do these pathetic wretches think they are?" she thought.

Finally, the event began and she peered on from the side of the dirt covered *stadion* inside of the *hippodrome*. The race was evenly matched as they approached the third turn. Then Cynisca's team fell behind, while the Thebans and Athenians pushed their mounts faster. Cynisca prepared her rider for this with mock races. He learned from her training methods that horses loved to compete.

"Let them yearn for it," she told him.

After the fifth turn, her horses became hungry for victory. Her rider sensed it as he loosened the reins and snapped his whip three times in succession. The horses quickened their stride, going faster, while they left those who trailed them in the dust. The crowd watched with the utmost intensity, cheering for their favorites, but when Cynisca's team passed both the Athenian and Theban racers by splitting them down the middle, they jeered and hissed. The Spartan chariot reached the seventh turn before anyone had reached the sixth. Her horses kept running faster and harder. The crowd fell silent. They were in awe. Never before had they seen or even dreamed a horse, let alone four of them, could go so long at such a pace. Her rider passed through the eighth turn and finished in first, nearly nipping the racer in last place with the end of his whip for fun. Cynisca raised her hand up and shouted, "Nike!"

Everyone heard her call to the goddess of victory, but only a small number of people cheered for her. They were Spartans, who weren't competing at the moment and wives of the pigheaded men, who were now eating their words. As for the women, she was their new hero. They hoped Cynisca's victory was going to give them more liberties when they returned home, like the Spartan women have had all their lives. Down on the stadion, the Athenian and Theban racers were so devastated by the loss that they took their own lives. They just could not bear the shame of losing to a woman.

The Olympics ended this day and the victors were gathered in front of the Wall of Champions during the closing ceremony. Many of them were Spartans, including Cynisca, who stood proudly alongside them as they waited to be honored with the prized olive wreath. The high priest of Olympia stepped to her last, and after she was crowned, Cynisca turned and faced the multitude of people attending.

"My fathers and brothers were Spartan kings! I have won with a team of fast-footed horses, and now I have this monument to honor my victory!" she announced and motioned toward the engraving on the wall.

The people were humbled, as she proceeded down the stone steps, which led to the main grounds. She was followed by her fellow Equals, and lastly, her rider. The throng moved aside to allow her to pass. She strutted through, triumphantly with her head held high. After she had gone, the people looked back toward the Wall of Champions. The monument read as follows:

*I say, I am the only woman in all Greece,*
*To have won this wreath.*

# BOOK IV
## THE ART OF DECEPTION

*A Spartan king agreed to a truce with his enemy. Soon after, oaths were broken and war resumed. Then, much later in life, the king saw his enemy whom he had negotiated the truce with. They were now allies and very much friends.*

*"But you did agree to the truce that day long ago," the man said to the king. "You did agree," he insisted.*

*"Yes, by Zeus I did, if it was right to. If not, and though I spoke the words, I did not," the king said.*

*The man took the king's meaning and grinned. "But surely kings should do as they please with just a nod of their head."*

*The king offered his friend a cunning grin and a nod in return. "No more so than those who approach kings should make proper requests that are appropriate to kings."*

# The Last Conversation

Save for the flicker of a small candle, it was dark, dismal and wet with rainwater, which drained off the filthy road. The smell was putrid from human waste. Flies and maggots accumulated in the corner by the piss pot. A rat would squeal in passing every now and again. Above, a circular grate at ground level was the only entrance to the underground cell, which the philosopher was confined to. Here, under the agora, Socrates sat in a rickety old wooden chair, as if he was at home, perfectly content. He was in deep thought, when the iron bars above opened and a knotted rope ladder was lowered down. The sun shined through, forcing him to squint as Plato and Crito came to visit him. It had been nearly thirty days since he last saw them at the trial.

Plato set his feet on the rank stone ground, making a subtle splash in a shallow puddle. Then he held the end of the ladder steady for Crito, who was nearly as old as the master philosopher.

"Plato, Crito!" Socrates said with enthusiasm. "Welcome to my new home! If you're envious, it will be vacant soon, I can assure you!" he joked, as his words bounced off the slimy walls.

Once Crito made it down, his face twitched from the malodorous air. He did not even offer Socrates a smile. He only expressed an extreme sense of urgency.

Socrates looked from Crito to Plato, noticing he wasn't in the mood for wit or humor either.

"We have paid the guards off. It is time to go," Plato said with the utmost seriousness.

"Where is it that we are going, that you would have to pay the guards?" Socrates asked.

"To escape this madness!" Plato replied.

"Oh, I see. And then what? Flee Athens? Live in hiding, only to be hunted down like some criminal? All that would do is deceive the principles by which I live. No, I will not escape fate. I am perfectly content, right where I am," Socrates said.

Plato was dumbfounded. "But you cannot stay he—"

Crito stepped forward, motioning for Plato to calm himself. "Socrates, we thought that you would take this opportunity to leave your confines, to perhaps, visit your wife and children one last time."

"And then you would escort me back to prison?" Socrates asked.

"Yes," Crito said hesitantly. "If that is what you want."

"Well that would defeat the purpose of my stay. If one could actually come and go from prison when they pleased, it would not be called prison."

Plato anxiously pulled out some bread, wine and water he held in a sack. "Here, eat and drink something. You are obviously not thinking rationally."

"Thank you, Plato," Socrates said, as he accepted the items. "I will be sure to enjoy this after our conversation."

"We have gone to a lot of trouble to free you, Socrates. Why do you think it has taken us so long to come and see you? Please, come with us," Plato begged.

"The last thing I would want to do is trouble my friends. So please come back and visit when it is better for you," Socrates insisted.

"But what of your children?" Plato shouted in frustration.

"I'm sorry, Plato, Crito, but my escape will disprove all that I stand for, which are the—"

"Principles of moral goodness and piety," Crito and Plato said redundantly.

"Exactly," Socrates said. "As for my children, they look to me as their teacher. My escape would only set a bad example for them. And so my death, will be the greatest lesson of all. You will see how Athens gains from it. My wife, well, I'm sure she will get over it. She is much younger and prettier than I, and can marry another. And we all know what a trying husband I have been," Socrates said with a warm smile, as he met their eyes.

Water pooled and dripped down their faces. They were grieved by his stubborn, yet relaxed disposition.

"What? Does my death unsettle you?" Socrates inquired.

"You know it does, you old fool!" Plato exclaimed. "They have been celebrating the Mission of Delos for the entire cycle of the moon. This is the longest they have ever celebrated it. The entire city is gone! They don't want to kill you! The Council, the Assembly, the executioners, the people, your friends, family…By the gods! Everyone, save Meletus, wants you to escape!" Plato was sweaty, winded and red in the face from his rant as he gazed at his unmoved teacher. He immediately realized that he could not persuade him. So he turned about and rudely brushed past Crito on his way out of the cell.

Crito glanced from Plato leaving back to Socrates. "Please, think it over. There is still time," he said gently.

Socrates looked at him plainly. "Same time tomorrow?"

Crito was devastated. "Yes Socrates, same time tomorrow."

∧

The ship honoring the ancient King Theseus returned from Delos at dawn and Socrates's execution was ordered. His closest friends were gathered. His wife Xanthippe and their sons had just left the execution chamber. The farewell was difficult for them. The chamber they left him in was just a larger cell, which was above ground in the southern part of the agora and away from all the trade and politics. Apollodorus, who did not have the stomach to watch Socrates's trial, arrived last. He wept upon entering. Socrates rolled his eyes at the sight of him and then he looked to Crito. "Where is Plato?" he asked.

Crito struggled to look him in the eye. "He is...feeling ill, Socrates."

"I see. Do tell him, that I hope he feels better."

"Yes, of course," Crito said.

His friends, twelve in all, stood staring at him and then they slowly began conversing. They discussed the relationship of the body and soul, the immorality of the soul, and the heavens in great length. It was interrupted with intermittent laughs and tears. They experienced both pain and joy, and through their exploratory conversation, Socrates proved that an unexamined life was a wasted life. When they had finished, Socrates glanced at the setting sun through the iron barred window. "Well, let's get on with it."

His friends hesitated, desiring more time with him.

"Crito," Socrates said. "Has the poison been prepared? If so, bring it in so I can have a taste."

"But you have until night and it is barely dusk," Crito said.

"What is the point of holding on to life for a few moments longer?" Socrates questioned.

"I refuse to go down that road with you," Crito said, holding back his tears.

"Well don't fuss about then, and do a favor for an old friend."

Crito snapped his fingers at his servant, who was outside the cell. The slave retrieved the executioner, who in turn, brought Socrates the cup of hemlock.

Socrates accepted it with an unusual cheerfulness. "Would it be inappropriate to pour a libation to the gods?" he asked the executioner.

"Best not waste any," the executioner said.

"I see," Socrates commented, realizing it may not work otherwise.

His friends couldn't believe that he was so relaxed, while they were so distraught.

"To city's orders!" Socrates said, as he raised the cup to honor Athens. Then he drank the hemlock in a single swallow. The philosopher had done it, and there was no going back.

Phaedo, Crito, Apollodorus and all the others broke into uncontrollable tears.

"Really, my friends! This is why the women are gone!" Socrates said sarcastically.

They composed themselves as best they could and watched Socrates stand up and pace around. He was previously instructed to do so, in order to move the poison evenly throughout his body.

"That should do," he said, and then he laid in the bed prepared for him.

His friends looked on with heavy hearts, admiring him, while he remained calm and courageous.

"You are an amazing man, Socrates," Phaedo said.

"Yes, I have been told that, but I don't know why," he said, turning their misty eyes into water. "Mm, I'm feeling a bit cold, nor can I feel my legs."

At that moment, Apollodorus broke into tears and stormed out of the cell. His friends called him back, but he just waved them off. He didn't have the strength. He truly loved the old man.

Socrates rolled his eyes again at Apollodorus and then he looked to his friends. "If anyone sees Xenophon, tell him I said goodbye."

"Yes, Socrates," Crito said with a sniffle. "Anything else?"

"Offer a cock to Asclepius, would you?" he added.

Crito was dumbstruck. "What?" he asked, and then he leaned over his friend, hoping for a response. "Socrates. Socrates," Crito called out. "What has the god cured you of?"

Socrates peered into Crito's eyes, penetrating his soul. The old philosopher's mind still labored. Then his eyes bulged from his crown and they settled back in. A warm, rosy cheeked smile followed, and at last, his eyes went dim.

# The Sea

The Ten Thousand pushed westward, entering the mountainous realm of the Taochi. Once again, they were in dire need of provisions. It had been two days since their last meal and they savored every sip of water rationed out to them. According to their Armenian guide, the Taochi worshipped the sun and the eagle, and they lived in great nests upon the mountain peaks. Soon enough, they came across one of these fortifications. It was as strange as their guide had said. It occupied the peak on very steep ground with no surrounding village.

Chirisophos took it upon himself to ascend the height with a sortie and search the stronghold for food. When they reached the nest, it was eerily quiet. Chirisophos ignored his fear of what may or may not be lurking inside, while he examined the threads of pine, which twined around in a circular mass and were bound with a stone mortar. There did not seem to be any direct way in. However, he did spot smoke funneling through the top of the nest in a perfect stream, as it was taken by the North Wind. There must be food, he thought, and then he peered through the crevices of the shelter. It was extremely dark, save for the orange glow of a cooking fire, which enabled him to glimpse many shadowy figures staring back at him. They had strange beady eyes, which seemed to gawk at him. Nor did they utter a word. He strained his eyes further, and to his surprise, he saw several cows and goats among them.

"We come in peace," Chirisophos said. "We only require food and water."

The Taochi did not respond.

"We only require food and water. Do you understand? We are starving! Please!" Chirisophos pleaded, and still, he received no response. His hunger drove him mad and he led an attack. It was brief, as it quickly proved futile.

There was only one side they could attempt to breach because the nest bordered three edges of the peak. Their weapons had little effect on it and nor did they want to defend themselves in an engagement in such a tight spot. It was certain death if you fell, and where the sortie stood, could maybe host ten wagons or perhaps fifty men crammed together. So they yielded in frustration, realizing the fortification was impenetrable. Chirisophos sighed. Then he took one last look at the giant nest and cursed as he tried to pull a pine out of the weave in anger. Again, it was futile.

The Spartan was vexed. He ordered the sortie to return to the army. On their way down the mountain, which was the only scalable side, the Taochi hauled a wagon out and dumped its load over the edge. Great masses of stones descended on the sortie, from rocks to small boulders. Not only that, their route of escape was covered with large pines. The Greeks scurried behind them to use as their defense. Three however, did not have Fortune on their side. One had his ribs broken after a stone pelted him in the back. The stone was only the catalyst though. When it hit him, he lost his footing and tumbled down, until a tree broke his fall. His midsection took the brunt of the impact, as his limbs wrapped around the trunk. The other two had their legs crushed from a single boulder, which rolled right over them, one and then the other. When the danger cleared, the sortie carried the wounded back to the army's position and reported their findings.

"We need that food!" Xenophon said in anger. He was starving and tired, just like everyone else. "All right, this is what I propose," he said, gathering himself. "Since they are atop a mountain with a deathly drop on nearly every side, it would be unwise to risk an engagement in such a confined place, as you have said Chirisophos. Especially, so close to heaven and the gods. We must prove to them that we mean them no harm and only want their food. To do this, myself, Chirisophos and another group of volunteers will approach as close as we can to the nest, while remaining clear of danger."

"But they will throw a great many stones down on us." Chirisophos insisted.

"Let them. Once we take the high position that is just out of their range. One or two of us will leap forward as if we're to make our move, but we won't. As soon as the Taochi dump their stones, our men will run back to us where it is safe. We shall do this until they've run out of their defenses. Are we in agreement?"

The captains and generals all raised their hands. The vote was unanimous and so they went about it. The volunteers ended their climb just short of the peak, where it was covered in pines, and they kept their eyes fixed above on the nest.

"I just want to go home," one of the men whined.

"Shut your cheese hole!" Chirisophos said, and then he looked at another volunteer. "Callimachus, get to it," he ordered.

Callimachus was a bit older than Xenophon. He was from Parrhasia, some hole in the south of Arcadia. He was good natured and he had a competitive streak about him. Back home, the

Arcadians and Spartans were fierce rivals, since the kings of old, but he enjoyed having Chirisophos as his superior. He found the Spartan inspiring and he thought their situation was comical, because if they were together in any other place than this, they would be reaching for the other's throat. He figured that it was just the nature of man to survive by any means necessary, so he had no quarrel with obeying his Spartan general.

Callimachus was to lead the men in another foolish risk, which seemed completely ordinary to him. He dashed seven paces out and looked above. The Taochi had already rolled out another wagon full of stones. The first wagon they emptied had already been moved to the farthest possible edge, opposite their nest and turned on its side to act as a defensive wall. When they dumped the second load, his eyes bulged at the terrifying and thunderous mass aiming to kill him. Callimachus quickly leaped and dove back into hiding with a laugh. "It's working!" he said, as he rolled on to his back.

Chirisophos and Xenophon assisted Callimachus to his feet, while he waited for the danger to clear. However, this time as he was preparing to go forward, his two friends, who he met on the journey, joined him. They also had competitive ways about them. Their names were Aristonymus and Eurylochus. The former was from Lusia and the latter was from Methydria. Callimachus looked over his shoulder at them. "You're on, my friends," he said, and dashed to the other side, far below the nest and clear of where the stones would pass.

Aristonymus and Eurylochus were surprised by his daring and became determined to match it as they watched the Taochi drop three wagon loads in succession. The mountainside shook, but no one was harmed. So instead of running back for cover where the army was, Callimachus ascended to a much higher position. "I'll reach the top before you!" he yelled, taunting his friends from across the gap.

It was an act of insubordination. They disregarded their generals' orders and the three were now in a friendly, yet deadly competition to reach the top first.

Aristonymus and Eurylochus leaped forward to bait the Taochi again, but this time, they hiked straight up the mountainside rather than going all the way across as Callimachus had done. Again, three more wagon loads were tipped on their side. The stones came barreling down like an avalanche, forcing Aristonymus and Eurylochus to get clear of the danger. At that point, Callimachus realized that he would lose the race, since he was farther out than his two friends. He needed to risk his life, if he was going to win. So he dashed back across the gap in the direction of his friends as the multitude of stones rolled down above him. His friends watched in awe, as a small boulder was going to smash him. Callimachus spotted it, but he couldn't stop or he would die, so he jumped as high and as far as he could. The boulder was coming down off a bounce and rolled directly under him, grazing his feet. Callimachus got tripped up in midair and he landed hard on his side. He then regained his footing and was now directly above his friends, smiling.

The volunteers, along with Xenophon and Chirisophos, could have cared less about their insubordination and they cheered Callimachus on for such an audacious maneuver.

It spurred all three climbers to do better, and as they looked up waiting for the next load to drop, all they saw were a line of empty wagons bordering the peak. So while Callimachus caught his breath, his two friends made their move and dashed up the mountainside, weaving around the trees and rocks impeding their path. Callimachus glanced at them and then back toward the top. It seemed safe and he assumed that the Taochi must have run out of their defenses, like Xenophon had said they would.

The race was on.

They moved nimbly up the ascent, unconcerned about the danger above. All they cared about was winning. Callimachus's friends were gaining on him, when he slipped on a pile of gravel and nearly cleaved his head on a jagged tree stump. That's when Eurylochus and Aristonymus passed him. Callimachus shrugged it off, forced himself to rise, and caught them at the peak. It was a tie. All three were victors.

Suddenly, they looked at each other, remembering their orders and crept down low behind the wall of wagons. Then they peered through the cracks in the bottom of a cart and watched the mothers of the tribe toss their children and infants off the other side of the peak. Callimachus was astonished as he looked to his friends who had seen the same thing. "What are they doing? We've got to stop them!" he cried.

They wormed their way through the wagons, yelling, "Stop!"

When the mothers saw them, they panicked and they all jumped off the edge at once.

"No!" Callimachus screamed. "We mean you no harm!"

Then, the men charged out of their nest, which they defended so valiantly, and followed their wives. All three of them were in disbelief. Callimachus attempted to stand in their path in an effort to stop them, but Aristonymus yanked him back and restrained him. "Let it be, Callimachus! Let it be!"

In that moment, Eurylochus saw a prize worth taking. The man must have been the Taochi's leader. He wore a feathered garment, which was studded with all kinds of precious stones and metals. It would have been worth a fortune back home and he desperately wanted it. He dashed toward him—possessed—and grabbed the man's arm as he went over. Then he planted his feet and leaned back to anchor himself. Callimachus and Aristonymus watched Eurylochus get towed off the mountain. It all happened so fast. They ran toward the edge, and when they looked over the drop, they watched their friend plummet to his death.

"Why?" Callimachus cried. "When we have come so far!"

Aristonymus was distraught too. He hugged Callimachus as he pulled him away from the edge, while the contingent below mounted the peak. It was a terrible ending for all, but the army got the necessary provisions and moved on.

∧

They were downhearted about the whole affair, which began as a game, and continued traversing the mountain range. For six days, they encountered more Taochi, who were eager to fly like birds. On the seventh day, after summiting another mountain, a trooper at the fore of their double column was routinely marching along as he had always done, but when he glanced up at the horizon, his mouth and eyes went wide. He couldn't believe what stood before him. His body tingled with hope and then he shouted, "The sea!"

The trooper next to him was in awe and he also shouted, "The sea! The sea!"

The message was passed back all the way to the rear of the army, where Xenophon and the baggage train were. In response, everyone broke file and ran down the last Persian mountain they would ever have to descend. The men were overcome with joy. Finally, they were so close to home. Tears flooded their faces. Hugs and celebrations swept through the ranks. It was total elation. All they had to do was sail home. How long had it been? A year's time? No. More like an age, they thought, as they reached the shore.

∧

Ten thousand perplexed faces stared at the sea. Why could they see masses of land on the other side? Why was this water so dark and murky? Their spirits sank the moment they realized they had been deceived. Eventually, a Thracian man came forward and informed Xenophon and the other generals that this was not their blessed Aegean. This was the Black Sea.

# Undefeated

With great pain and determination, Xenophon was attempting to rouse the men with a dramatic oration. He was trying to convince everyone that it did not matter that they had been deceived by the sea because they had been deceived since their campaign first began. He reminded them that they were going to rid Cyrus's land of the Pisidians, which never happened. "But what did happen?" he asked them on the shore with the Black Sea to his back. "We defeated the Great King in battle!" he exclaimed. "Then what happened?" Xenophon asked them rhetorically. "Tissaphernes deceived our generals!" Then he eyed the men and he could tell that he was getting through. "And what did we do? We marched through as far east and north as the Persian Empire reaches! We have gone where no Greek has ever gone before! And we have remained, undefeated!" he screamed with all of his might.

The men shouted, as they banged spearhead to shield in a raucous.

Xenophon continued, pouring honey on top. "So it does not matter if we are not home. We can go anywhere we want! You can live here, like a king, if you so choose! By the gods, man! I might found my own city!"

At this point, the men became uncontrollable as they boasted their confidence with shouts of self-praise. Chirisophos gave the philosopher a nod for such an outstanding speech. No one else could have done it better.

"Generals!" Xenophon said. "Square your men, and let us go home!"

"Only the gods can strike us down!" one Greek yelled.

"But they won't, because they are with us!" another cried.

The Ten Thousand couldn't be contained as they fell in line and headed west—elated, injured, motivated, maimed, baggage and all.

Λ

They were so close, yet so far from home. But all they had to do, according to the Thracian, was to keep the Black Sea to their right and follow it to its end. Despite this man's savage origin, being from Thrace, where it was rumored they ate other men after killing them in battle, they trusted him, because when he said something was so, it was, and when he said something was not, it was not.

A moon went by and there were many more Persian mountains to conquer. Things proved slow and tedious. They pushed through heavy winds and miserable rains. The Black Sea seemed endless and ominous. Old worries returned. How much farther till we reach home?

Xenophon overheard their chatter and he ordered the ranks to sing the paean to occupy their minds. He was proving himself to be a marvelous general, but really, he had no other speech on hand.

Another day passed and the army came upon a river, which was necessary to cross, when they were ambushed by the Macrones. It was the paean that gave them away. The Macrones were beastly looking savages, who wore tunics made of animal fur. This tribe's weaponry consisted of the spear, axe, and shield, and they were just as good at killing as their neighbors, the ferocious Scythians. The Ten Thousand were completely surrounded on both sides of the watercourse and their baggage was cut off. Just as the skirmish was about to commence, a trooper, who was a former Athenian slave, claimed that these were his people. He knew their language, even though he hadn't spoken it in ages. He assured his countrymen that the army was not invading and just passing through. Terms of peace were met. Gifts were exchanged. Sacrifices were made and oaths were sworn to both their gods, as was the Macrones's way. After, the Macrones displayed how friendly they were by mingling within the Greek ranks as they guided them west, out of their territory. It was difficult for the Greeks to believe. Many of them hid their fear at the sight of these muscle bound, yellow toothed tribesmen, and they felt tremendous relief when they parted ways.

The Ten Thousand marched on. They remained undefeated, as they entered Trapezus and sacked every village they came upon. The harsh weather vanished and the sun showed her glorious face. Her warmth soothed the men. Everything was beautiful. Night came and they camped at an abandoned village. They were feeling so good, that they resumed their undefeated bragging rights.

"We have never lost a battle!" one man said, as they huddled by the fires.

The army shouted their war cry in response and then simmered back down.

"Undefeated!" another said.

The men responded again, bellowing their cry.

"General Xenophon, tell us of our bravery. Tell us how no man or any land in the Persian Empire can defeat us!" a trooper requested.

All nearby eyes fell on Xenophon, but he was preoccupied. He was looking straight up above the campfire, trying to figure out what was hanging overhead. "It cannot be," he thought. "Shit on Styx, it is!" He was certain of it. He looked around at the other trees and saw similar dark formations hanging. Everywhere he glanced, he saw them, hundreds of them. Then Xenophon sprang to a stand and looked at his men. "I shall tell you of something more glorious than you, something that all Greeks cherish more than women and wine!"

"What is it, general?" a man shouted from afar.

Xenophon paused and then he pointed to the trees. "Honey!"

They looked to the trees with and without the aid of torch fire. "By Zeus!" several of them shouted, and a frenzy began for their first delicacy since they left home.

Most of them used their spears to knock the hives down to the ground, while others climbed the trees to do the same. One man fell a good ways off a branch during his effort, but he was unharmed. The men watched it happen and laughed at him, as he cheered himself on. When they cut the hives open, they thought it was strange that no bees flew out to protect their nests, but they didn't bother themselves with it and extracted the comb. The troops sank their teeth into the sweet goodness, which they had long forgotten about. Honey dripped all over their faces and hands.

"It's delicious!" a man cried, eating from one hand and then the other.

Meanwhile, Ariston approached Xenophon, who was standing next to Chirisophos. The Spartan wanted no part in the festivities.

"Xenophon, share this with me," Ariston said and he extended his hand.

"Where have you been, Ariston?" Xenophon asked, as he took the piece of comb offered to him. "I feel like I haven't seen you since the last moon."

"Just keeping to myself. It helps to pass the time," he said, sounding a bit down.

Xenophon nodded and then he tried a small bite. "We are almost there. I can feel it."

"Do you really believe that?" Ariston asked, meeting his eyes.

"I do. We just have to keep safe and avoid any unnecessary calamities," Xenophon said.

"I'll see this through with you, to the end," Ariston replied, when they became distracted by the men.

All around them, the ranks began dancing and singing as if they were mad on wine.

It gave the three a laugh.

"I'm going to go get some more. Would you like some, general?" Ariston offered.

Xenophon craved more of the sweet nectar, but as he glanced at the reserved Spartan and then back at Ariston, he shook his head.

"I'll be right back, then," Ariston said with a parting glance.

Xenophon met his eyes in that moment and he sensed that his friend was not well. He watched Ariston disappear into the throng, when suddenly, a man fell where he was standing, and then another. Xenophon took notice. As he observed them closer, he saw their dance and song had become more of a stumble and slur. Nearly the entire army was moving about without any control of their limbs, and eventually, they toppled over. "What's with the men?" Xenophon asked Chirisophos, but when the Spartan turned to look at his Athenian friend, he had already fallen down.

"Xenophon!" Chirisophos exclaimed. Then he lowered down to him. Xenophon's eyes were shut and he did not move. The Spartan placed a hand over his chest and he felt several thumps in succession. "Poison," he declared bitterly. "Put the honey down!" he ordered, but it was too late. All who had a bite, had succumbed to its toxic effect. The Spartan could do nothing, except watch and pray.

Λ

Three days passed, while Chirisophos and a thousand or so others kept a careful eye on their slumbering men. All they could do, save for waiting for them to wake, was to move their cloaks and tunics away from their bodies, so as to prevent each man from spoiling his dress with his own waste. On the third night, those who woke, did, while those who didn't, remained down forever. Ariston was of the latter. Xenophon wept for him, while the rest of the army regained their strength.

The next morning, Xenophon held an assembly with the entire army. "We are morons!" he declared. "Myself included. It is senseless for us to take such foolish risks. Swear an oath! Swear an oath right now that you will use caution until we reach home! The man by your side is counting on you!"

No one spoke a word. They had all lost a friend or knew a friend that lost one. It was a horrific tragedy. They silently swore their oaths to use caution and the assembly adjourned. After they buried the men, sacrifices were made to Zeus Savior for forgiveness and to Herakles for a safe return. They didn't linger and pushed west.

They kept the Black Sea to their right for another four moons and reached Chalcedon. There was much opposition along the way, but they remained undefeated. From here, they managed to sail across a narrow channel to Byzantium, the easternmost point in Thrace—the edge of Greece. The men were beaten and battered, when they reached the Spartan garrisoned city, as their journey had finally come to an end. There were no cries of celebration, just relief. Xenophon joined Cyrus's army as a puny philosopher and he came out as a callous and brilliant war general. Word had spread to all reaches of the known world of the mighty Ten Thousand, and for the Spartans in Byzantium, their arrival provoked concern. The Spartans were outnumbered against a proven fighting force. They permitted the mercenaries to stay, but they assigned them to a separate quarter, so as to keep an eye on them. Recover and then disband was the message.

That night, the Ten Thousand celebrated their return from the depths of the underworld, while Xenophon took advantage of some time to himself. He missed Chirisophos, who did not sail with them. Since his banishment from Sparta, he swore to himself that he would never face his fellow Equals again because of his desire to return home. So he disappeared back into the vast lands of Persia. Xenophon did not know if he would ever see him again.

During his stay, he learned of Socrates's death and contemplated his return to Athens. Xenophon had mixed feelings. He broke his father's heart when he left, his mother's too. He wasn't sure if they even wanted to see him. Additionally, there was a strong chance that he had been banished from Athens and branded as a traitor for marching with Cyrus. If this was true, and he did return home, he would be put to death.

Many more days went by at the garrison, and once again, Xenophon became entranced with the Spartan way of life. He joined them daily for their morning gymnastics. For some reason, it kept reminding him of that conversation he had with Socrates, when he said that he favored Sparta over Athens for their incorruptible form of government. Xenophon laughed. He went on tour and managed to stay alive. He did not know where his life was going, but he was finally beginning to feel at peace with himself.

# Masters of War

The king deliberately lingered in Ephesus for a good deal of time, so that word would spread far and wide of the Spartans' arrival. This was a typical military strategy used by the Spartans to invoke fear in their enemy. During that period, Agesilaos reassigned Lysander to a Spartan garrison near the Hellespont. There, Lysander's hatred toward his longtime friend and the law, regarding hereditary kingship, consumed him like the plague. On this day, a Persian messenger arrived in Ephesus to see the king. He was escorted inside the Spartan camp alone. Agesilaos met with him out in the open near his thirty knights, amid their morning regime at their makeshift gymnasium. Their athlitika, sands, pitch and trek consisted of just the men on the open campground, wherever they happened to be. The only thing missing was the luxury of their machines. Not a man was clothed in the scorching sun. All of the Equals looked like lean slabs of tanned meat, while in contrast, the messenger was covered from crown to toe with several layers of silks, linens and jewelry. Among the Equals, Demaratos and Theras shouted and grunted as they challenged one another to see who could push themselves off the ground the most.

"Should we not speak in private, King Agesilaos?" the Persian messenger asked in Greek.

"I've nothing to hide. Do you?" Agesilaos countered.

The Persian was caught off guard by his blunt response. He then cleared his throat as he momentarily glanced at the nude Spartans performing their gymnastics. Fear struck him upon witnessing their powerful bodies and impressive movements. Then he turned back and nervously eyed the king. "Tissaphernes, I, I come on behalf of, Tissaphernes," he stuttered. "He demands, to know why you are here."

Agesilaos laughed. "Is that so? Tell your master, I have come to free the Asiatic Greek cities from the Persian yoke."

"I see," the messenger said routinely. He did not seem to take Agesilaos's response personally at all. Then, he fished through a leather sack on his person, which held several scrolls, and he chose what seemed to be the most appropriate one to read as a reply. "If you will agree to a truce, so that I may send to the Great King your terms, I believe you will be able to achieve your purpose and then return home." The messenger then lowered the scroll from his face after he finished reading to hear the Spartan's response.

"I did not know we were at war," Agesilaos said defiantly.

Frightened, the Persian clumsily shoved the one scroll back into his sack and feverishly searched for another.

Agesilaos rolled his eyes. "By the twin gods, find me a Persian who can take a joke," he commented, and then he spoke directly. "Tell your master, I will agree to his terms so long as I am not being deceived."

The Persian hesitated to look over and then he felt a bit of relief, when he saw that the Spartan king was not angry with him at all. "I will do so, King Agesilaos. Thank you," he said, and he gave a slight bow, which was more out of fear than respect.

Agesilaos watched him rush out of camp and then he turned around to his knights. "Did you see that pathetic sack? That is who you will be fighting!"

The Equals sounded off their war cry for their king as they continued their gymnastics.

Agesilaos then ordered Megillus, Dercylidas and Herippidas to follow the messenger without being seen. Herippidas was the ugliest Equal in the Five Villages. The only thing he could do to pretty himself was to keep his beard styled in the old fashion to compensate for his scarred, bald crown.

For two days, they remained out of sight and reached Lydia's main populace. They snatched a native while en route to translate for them, and when night came, they crept to the outside of Tissaphernes's palace. There, they spied on him for the entire night just outside of a window. They learned that Tissaphernes would be asking Artaxerxes for reinforcements to rid the Spartans from the Asiatic coast, so that he could redeem himself for letting the Ten Thousand slip through his clutches.

The knights dispatched their translator on their way back to Ephesus and left him face down in the dirt for the birds. They reported at once to Agesilaos what had occurred.

Since Agesilaos became king, he thought it was wise to conduct all his affairs out in the open, no matter who was around. This proved to his knights that he had no ulterior motives, and inadvertently, it made the Equals feel like his equal. He looked to them after they all heard the news. "We shall wait three days, and then we shall teach this Tissaphernes of war!" he said, rousing the men.

During that time, a Greek native came to the Spartan camp, hoping to get in Agesilaos's good graces. He informed him that the

Ten Thousand were going after the Great King. "By the twin gods!" he thought. "They're going to steal my glory before I ever get the chance." Agesilaos prayed for the three days to pass quickly, so he ordered his army to hold mock battles for the next two days. On the third day, after their morning gymnastics, Agesilaos gave his men the day off for rest.

As Theras walked with Demaratos back to their tent, he tried to convince him to take a short tour of Ephesus with him. The foreign land intrigued Theras and he was very eager to see more of it, while Demaratos refused to go anywhere unless it was absolutely necessary. Theodoros approached them at that moment with watered down cloths and oil, so they could clean up after their gymnastics. He was one of the freed helots enlisted in the army, but he was still required to serve Demaratos as he had always done. The Equals respected him, even through Ox's death, because he saved Cheese. Before he set sail to go on campaign, he even taught Red how to tend to Cheese's wounds to ensure his recovery.

"Thank you, Theodoros," Demaratos said, now that he was free.

Gratitude was a foreign concept to Theodoros. It struck him as odd, just to hear those two words directed at him.

"How does it feel?" Theras asked.

Theodoros looked at him questioningly.

"Your freedom," Theras added.

"Oh, no different, sir," Theodoros said like a slave, and then he dismissed himself.

The boys chuckled momentarily as they watched him leave because there really was no difference.

"Come with me," Theras asked one more time, as he finished anointing his body with oil.

"Not a chance," Demaratos said. "And you'd be wise to use caution."

Theras wasn't concerned in the slightest. He draped his crimson over his shoulders and clasped it around his front. "Suit yourself," he said, while sheathing his blade and then he departed camp.

Theras was the only one with a crimson and a muscled, bare chest as he walked through the main roads. Least to say, he did not go unnoticed during his survey of all the different merchants, who lined the city with their assorted shops. They stood, selling strange foods, clothes and other goods. There were so many of them all crammed together. It was unbelievable to him. The smells were nothing like he was used to either. Nor had he ever seen so many different shades of men. His mind spun as he took it all in, when soon enough, he found that he had entered a different quarter.

It was filthier than the others by comparison. Men were drinking hard in the day, women flaunted their bodies and children were being auctioned off as slaves at the far end. Theras realized that he should turn around and go back the other way, when two women with linen robes on, ones that you could see through, approached him. They clung to his sides, whispered in his ears, and pressed their curves against him. Their Asiatic accents made their Greek difficult for him to understand. The one lady realized this, so she spoke slower.

"I'll, give, you, pleasure," she repeated.

This time Theras clearly understood her and temptation got the better of him. That day at Pitana Grove with Eirene was all that he could think about. He hoped she would still marry him. Or, if she did get married to another by the time he returned to Sparta, perhaps her husband wouldn't mind if she gave him a son as well.

Nonetheless, he desperately wanted to couple. So he allowed the prostitutes to escort him across the road toward a brothel, when several men, who ran the dirty dealings in this quarter, surrounded him. These men embraced the Persian yoke, despite being Greek, because Tissaphernes allowed them to do as they pleased, so long as they paid their annual tribute to him. When the Council of Ten ruled, these practices had been outlawed from Ephesus. Now with the arrival of the Spartans and a bit of coin on their person, they felt their livelihood was being threatened, and they weren't willing to give it up so easy.

"You there, Spartan!" one of them said.

Theras shook the ladies of joy off of him and he defiantly stared at this man and the other six ruffians surrounding him. They all held blades or clubs.

"You pay first!" the man said to him intensely.

Theras remained silent and vigilant, as he had yet to draw his iron.

"But you have no coin, do you Spartan? Spartans don't know what coin is!" he said, and then he raised his sword. "Kill him!"

Theras drew his blade. It was short in nature and it required one to get in close. He stepped forward and blocked the sword strike from the man who insulted him. Then he kicked him with all of his might. The bottom of Theras's foot engaged the man's torso and he flew back several paces, crashing into the front of his own brothel. Theras quickly turned to his right and grunted as he extended his blade forward. It plunged through his adversary's throat. Immediately after, he spun back around to his left as one of the men charged toward him with his club held high. Theras lunged to his side, allowing him to pass and then he stuck him in his lower back.

The last three attacked Theras from behind as one. First, he shifted to the outside of the enemy on his left. Then, he grabbed him from behind and slit his throat. The man dropped. Theras moved so swiftly, the middle attacker had yet to turn and he had his spine severed. Iron penetrated all the way through his chest. At that moment, the last foe saw his opportunity to end the contest. He swung his sword across, left to right, aiming for Theras's neck. Theras pulled his sword out of the cavity, shoved the corpse forward as he dropped to a squat, and dodged the moving blade. Only a few hairs on his head got trimmed and Theras was now directly underneath the attacker at a slight angle. He rose to a stand as he drove his blade up under the man's chin. The tip of his sword poked through the top of his crown. Theras retracted the bloodied blade and let his dead enemy brush against his body as he fell to the ground. He now stood where the fight had started and faced the man who disrespected him.

His enemy stood, confident and unfazed by his fallen men, while Theras glanced around, laboring for air. He noticed more ruffians had arrived. There were about twenty-four in all and they surrounded him. So be it, he told himself. I'll take as many as I can with me.

Suddenly, one of their men jerked in his stance and blood gushed from his flaccid belly. Theras took a closer look and he saw Laconic iron extending through his foe. Then, Demaratos revealed himself by standing tall over the man's shoulder. "I changed my mind," he said to Theras, as he tossed the ruffian aside.

Theras nodded. "Glad to hear it, brother."

Demaratos screamed a murderous cry as he attacked and slew one and then another. Theras responded with a shout of his own and resumed fighting. The two budding Spartans took on the entire district of ruffians. They fought their way toward one another and pressed their backs together as they each took another life. The enemy now approached them slowly, as half their men lay strewn upon the city ground.

"The king will have our heads, if we get killed," Theras said.

"This way," Demaratos replied, as he charged through the gauntlet, taking two more down. Theras was directly behind him and they dashed out of the dirty quarter. The ruffians gave a short chase and backed off, but that didn't stop the boys from creating as much distance as possible.

When they arrived back at camp, the men were already in full kit and the line was squared, while Agesilaos was approaching the fore of the army. Demaratos and Theras grabbed their lids, eights and twenties from their tent and hustled to their positions. The king eyed them, wondering where they had been, as they tried to calm their breath. He didn't bother pressing them about it and addressed the men.

"A Persian messenger arrived today. I was informed that Tissaphernes officially declares war on us. Not to worry…He has broken his oath and waits for us on the field of battle. They have already been defeated by the Ten Thousand. So let us show them what eight thousand can do!"

The allied troops shouted their war cry, but they were all concerned about being so vastly outnumbered.

The king continued. "I have sacrificed for the last three days and the signs are in our favor. We shall have our victory!" Agesilaos said without a doubt. He then eyed Herippidas.

Herippidas crossed over to the king's tent, entered, and when he came back out, he roughly escorted the Persian messenger to the fore by Agesilaos. The Persian had been listening to the king's speech the entire time. His hands were bound behind his back. He had been beaten, stripped naked and his brown face didn't compare to his pale, scrawny body.

"This is your enemy! This is who you will fight!" Agesilaos said.

The army examined the nature of this man. The Persian was humiliated and he refused to look up. The Greeks thought only very old and sick men could look like him. His breasts and stomach, although not large, sagged. He had not one bit of muscle, anywhere. One of his testicles never descended and his stick was so short it was consumed by the hair. Jokes and laughter erupted throughout the ranks, while Demaratos and Theras eyed one another, shrugging off their earlier adventure.

"This is the wretch who informs me that Tissaphernes declares war, if we do not leave. How dare he! We are the masters of war! We decide, not our enemy!" the king said.

The men bellowed their cry again.

"I've learned that Tissaphernes's home is to the south of us in Caria. I'm sure he has much to plunder," Agesilaos said intentionally, as he eyed the messenger, who now found the courage to look up at him. Then the king gazed at his mercenaries who were hungry for gold, and then to his knights who could care less for riches. "Megillus."

"Yes, my king," Megillus said obediently.

"Send a messenger to inform all the cities en route to Caria, that they will need to ready their markets and shops for us."

"Yes, my king," Megillus said, and he obeyed.

"Dercylidas."

"Yes, my king," Dercylidas said.

"Send a runner to our posts in Ionia, Aeolis and the Hellespont. Tell them we will need all available troops, immediately."

"Yes, my king," Dercylidas said, and he obeyed.

Agesilaos then confronted the Persian messenger. "Please tell Tissaphernes that I am indebted to him. By breaking his oath, he has made the gods our allies, rather than his."

The Persian was mortified. He couldn't look the Spartan king in the eye any longer, so he acknowledged him with his gaze set low. "Yes, King Agesilaos."

"Herippidas, free the prisoner," the king said.

Herippidas obeyed.

Agesilaos watched the Persian messenger run out of the Spartan camp without a shred of cloth to cover his loins. He then turned back to his army and found them all standing at attention. "At ease, men," he said, and then he paused, eyeing every one of them. "If there is one thing that vexes me more than anything, it is a perjurer. I will not tolerate deception from our enemy. Are you ready to teach the Persians of war?"

Again, the army shouted their enthusiasm.

"Good," Agesilaos said. "Because we are going north, to Phrygia!"

# Ways and Means

The Persian messenger staggered into Tissaphernes's camp two nights later. He was emaciated and still mortified by the way the Spartans had treated him. He managed to cover himself with old oddments of linen, which he found along the city roads, and clearly, he did not look like the man Tissaphernes had sent out to represent him. When he told his master all that had happened, Tissaphernes thanked him for the message and then he had him executed for the shame he brought to his reputation.

With Agesilaos's declaration of war on Caria, Tissaphernes became very concerned. He was a wealthy man. While he had many palaces across Lydia, Caria was his home and place of birth. If he lost his personal property, he would not be able to redeem his reputation as a great military leader in the eyes of the Great King. He also knew Artaxerxes would never forgive him for a second failure and he felt compelled to defend it. They left their camp near Ephesus and ventured south. He took the position just north of the River Meander, which bordered Caria. It was an advantageous location in his view because of the open plain. He was aware that Agesilaos did not have a significant cavalry and he assumed that he could run his army down, since they were such a small force. However, after much time, the Spartans never appeared for the engagement. His men, while they would never speak of it to him, began to talk behind his back. It was humiliating for Tissaphernes to be deceived, when finally, after many days, he learned from one of his scouts that the Spartans headed north.

North to Phrygia meant they had to venture through Lydia, which was Tissaphernes's domain. The Great King placed him in charge of this vast portion of his empire and he had left it undefended. Tissaphernes desperately needed results, and with the Spartans on foot and his men born riders, he figured he could catch them before it was too late.

Λ

When Tissaphernes broke his oath, Agesilaos considered his act of deception to be honorable. His allied force went uncontested, capturing all the Asiatic cities in his path. Colophon, Clazomenae, Smyrna, Magnesia, Phocaea, Cyme, Atarneus, Adramyttium, Antandrus, Troad, Ilium, Abydos and Lampsacus were all taken.

To take a city in the Persian Empire was much different than in Greece. All that was required of Agesilaos, was for him to approach the city wall from a furlong away. His entire force would be assembled in plain view of the enemy, but out of an archer's reach. Then they would wait. Somewhere between immediately and day's end, the city's governor and his small contingent of guards would appear and they would hand their city over to him. Any city that was unsuitable, meaning it could not provide for his army, he would have reduced and the surrounding land would be devastated with fire. He also freed all the natives, instead of enslaving them. They loved him for it. The newly freed people embraced their liberation and they welcomed the opportunity to care for their saviors. However, all men of age were conscripted into the king's army, trained on the move, and put to their new labor. The governors, typically through a translator, would tell him all he needed to know about the region. Namely, where Agesilaos was positioned within the empire, where the Great King might be, where Tissaphernes was, and where the next suitable city was to take.

Although Agesilaos wouldn't mind killing Tissaphernes, he didn't care at all about him. That's why he bypassed Lydia and edged along the Asiatic coast, because his objective was to prevent the Great King from invading Greece and that was exactly what he was doing. He thought if he could keep Persia preoccupied through the warring season, meaning give Artaxerxes enough trouble on his own land, then he would never have the time to set sail and land in Greece before winter. If by chance, Agesilaos does get to engage Artaxerxes in battle, then all the better for him. He will have satisfied a personal whim.

Moons had passed by the time Agesilaos arrived in Phrygia, and with the additional troops from Ionia, Aeolis and the Hellespont, the army numbered well over fifty thousand. The Equals were pleased about this, so that the burden of war would be distributed evenly and not rest solely on them. They praised their king and called him wise for his strategy. The freed helots were honored with a promotion. They were put in command of the Persian and Asiatic Greek natives, who were conscripted into his force, so that former slaves commanded slaves. The Greek allies got the gold they were promised, as there was much booty to plunder. Simply put, everyone was happy.

The natives of Phrygia were also greatly surprised when the Spartans arrived. They had expected another tyrant, but they were delightfully mistaken when Agesilaos freed them from the Persian yoke in exchange for fertile land. They were so pleased by the notion, they began to think of him as their father. So while Agesilaos had a new camp with free provisions supplied to his army, he decided to take the rest of Phrygia.

The land of Phrygia was immeasurable. It was divided into two domains, Phrygia and Greater Phrygia in the east. The former was easy to take. Keeping his army moving also meant more frustration for the Great King and more ground for Tissaphernes to cover before he could engage them in battle. So far, he had taken the entire Asiatic coast north of Ephesus without a man fell. On his next march, he sacked another suitable Phrygian city. Now they too worshiped Agesilaos, as the Asiatic Greeks and Persians worshiped Lysander during the Great War.

Inevitably, he accumulated so much wealth from plundering missions that it slowed his campaign to a halt. He had to unload it, save for what was necessary for the campaign, and what better way than to give it back to the people he freed. This way, Persians and Asiatic Greeks, who were formerly dominated, now owned their former masters' property and land. It was a devastating effect on these former governors of Phrygia and the Asiatic territories to witness their past subjects wearing their silk robes and gold, while walking in and out of the palaces they once lived in. It all came back to Artaxerxes, which in turn, made Tissaphernes look worse. The Great King was losing his empire and his most trusted satrap was failing him.

Agesilaos's kindness also extended to orphaned children and elders of the cities he razed. He did not want them to fall victim to the slave trade. He was against those dirty dealings. There was much of it throughout the empire and it truly disgusted him. So he ordered the natives to care for the wandering orphans and elders, placing them with families who now had the means. Word of his good nature continued to spread throughout the western half of the empire. He was known as a man of quality and he became trusted by all. Persian deserters came to him with all sorts of beneficial information. The most common reports were where there was another city worth taking. Some cities weren't worth an obol, but the natives had families there and served Agesilaos now, so he would occasionally take one of these cities and free the people out of kindness.

Agesilaos's generosity increased his power and reputation. It was unavoidable and overwhelming. He handled his fame with such grace though. Wherever he was, he would allow anyone, whether native or Greek, to flock around him, just so they could tell their peers later that they had spent time with the Spartan king. He was perceived as a great man who was incorruptible to gold. He also maintained his plain dress, never forgetting his humble origins. Additionally, Agesilaos continued to deal with all of his affairs out in the open for everyone to see. He claimed it made himself and those around him more virtuous. He was right. Many men began modeling themselves after him, while those on campaign with him, were at the point where they would die for him without a moment's hesitation.

The army ventured farther east into Phrygia, unopposed, until the terrain deceived them. The land was endless. So much so, that after seven straight days of marching, the mountains on the horizon were no bigger than they were on the first day. The sun was relentless. The men burned and blistered, and without any signs of life anywhere, Agesilaos decided to make sacrifice. It did not go well. The liver was without lobes and they decisively marched back toward the coast.

Once they arrived in the coastal city of Troad, which was far north of Ephesus, news finally arrived that the Ten Thousand had returned. Agesilaos learned that they had never gone after the Great King. He was grateful for that and then he listened to several tales about the legendary army led by an Athenian scholar. He was so fascinated and amused, that he called Theras and Demaratos over to him and gave them a direct order.

"Bring me this Xenophon."

# Book V
## Manly Virtue

*A man drew the Spartan king's attention. He pointed to a new wall built around his city, which he claimed was more formidable than any other of their time. It was easily six men tall, two wagons' breadth and made of stone cut from a quarry. "Does it make a favorable impression on you, my Spartan king?" the man asked.*

*"By Zeus!" the king said. "Favorable for a woman to dwell inside of, but not a man."*

# Men of War

"My king, it is a great honor," Xenophon said, bowing his head to Agesilaos.

"Pick your head up, man," Agesilaos said cheerfully. "You need not bow to me."

Xenophon did as he was ordered and smiled out of surprise due to Agesilaos's unexpected charm. His height too was a surprise, as he stood half a head shorter than him. The Spartan king was not at all who he expected him to be. Even his limp and scars caught Xenophon's eye. "How could one man accumulate so many marks from war and still be alive?" he wondered.

"You are probably wondering why I brought you here."

Xenophon cleared his mind and nodded. "My king."

As they began walking through the city of Troad together, they were not alone. Demaratos and Theras remained close behind without intruding, while the rest of the army mingled with the Ten Thousand. Demaratos and Theras hardly spoke to Xenophon during their march south together. The Athenian was not at all whom they thought him to be. Theras assumed prior, that he was going to be plump and weak of sight, and carrying countless papyrus scrolls on his person. Demaratos thought more or less the same, but that he was going to be a typical scrawny philosopher whose body was swallowed up by his own tunic. However, when they had arrived to escort him south, they found him doing gymnastics. He was training alone and as hard as the Spartans in Byzantium. His body looked like an Equal's. He even had some decent scars, which proved the legendary tales of his Persian campaign true.

When the Ten Thousand heard Xenophon was ordered south, they insisted that they escort the three. He was their general and friend. Their loyalty to the philosopher knew no bounds after all they had been through, and nor would they see him mistreated like they were by the Spartans in Byzantium. It turned out that the surviving Ten Thousand got along well with Agesilaos's allied force. Many of them knew each other. Least to say, there was much happenings in the city as the king and general strolled through.

"Your knowledge of the land is quite valuable to me," Agesilaos said. "Will you join me on my campaign?"

"Of course, my king. Without question," Xenophon said enthusiastically.

"Good. So then, what do you know of Tissaphernes?" the king asked Xenophon, as they made their way through the marketplace.

"He killed our generals. One of them a good friend, the other a Spartan, my king," Xenophon said.

"Clearchus?" Agesilaos asked.

"Yes, my king."

"Ha!"

Xenophon found it peculiar that his death pleased him, but he knew it wasn't his place to question it. "Without Clearchus and Chirisophos—" Xenophon began to say.

Agesilaos eyed him, curiously yet heatedly.

So Xenophon rephrased. "Without Spartan influence I would never have become general of the army, nor survived such a blasted catastrophe. My king, what I am trying to say is that I have come to love the Spartan way of life."

Agesilaos stopped and faced Xenophon. "I do not doubt you. Our ways have been known to seduce a foreigner or two, but what I believe you are in love with, is manly virtue."

The philosopher was perplexed.

Agesilaos saw it. "As I hear it, you were a pupil of Socrates?"

"Yes, my king."

"Did he not prove to his countrymen that he stood by his principles in the face of certain death?"

"That is how I heard it."

"Is that not what a virtuous man does?"

"Yes, my king," Xenophon said, feeling like he was with his former teacher. "Uh, my king, you sound like a bit of a philosopher yourself."

Agesilaos eyed him hard, making him feel nervous. Xenophon did not intend to offend him as an uncertain moment passed, and then, Agesilaos curled his lips.

Xenophon felt a rush of relief.

"Don't tell anyone, or they'll think I'm girlish," Agesilaos joked, and then he motioned for him to continue walking by his side. "Return to Tissaphernes."

"Yes, my king. After our victory against Artaxerxes, our generals were invited to his camp to discuss terms of peace. They were deceived and beheaded."

"Persian loyalty."

"Yes, my king. I would like to see Tissaphernes dead. I despise the man and every Persian on this forsaken land."

Agesilaos laughed. "Ha! I think we shall get along well, Xenophon."

# Λ

Winter had come and gone as the cost of war remained on Persia. Xenophon and Agesilaos were now inseparable. Wherever the king was, so was he. During his first few days in Troad, Xenophon was introduced to all the men, including Agesilaos's new Persian informant.

Lysander had returned from the Hellespont with a man named Spithridates. He was the handsome, yet cynical looking cavalry commander in the northern region of the empire, who served the satrap, Pharnabazus. He had defected over rumor of an insult. Really, there was no evidence that Pharnabazus insulted him in regards to his lack in horsemanship, but Spithridates, like all Persian riders, prided himself on his ability, and he knew Lysander was a man of honor. So if Lysander said it was so, then it must have been true. The Persian brought with him two hundred of his cavalry. Agesilaos was grateful to Lysander for turning him and he made every effort to mend their lifelong friendship. He couldn't allow one argument to ruin it all, but Lysander was consumed with envy and his mind had been corrupted with forbidden ideas during all his time abroad. Least to say, it proved unsuccessful.

The next morning, Agesilaos received orders from the ephors, informing him that the Spartans' one year term was up and they must return home. The one year term was a preventive measure to ensure their precious men of war were not corrupted by foreign ideology. The thirty knights were going to be replaced by a new thirty. However, the king put in a special request, well in advance, to keep Demaratos, Theras and Herippidas abroad, and it was fulfilled without question. Agesilaos did the same for Lysander, but he withdrew the offer, since he was not willing to remain friends. Unfortunate as it was, the king dismissed him. The legend of the Great War departed Ephesus just as bitterly as he had the first time, but this time, he vowed to overthrow the constitution from within, in his effort to strive for the crown.

While Xenophon was in awe of Lysander, the man who brought Athens to plague and ruin, he hated Spithridates from the start, and the Persian knew it. Spithridates had his own aims to reach with the king, but why not have some fun while he was at it, he thought. Spithridates would intentionally linger about, smile cheekily at him for no reason, and joke with the king whenever Xenophon was in their company. Even worse, the Persian spoke Greek, which really got under the philosopher's skin. Everything the Persian did, seemed to be out of spite. Go back to your desert, you filthy sand rat, Xenophon would say to himself. Nor could he bring himself to address his grievance to Agesilaos or he would come across like every other sniveling, girlish Athenian. Then, four moons went by and the Persian hadn't shown his face.

"Xenophon, are you with me?" Agesilaos asked.

Xenophon was catching his breath, as he and the king were doing their morning gymnastics just outside the city walls at their makeshift athlitika. He was thinking about how great it was without the pesky Persian around and then he snapped to. "Yes, my king."

"So you see...My sister took the olive wreath at last summer's games over the men because of her means, not her skill," Agesilaos said with a laugh. "I told her anybody with coin could do it!"

Xenophon forced a laugh for Agesilaos even though he had not been paying attention, when Spithridates approached from out of nowhere in haste. It was like a dark cloud cast over Xenophon, and only Xenophon.

Spithridates was covered in dust from toe to crown as he dismounted his horse. "Spartan king! Pharnabazus lies in Dascylium. We must respond quickly, before he departs. He will know where to find the Great King."

"Well done, Spithridates," Agesilaos said and he dismissed him.

"Spartan king," the Persian replied with grace, and then he eyed Xenophon with another cheeky grin before walking back to his mare.

"Are you sure you can trust him, my king?" Xenophon asked.

Agesilaos smiled. His mind was elsewhere, so he didn't bother acknowledging his question. "For the coming engagement, I'm putting you on the right wing next to me."

"Yes, my king. It would be my honor."

"Your men will fight alongside mine on the right wing as well. If you defeated the Great King with ten thousand, imagine what sixty thousand will do. Ha!"

∧

They reached Dascylium, which was directly east of Troad, in eleven days courtesy of the Great King's Royal Road. Xenophon was now on tour with the Spartans. What had started as a philosophical conversation with Socrates had come true, but the philosopher in him died long ago and a warrior had been born. Xenophon did loathe the idea of marching back into Persia, but he couldn't pass up on the opportunity to campaign with Agesilaos and his thirty knights.

The army halted in a low lying plain under a clear summer sky. Agesilaos's personal cavalry was small. He had with him fifty riders and they were dispatched to scout the dirt hills ahead. It was there, that Pharnabazus had been seen. Xenophon was among those waiting. He looked over to his left at the Persian cavalry contingent and spotted Spithridates. He was already glaring at Xenophon with another maddening expression. To Styx with these Persians, he thought, and then he shook his head as he faced back forward. The army watched as the Greeks rode to the top of the hill, when a contingent of Pharnabazus's cavalry unexpectedly came up from the other side and met the Greeks. Agesilaos's riders didn't hesitate. They charged in a galloping phalanx, while the Persians, who were twice the Greeks' number, remained in a double column. Every Greek hit their mark and broke their spear. As they wheeled their mounts around for another charge, the Persians counterattacked and twelve Greeks fell.

As soon as Agesilaos saw them fall, he gave the order. The trumpets sounded off and the king's mora, as well as Spithridates's cavalry, charged the hill. The enemy retreated back down the other side, when they saw them advancing. So by the time the allied force reached their troops, the Persians had vanished. Not a single rider was seen in any direction.

Agesilaos looked to Spithridates questioningly.

"They have gone, Spartan king. It is how I have taught them to ride," Spithridates said proudly. "You will not be able to find them on foot."

The allied force was disappointed that they did not get to spill Persian blood, and once again, they ventured back to Troad. From there, they headed south along the coast and returned to Ephesus. As their second winter arrived, the warring season concluded, and thus far, the third Persian invasion had been quelled.

Along the way to Ephesus, the army stopped at all of the newly conquered Spartan cities and the king sent to every wealthy man a proposal. Agesilaos offered them exemption from military duty, if they could provide a horse, rider and the means to maintain them. The wealthy did not hesitate to accept his offer and it was another cost that Agesilaos did not suffer.

The Ephesians, on their own accord, had run the dirty dealers out of the city. They decided there would be no more slave trading or prostitution in the king's new capital. This pleased Agesilaos greatly upon his arrival. It told him that his leadership was influencing everyone in the best possible way. Not only that, when the natives saw the size of the Greek army and the additional four thousand cavalrymen Agesilaos had conscripted into his force, they expanded the city to encompass the camp.

Ephesus turned into a workshop of war. The army's camp was now the city, and anything and everything the hoplites, peltasts, slingers, archers, cavalrymen or horses could need, were available to them. Tailors, craftsmen, metal workers, food and doctors for the men and horses, sleeping quarters and even amusement were all at the army's disposal. Every day when the sun was at its zenith, Agesilaos and his thirty knights would parade the city with their garlands on. It had great effect. Everyone they passed strived to be champions, like the mighty Spartans. The army trained daily. Mock battles were held and the king's new cavalry refined their maneuvers. Any Persians who came wandering into the city or anywhere near it, were seized, stripped, tied to a post, and put up for sale. No one actually bought them of course, but Agesilaos wanted to remind his men who they were fighting. Finally, summer was arriving and the time was nearing to go after Pharnabazus and the Great King, and kill them once and for all, so Agesilaos held games to boost their morale even further.

The events consisted of the best cavalry maneuvers, test of strength and speed among the hoplites in full war kit, and also javelin throwing, slinging and archery among the light armored troops. He even held a pankration event for all, which was a mix of boxing and wrestling.

In this latter event, Demaratos met Theras in the championship round. The match went on for a great length of time and they beat each other bloody. The entire army watched in awe because they knew they were the greatest of friends. However, they were taking it too far and Agesilaos became concerned. He couldn't afford to lose his most valuable knights, so he stopped the fight. As he stood in between them, he stared proudly at them both, while regarding their competitive nature, which Sparta had blessed them with. Their faces were unrecognizable, but Theodoros would take care of that later. Then the king grabbed both of their arms and he raised them to the heavens, declaring both Theras and Demaratos victors. All of Ephesus cheered for them. They were the elite members of the army and heroes to the men of the ranks.

At the end of the games, all of the champions were honored with garlands. The army roared and applauded, but during the course of things, something happened. The men began emanating their Persian hate. They shouted insults about their enemy and boasted how many they would kill. Their exhilaration could not be contained. It led to disorder. Some took turns pissing on the Persian prisoners, who were tied up for sale. They would have been raped and killed by some, but they knew the king would not permit that. Agesilaos looked around at all of his men, smiling. He had them exactly where he wanted them, bloodthirsty, and ready for war!

# Tissaphernes

Tissaphernes was struggling. While retiring in his Lydian capital, Sardis, for the winter, Artaxerxes had summoned him to his palace in Babylon. Tissaphernes was in his middle years and age had begun wearing on him. His girth had increased considerably and he was exhausted by the journey, but he was determined to get back on level ground with the Great King. He also knew Artaxerxes was informed of his humiliation by the Spartan, but he felt the king was probably more concerned with the loss of the western region of his empire.

When the satrap arrived, the Great King was sitting on a stone carved bench and gazing at a shallow pool, which hosted all sorts of exotic, colorful fish. "Do you not want to please your king?" he asked, without bothering to look back at him.

Tissaphernes stood behind the king and stared at the back of his crown in the middle of the Hanging Gardens. During Darius's rule, he always took the opportunity to visit his master here so that he could enjoy the majestic beauty and serenity this palace offered. However, at the moment, his nerves were rattled and the lush garden looming over him instilled fear. It was as if the plants were arms and their hands were reaching for his throat. "Yes, Great King, of course I do. I live to serve you."

"Then how could you fail me so miserably now? You served my father well and guaranteed me the crown. What is the problem?"

"Great King, I am without an excuse. I underestimated the Spartan and was made out to be the fool. Please, offer me the chance to correct matters."

Artaxerxes chuckled. Then he turned and looked back at him with a deceitful glare. "Pharnabazus informed me that he prevented the Greeks from penetrating farther east with his cavalry. He will assist you." The king paused to stare at his satrap's consternation. He was truly enjoying the power he wielded over his subject. "I am still your friend, Tissaphernes," he said reassuringly.

"Great King," Tissaphernes said with a bow. "I will not fail you," he declared, and then he immediately returned to Sardis.

Once there, the warring season commenced and a messenger arrived from Agesilaos, stating that he would be marching on Sardis should he like to meet him in battle. Tissaphernes killed the messenger. He was at a loss. He couldn't be sure if Agesilaos was being truthful or not. In the end, he decided it was another act of deception and he took his army to defend Caria instead. Pharnabazus warned him otherwise, but he was ordered by the king to obey Tissaphernes, so as to measure his worthiness. Together, with their armies, they departed, which allowed Agesilaos to take Sardis without any opposition. The Spartan now had control of the satrap's entire domain.

Tissaphernes soon realized that he made a fatal error and he headed back to Sardis in haste, but once again, he was too late. The Greeks freed the natives and left their city intact. They also plundered Tissaphernes's personal property, claimed his resources as their own, and laid waste the surrounding territory before advancing farther east after the Great King.

Pharnabazus, by secret order of Artaxerxes, broke his cavalry off and went after the Greeks, leaving Tissaphernes to figure out his next maneuver for himself. Pharnabazus managed to attack a contingent of Agesilaos's peltasts, who were on a plundering mission far to the east of Sardis. The Spartan king, when he heard they were trapped by a watercourse and escape was difficult, responded swiftly. He sent his new cavalry to the rescue. The Asiatic Greek and Persian riders were trained over the winter by Spithridates and refined by the Spartans. The cavalry killed twice their lot and they forced Pharnabazus to retreat. The Persians were dismembered and left to rot on the river bank, so as to leave the Great King a message to beware of Greeks. However, after the Greek survivors were rescued, Agesilaos feared that Pharnabazus would cut off his resources and he decided to march back on Sardis. So while the Greeks were the victors, Pharnabazus again prevented them from penetrating deeper into the empire.

The Great King could do no more to save his friend and he was deciding who Tissaphernes's replacement should be, when Tithraustes, a member of the Great King's royal guard, requested an unexpected audience with him. It was a daring move for a mere nobody, but unlike all the other guards, he had ambition, and he got his chance to speak with Artaxerxes. He suggested that it would be best to rid the Greeks from his land by creating trouble for them on their own land. Artaxerxes was pleased with his proposed strategy and he silently praised Ahuramazda for not allowing him to pass over on seeing Tithraustes. That's when the candles on the corridor walls flickered. The Great King perceived it as a very good omen, so he honored Tithraustes by appointing him as his new satrap of Lydia.

"Do not fail me," Artaxerxes said to him.

# ∧

Tithraustes rode hard to Caria with only a small number of Immortals, who were posing as his personal guards. The soon-to-be former satrap was lounging on his side, stuffing a roasted ostrich leg down his throat, when Tithraustes stepped inside his palace unannounced with his assassins. "The Great King no longer requires your service," he said.

Tissaphernes was caught unaware and he jumped to his feet. His hand still clutched his meal, as if it was his sword. "Guards!" he yelled with a greasy face.

No one came to his rescue because Tithraustes showed his guards the Great King's official orders upon his arrival. It was just a rolled up piece of papyrus with a few words on it. The scroll was sealed in red wax, which depicted the symbol of the Persian archer.

Deep inside, Tissaphernes was tired, and he was expecting this, but he hadn't yet come to terms with his execution. The ostrich leg then fell from his grasp. "Leave my family unharmed," he requested, as he willingly turned his back to them and kneeled.

"Of course," Tithraustes assured him, as one of the Immortals approached with his blade held high.

The feeling was crisp, cool and quick, and his exhausted body retired on his severed head.

# Cynisca

Two winters ago, Kleora dashed to the base of Mount Taygetus to watch the old seer above. Her insides squeezed and choked her. She felt ill as she prayed her infant would live.

"Twice, I've stood here," Cynisca said, as she approached without warning.

"Cynisca!" Kleora said with surprise.

"They say it is forbidden, but the council knows of a mother's will, let alone a queen's."

"Please, tell no one I've come," Kleora begged.

"I've come to support you child. What do you take me for?"

Kleora forced a quick smile and then panic riddled her face once more, as she looked back up toward her newborn's inspection. Cynisca held her close, consoling her, and finally, it was done. The seer turned from the edge of the peak with her infant in his grasp. Kleora sighed and her body tingled with relief. She then looked to Cynisca. Both of their smiles glowed brilliantly.

"Get back to your house, before they do," Cynisca said.

The queen gave her a kiss on the lips and she ran off. Occasionally, their friendship was a bit more. It was commonplace in the Five Villages with the men always gone.

Kleora had maintained her gymnastic training through her pregnancy and she was able to push through her fatigue from giving birth the night prior. She made it back just in time, having to take the long way so as to not be seen, and she crept through the back of her house as the old seer and several Elders and ephors approached the front door. She quickly removed her tunic and used it to wipe her sweat off. Then she grabbed a clean one and slipped it on as they knocked on the door. Kleora slowly opened the door and presented herself as she tried to control her breath.

"Archidamus, son of Agesilaos, will live, my queen," the seer said and he handed the boy to her.

She cradled Archidamus, while containing her enthusiasm to only a smile.

Cynisca lived nearly next door and she met her soon after the council had gone. They paraded the Five Villages together to show the king's boy off. They started in Limnae and went to Mesoa. From there, they went to Pitana, then to Cynosoura, and lastly, south to Amyclae. She did this nearly every day, and with her husband still gone, Kleora spent a lot of time with Cynisca.

A year went by and they were walking through the agora together, when Cynisca spotted Lysander speaking to Pythagoras from a distance.

Kleora saw Cynisca's consternation when she saw him. "He returned the night prior. You did not know?" the queen asked.

Cynisca didn't respond.

"I've much to tell you then, about your Lysander."

∧

Lysander was at his wit's end as he sat inside his house at his oaken table. He had refused to sail from Asia Minor during the cold season because his former naval experience taught him that the sea was unforgiving during that time of year. The land proved treacherous too. It took him and the other twenty-six knights all winter to walk home. They were delayed in Thrace and then again in Macedonia with unprecedented snowfall. As he sat with a scowl across his brow, he had ordered Myron to fetch him several pieces of papyrus, ink and a pen. Lysander spent the entire night writing his own version of the Spartan constitution as his earlier conversation with Pythagoras echoed in his head.

*"Agesilaos has made quite the king, Lysander," Pythagoras said.*

*"He has," Lysander responded, as more councilmen approached them.*

*"It seems that you have interpreted the Oracle's prophecy, most accurately. So much for a crippled kingship," Pythagoras said with a smile.*

*Lysander nodded, as he vented through his nose to conceal his animosity.*

*"We welcome you home."*

*"I am overjoyed to return."*

Lysander finished his rough efforts as a scribe by dawn, when a pink-violet hue breached the horizon. Myron remained in the corner, ready to serve his master the entire time. His mind was burdened with guilt though, as he watched Lysander stow the document in between two flat pieces of timber, which he then nailed to the bottom of his table. Lysander couldn't allow anyone to know of it, nor could he propose it to the council, until he met with Leotychidas and the other supporters.

Cynisca knocked on the door as expected, just as he had picked himself up off the stone floor. He tossed Myron the mallet and dismissed him as he went to answer her call. Cynisca was freshly bathed and smelled of honey and sweet almonds. She learned from Kleora, who learned from the other women, that her brother was no longer friends with her former lover. This distressed her greatly.

She loved Agesilaos and she intended to remove any and all potential threats to his rule. Cynisca gazed at the scar she inflicted on him during their previous relationship and then she peered into Lysander's eyes, as he invited her inside.

She kissed him upon entering. It was their first kiss, since she struck him with the blade years ago. He had already proven once that he could sway minds with gold. She would not allow him another chance to do anything else of the sort. They made their way to his bed, dropping what they wore along the way. He slammed her down gently and then penetrated her. As they coupled, her hand found the hilt of a blade underneath his bed. Myron had placed it there in return for a new life. She swore to Athena of the Bronze House that she would go before the council and request his freedom once the deed had been done, and only if the deed had been done. Myron was quick to comply.

Lysander continued his motions. "I have longed for this day."

She pulled the hilt from underneath the reed sack part way out and held it firm. "I too."

"I have been given orders to campaign in Arcadia with only a sortie, the day after next. There will be many against us. It will be fierce and I am unsure if I will return," he said.

Her eyes widened and she let go of the hilt. "Even better," she thought. "Let him meet death in war." Cynisca slid the blade back into hiding and then she rolled her lover over. "I will offer a ram to Zeus and pray for your return," she said.

Lysander clasped her face and kissed her passionately. "I have always loved you, Cynisca."

# Meletus

Aristophanes, son of Philippus, was a renowned comedic dramatist. His satirical play, *The Clouds*, just concluded for the tenth straight night at the Athenian theatre. His masterpiece was two years in the making. He played the role of Socrates, where he walked on clouds as if he was a god in the heavens, looking down on his mortals, while proving the truth in all things. Meletus had attended only to please his fellow councilmen and he was the only one who did not offer a standing applause, because somehow, killing Socrates immortalized the philosopher.

Earlier that morning on the way to court, he walked through the agora as usual, and everywhere he looked, there was someone pretending to be Socrates. It had been this way since his execution. He thought it would only last for a day or two, but Socrates was now more famous dead than he was alive. Even the merchants at the agora expanded their goods to include new writings based on his philosophical conversations. The effect was great and unavoidable, which made Meletus even more miserable than when the old man lived. While navigating through the throng of Socratic imitators, he took a glance at several of the writings and he found that every single scribe was a pupil of Socrates. The most popular seemed to be written by Plato, Crito, Apollodorus and Phaedo. When they witnessed how brave Socrates was at his end, they vowed to continue his duty to his god by becoming teachers of the young. Meletus couldn't believe what was happening. While he and his cohorts were trying to reestablish Athens as a great military empire, as it had once been, the people were going in a different direction. They wanted to be educated.

When Meletus finally reached court, he was informed that it was now prohibited for the accused to sing high praises to the Council and jury as a method of defense. The accused must now defend themselves with physical or oral proof to be vindicated of their charges. Meletus wasn't happy about it because this was Socrates's doing. As the first trial of the morning got underway, a farmer stood accused of murder and he defended himself as others had done for so long. He offered his praise to the men of the court, calling them noble upright citizens of Athens, instead of defending himself against the crime, which he was being accused of. In the end, he was found guilty due to the unexpected change in policy. His execution was ordered and it was going to be carried out the next day. As the second trial started immediately after, the accused learned the fate of the farmer, as well as the change in policy, and he did his best to speak his defense. It was the first true trial in Athens. The reform had begun. It forced the Council and jury to use their minds, and to think with reason. The Athenians were at the dawn of a new age, an age of intellect and wisdom, and it all created an immense pain across Meletus's brow.

After such a long dreadful day, Meletus snuck away after Aristophanes bowed out and left the stage. He heard *The Clouds* was going to be performed for the next twenty days by popular demand. It made him sick to his stomach. When he arrived home, his wife and young daughter of nine years were waiting for him to eat their evening meal. He sat down and sighed, as he was grateful for peace and solitude from the city.

"How was your day?" his wife asked and she served him food.

Meletus swallowed an entire cup of wine. "Socrates, Socrates, Socrates!" he exclaimed. "It is all I hear out there!"

His wife didn't dare mention the philosopher's name for fear of a beating. So she sat down and they began to eat. "Have some more wine. It will calm your nerves," she said in a soothing manner.

Meletus did, and as he drank another cup, he eyed his daughter. He had ignored her since he walked in the door. It wasn't right and he knew it, so he attempted to make a face by curling his lips and bulging his eyes to get her to smile. There was no response from the little girl. She just stared blankly as she chewed her food. He then looked to his wife, who in turn, shrugged her shoulders. She had no idea what was wrong with her.

"What's the matter, my child?" Meletus asked in a soft voice.

"I'm thinking," the young girl said.

"Thinking of what?" Meletus asked.

"An unexamined mind is a wasted life, father," she said with a Socratic tone.

Meletus rolled his eyes in a huff. The last thing that he needed was for his daughter to become infected with philosophy. His wife remained indifferent by focusing on her meal, but when she peered out of the corner of her eye and saw that her husband resumed eating, she smiled at her daughter and gave her a wink.

# Free Men

There were stacks of chests and heaps of gold, jewels and countless foreign goods at Agesilaos's treasury in Sardis. Rows of statues, dating back to the Assyrian Empire bordered the stone walls of the underground chamber, which was lit with torch fire. So much wealth had been accumulated after taking Sardis and the surrounding cities that Agesilaos found himself mulling over what to do with it all.

Meanwhile, hordes of freed natives flocked outside the palace entrance in hopes that they would get a word in with the king. One of them however, stood out. He sat off to the side in better than modest attire. He found it humorous that freed Persians would rally in an effort to serve their new king, rather than take advantage of their liberty and serve themselves.

As for Agesilaos, he would have preferred to have been outside, but the natives became overwhelming. The endless requests and offerings never permitted him a moment to himself. They came at him for everything, from sharing a meal, to kissing their child on the cheek for good fortune, but most just wanted to say that they walked or talked with their great father. It was just like Phrygia, only more intense.

Xenophon pushed through the mob, passed through the guarded palace gates, and found the king pacing around the spilled coins, which depicted the infamous Persian archer. "It is madness out there, my king."

"Tell me something I don't know," Agesilaos said. Then he looked at Xenophon. "What should I do with all of this?"

"You are not to keep it for yourself, my king?" Xenophon asked hesitantly.

Agesilaos laughed.

"Socrates was right again," Xenophon mused. "They really are incorruptible." Then he glanced at the mass of wealth and suggested, "Goodwill?"

"I've done that. This is the remainder."

"Goodwill in Greece, my king," Xenophon followed up.

Agesilaos truly hadn't thought of that. "Done," he said. "Tell Herippidas to send a tenth to Delphi and a tenth to Sparta. We'll think of what to do with the rest later. Now, Xenophon. Tell me something, *I want to hear.*"

"Well, there is word of a rebellion."

"Against who?"

"The Great King, my king."

"Good. Let them have a go at it. What else?"

Xenophon thought for a moment. "I did see someone outside. He seemed different from the rest."

"A Persian?"

"Yes, my king. By his dress, very wealthy."

"Bring him to me."

"Yes, my king."

Xenophon pushed his way back through the boisterous throng outside the palace gates and approached the man he glimpsed off to the side on his way in.

"You, do you understand my words?" Xenophon asked loudly.

"Perfectly," the Persian said in Greek.

"What is your business here?"

"To see the Spartan king," the man said confidently.

"Well?" Xenophon questioned, motioning for him to follow. "This way!" he ordered, as he was frustrated by the noisy mob. "You can tell me who you are on the way in."

Tithraustes nonchalantly shrugged his shoulders and he followed the agitated Greek. After murdering Tissaphernes's family and claiming his property as his own, he immediately departed Caria for Sardis to reclaim his domain. During his wait outside, he observed the Spartan king's genius. Every city Agesilaos freed, he made useless to the Great King because they both knew that Persians were born slaves. They did not understand the concept of freedom and it was evident that they did not know what to do with it. Tithraustes however, was determined to reverse matters. *Enjoy your time, while you have it, slaves. It won't last long*, the satrap thought, as he pushed his way through them.

They made it back inside and met with Agesilaos in the main hall.

"My king, this is Tithraustes. He claims to be the satrap of Lydia and Phrygia, and he would very much like his dominion back."

"Ha!" the king laughed mockingly. "And where is your master, Tissaphernes?"

"Our common enemy has paid the penalty, Spartan king. My king now proposes that you return home and he swears an oath that the Asiatic Greek cities will maintain their freedom, so long as they pay their tribute."

"His words smell like skata," Xenophon said outright.

Agesilaos grinned at Xenophon and then he looked back at Tithraustes. "Tell your king, I said no."

"How far do you think your boundaries stretch, Spartan?" Tithraustes asked disrespectfully.

Some of the king's knights were standing by with Xenophon. They immediately stepped forward and slammed the butts of their eights down on the marble floor. Agesilaos in turn, signaled for them to hold.

At that instant, Tithraustes felt that he had obtained some respect from the Spartan king, since he did not allow his men to harm him.

Agesilaos eyed the Persian thoughtfully for a moment and then he walked over to one of his knights, grabbed his eight, and brandished it. The point kissed Tithraustes's nose and scratched the skin. "As far as this can reach," he said with fire in his eyes.

Tithraustes leaned away from the spear, hiding his fear. "Forgive my rudeness. I thought it was the way of Greeks. I would truly like for us to be friends," he claimed, as he attempted to begin again.

Agesilaos lowered the ash. "Very well. Tell your king that I will go nowhere, unless ordered to do so."

"But surely a king can do as he pleases," Tithraustes appealed, which angered the knights once more.

"Your king has spoken!" one of the Equals said.

Agesilaos motioned to his men again for them to remain calm, while he faced Tithraustes. "A king must abide by his laws, not his desires."

"Well perhaps you could move your army to Greater Phrygia, to the domain of Pharnabazus, until you hear from your master,

Spartan king. Once there, this will put you closer to the Great King. This is what you want. Is it not?"

"Two for the cost of one," Agesilaos thought, and then he replied. "Thirty talents to cover the journey."

"Agreed," Tithraustes said. "And let us be friends."

"Done," Agesilaos said, and the satrap made for his leave.

Xenophon was in shock that the king agreed to the proposal as he looked to him, when Tithraustes stopped and turned back.

The Persian had realized that if he could be the Spartan's friend by handing him Pharnabazus and the Great King, with a little patience, the empire could be his. "Make time to visit Paphlagonia, Spartan king," he said without explaining why, and then he departed.

"He betrays his own people with treason!" Xenophon exclaimed. "You cannot trust him, my king!"

Agesilaos was far from concerned as he looked at his friend with a baffled smile. "Such extraordinary men these Persians are. They make fine slaves, but are truly worthless when freed."

Λ

The ship with the Greek donation reached its destination and returned with the Spartan naval fleet. They massed their triremes on the eastern side of the island of Lesbos in Mytilene. Agesilaos had taken the remainder of the treasury at Sardis after receiving the thirty talents and he marched with his army back toward the coast. From there, they ventured north to the plains in Cyme, which was just east of the navy, when he received a skytale from a Spartan messenger. He was notified that the council was so pleased with his campaign that he was given charge of not only the entire army, but the navy as well. This honor was a first for any Spartan king.

"By the twin gods, I've made history!" Agesilaos shouted.

The Spartan messenger was honored to be in his presence during his excitement. "Yes, my king. Everyone looks forward to your return home as well. They all sing songs of your conquest."

"I am honored by your words," Agesilaos said.

"Thank you, my king," the messenger said with a bow.

"How long before you reach the navy?"

"Well before day's end, my king."

"Tell Peisander. Do you know of whom I speak?"

"My king, he is your brother-in-law. He is as fine an Equal as any on the sea."

"Tell him, he is in charge of the fleet, while I am on land. His first orders are to build one hundred twenty triremes and destroy the Persian fleet at Phoenicia. I'll send him coin."

"Yes, my king," he said with a smile.

"Dismissed," Agesilaos said, and then he turned to his men, who were waiting to resume the march back to Phrygia. His eyes glowed. He had obtained unobtainable glory and he desired only one more thing. His fellow Spartans loved him. The Greeks and Asiatic Greeks loved him. The Persians loved him. He commanded their entire world. What he said was law. Whatever his spear touched was his. He knew there were others in the navy more qualified than Peisander, but he wanted to please his wife, to make her proud on both sides of her family. Favoritism was against the Laws of Lycurgus though. He should have chosen what was best for Sparta, not for him, but so what, he thought, and shouted to his men. "Are you ready to kill the king?"

# Ill Will

Cynisca learned that Lysander was victorious on his Arcadian campaign. He and his sortie had routed ten times their lot in a brief engagement in the northern Peloponnese. It disappointed her greatly and she had no stomach to let him inside her again. If she did, she would kill him and then she herself would be executed for the crime without any proof that he was indeed a threat to Agesilaos's reign. Nor could she risk jeopardizing her family's name, the king included. They could all lose their status and be sent into exile. She knew he conspired though. She could feel it, but over what, she did not know.

Lysander had spent the last year in Arcadia to ensure Spartan laws were enforced and he was expected to return by nightfall. When Cynisca heard this, she ordered her helot to run north and find him. He did and he expressed Cynisca's desire to see him this night. Lysander responded agreeably. Then her helot returned and informed her of his response. After her evening meal, Cynisca knew it wouldn't be long before he would arrive, so she strutted through the gymnasium and grabbed the first Spartan she saw, who she was certain was of low nobility. She demanded that he come to her house for an engagement and he willingly complied. As planned, during the course of their coupling, Lysander made his visit to the back door of her house.

She stood unclothed at the entrance with beads of sweat dripping down her chest. "Yes, Lysander," she said, still calming her breath.

"You desire to see me, my lady?" he asked, and at that moment, he realized she was with someone else.

"No, I don't, ever," she said vindictively.

Lysander peered behind her to see who she was with and he knew him. The man had lost his status because he couldn't afford his tribute to his mess. Then he looked back at Cynisca. "You invite me over to witness this? He's not even an Equal! Are you expecting me to be envious? Fuck all the Five Villages, for all I care!" he shouted, and then he stormed away.

Cynisca became enraged and she stepped from the doorway. "One whisper of conspiracy against my brother, and I'll kill you myself!"

∧

Myron did not accompany his master in Arcadia and he was still upset that Cynisca did not follow through with her assassination. At the same time, he had absolutely no one to complain to. It was the life of any helot. So to feel better, he decided to ensure that he was still in Lysander's good graces. When his master walked through the doors of his house that evening, he informed him of Peisander's new promotion.

"Perfect, Myron. Continue to come to me with news of this sort, and I shall see about your freedom," Lysander said.

Hope was a helot's worst enemy, but it struck a soothing chord in Myron's heart. "Yes, master. Of course I will."

The next morning, Lysander went to the agora and confronted Pythagoras. He whispered unheard words in the old man's ear.

Pythagoras was stunned. "To please his wife, you say? It cannot be."

"I assure you it is so, and worse, there is more."

# Persian Loyalty

The army returned to Phrygia and then they proceeded north to Paphlagonia, as Tithraustes suggested. Xenophon knew the area bordering the Black Sea well, so he served as a guide for Agesilaos. It gave him some breathing space from Spithridates. On the third sun, they finally found King Cotys, or rather, his army found them. They consisted of two thousand peltasts and one thousand cavalrymen. They were fearlessly massed with their city to their backs against Agesilaos's sixty thousand. Cotys and his people were all a bit mad, but once he realized they were Greeks, he welcomed them with open arms.

King Cotys had rebelled against Artaxerxes after hearing of the Ten Thousand's feat. He felt even more confident about it after Agesilaos invaded, so he hadn't bothered to pay his tribute to the Great King in several years. Artaxerxes inevitably sent for him because of his insolence and Cotys refused to acknowledge. So now, he was at war and he was grateful for the Greeks' arrival. They were quick to form an alliance and they marched south together into Greater Phrygia, the territory of Pharnabazus. They laid waste his land and then they ventured farther east to the Cayster Plain. Sandy rock lay in all directions. But here, in the vast emptiness, they caught some of Pharnabazus's men along their route and tortured them for information. It led them closer to

Agesilaos's aim, and finally, the last breath of a flogged Persian prisoner revealed his master's location. A scouting party was dispatched. They searched every ledge, crack and hole without any success. It was the terrain. Spithridates knew Pharnabazus's tactics and habits well though, and he suggested to Agesilaos that he do the scouting personally. Agesilaos agreed. Spithridates and the king's knight, the Equal named Herippidas, embarked with a mixed sortie of Greek and Persian cavalrymen to seek him out.

The next morning under a searing sun, the sortie dismounted from their horses and crept around the bend of a mountain on foot. Spithridates led them to where he thought Pharnabazus would be and they actually found him bathing all alone in one of his favorite rivers. Pharnabazus was a private sort of man and he did not like to be seen when he bathed or when he relieved himself. So his army was out of sight, but Spithridates knew they were nearby.

Herippidas reversed his head back behind the mountain and looked at Spithridates. "Hey Persian," he whispered. "How would a modest man feel without cover?"

"Very good, Spartan," Spithridates said with bulging eyes.

Pharnabazus kept a small tent, which was big enough for one man. It was fifty paces from the river bank. His clothes and other personal property were inside it while he bathed. Herippidas and Spithridates crept across, while the satrap's back was still turned, and they stole everything inside his tent. Then they returned around the bend where their men were and shared a laugh.

"I want his staff and ring," Spithridates said in between his cackling.

Herippidas dropped his smile and he looked at him crossly. "All plunder goes to the king. Those are my orders."

Spithridates was offended. "He is not my king. He is yours, Spartan."

"You'll follow the king's orders, you sand crusted desert rat!"

Spithridates placed his hand on his hilt, when Herippidas beat him to it. "Go on then, make your move," the Spartan said.

The Persian dropped his guard. He was vexed. He knew the Spartan would open him and his riders up single-handedly. Then Spithridates mounted his horse and he rode back to the remainder of his cavalry, who was with the main army. Without a word to Agesilaos, he rode off with them and vanished in the endless sands.

Xenophon grinned as he watched his departure.

Shortly after, Herippidas returned with his men and he approached the king.

"What has happened?" Agesilaos asked, as he eyed the goods the sortie returned with.

"Pharnabazus bathes on that side of the mountain, my king," Herippidas said, pointing. "His army is to the far side."

"And what of Spithridates?"

"He claimed what was not his, my king."

Agesilaos nodded thoughtfully. "Well done." Then he looked to Demaratos and Theras. They had been promoted to polemarch along with Herippidas and three of the other Equals. "Assemble the men in the face of that mountain."

"Yes, my king," they said.

The army formed up in silence. Sixty thousand parched men waited in the scorching heat. The horizon was blurred, and when the sun had peaked, Pharnabazus walked out of a cave in the base of the mountain alone. He valiantly made his way toward the Greeks, wearing someone else's clothing. He did not look like nobility in his current dress, but he very much presented himself as such, while above, thousands of his archers appeared across the rocky mountain top. Agesilaos crossed over the gap of sand and scraggly grass and he met Pharnabazus halfway, while the armies remained at a standoff.

They stared at each other for a good while, measuring one another. It put their men on edge. The Greeks gripped their spears and shields, praying for war. While overhead, the Persian bows were drawn and their missiles were ready to be released with an unrelenting force.

"You are, Pharnabazus?" Agesilaos inquired politely.

"Yes," he said in Greek.

"I am Agesilaos. Please, let us sit," the Spartan king said, and he sat down, while gesturing for Pharnabazus to do the same.

The satrap hesitated and then he finally sat. It was against his custom to do so without something to protect him from the dusty earth. Agesilaos laughed inside, realizing this, as he allowed Pharnabazus to speak first.

"I want to remind you, that when you Spartans warred with the Athenians, I was your ally, and most importantly, your friend, Agesilaos. I was the one who provided you with the coin to destroy their fleets. I was the one who drove the Athenians into the sea with my cavalry. And nor did I deceive you like Tissaphernes. And you, you have made me an exile in my own domain. I cannot find any food, unless you leave it behind. You have destroyed my palace, burned my land, and cut down my trees."

Agesilaos nodded, confirming that he understood. "I am still your friend, Pharnabazus. This is just the way of men and war. I must treat everything your king possesses with hostility. I cannot advise you to leave your king and be my ally, but if you did, you would be rich, and free."

Pharnabazus reflected thoughtfully on his words. "You have spoken honestly, as have I. Now, I will speak directly."

Agesilaos nodded.

"If the king replaces me for my failure to stop you, as he did with Tissaphernes, I shall very much like to be your ally. But, if the king gives me the command of his army too, then I shall do my very best to war with you."

Agesilaos extended his hand with a smile. Pharnabazus clasped it, and he realized at that moment, Agesilaos was a man of honor.

"You are a good man, Pharnabazus. I shall pray for the best outcome," he said, and he began to rise.

Pharnabazus smiled, as Agesilaos assisted him to his feet. "I look forward to the future, Spartan king."

They respectfully eyed each other, as they were about to part ways.

"Allow me to return your property," Agesilaos said.

"Keep it. It is a gift," Pharnabazus replied, and then he walked back into the cave, while above, his archers disappeared.

Pharnabazus cut through an ancient tomb in the base of the mountain with a torch. He passed by many Assyrian dead, who lined the cavern walls. Their bodies had decayed to bone and dust. He perceived it as a sign of defeat. When he walked out the other side of the tomb, his army was waiting for him on horseback. There were many men, easily thrice the number of the Greeks. Pharnabazus mounted his ride with the assistance of his slave and then he looked to the man by his side. "They look for you, Great King."

Artaxerxes's eyes perked.

"But I must warn you. If we war with the Greeks, your empire will be lost. I am certain of it. It is best to wait for your golden archers to send them home."

Artaxerxes nodded. "I have great trust in you, Pharnabazus. You have served my father well and you are one of the few great men in this land. A true hero of Persia."

"Thank you, Great King," Pharnabazus said. Then he signaled the army in silence and they rode off, vanishing into the endless sands.

Meanwhile, on the other side of the mountain, Agesilaos had crossed back over to his army and approached his polemarchs.

"Your orders, my king?" Demaratos asked.

"My orders?" Agesilaos questioned under his breath. "My orders, have not changed."

# Book VI
## Kill the King

*Long ago, three hundred Spartans and their allies held a pass. It was the only possible route into Greece, as the Persian horde massed along their coast and funneled their way up the mountain to engage them. A million was their number. While the Persians were forced to fight and die for their king, the Greeks were prepared to fight alongside and die for one another. The heat was stifling this day and the tension was heavy because the freedom the Greeks fought so fiercely for had been threatened.*

*They stood, ready to do battle, when an enemy messenger approached the center gap and waited to deliver the Persian king's terms. Of the Greeks, a slave from their baggage train was sent to meet him. He knew their foreign language and accepted the message. Then he returned to the front line of his army and stood before the Spartan king to read it aloud.*

*"Deliver up your arms."*

*The king set his shield down to rest against his leg and then he extended his hand. The slave gave him the papyrus and a pen which was already wet with ink. He took no time to write his response and the message was delivered back to the enemy.*

*The Persian messenger crossed back to his army and disappeared behind the masses. He then took a snaking goat path, edged along a narrow cliff, and trekked high up to an isolated peak. Here, the Persian king sat on his golden throne to observe the coming engagement. The messenger kneeled before him and read aloud the Spartan king's response.*

*"Come and take them."*

# Pausanias

Pharnabazus, by order of the Great King, had sent Timocrates of Rhodes to Greece with gold. He met individually with the most influential men of Thebes, Corinth, Argos and Athens. The Persian king's terms were simple. War with Sparta, and the coin is yours. They readily agreed and swore their oaths. Over thirty thousand gold coins were distributed equally among them, save for Athens, as they needed no encouragement. These cities had already been complaining of the lingering effects of the Great War. It affected them all. The Spartans had taxed them by claiming portions of their crops, establishing garrisons in their cities, and enforcing their laws upon them. During the Great War, Sparta had claimed freedom for all, if they revolted against Athens. But now that the war was long over and Sparta reigned supreme, she revealed her true face. Their freedom was really servitude. So with this coin, the leaders of these cities met. They desperately wanted an end to the internal strife after such incessant war. They swore oaths of loyalty to one another and made sacrifice. Thus, the Quadruple Alliance was born.

Thebes took the initiative and acted first, as their hatred of Sparta infected them the most. They decided to make war with Sparta justified by pitting Phocis and Locris against one another. As all cities north of Boeotia and south of Thessaly looked to

Thebes for leadership, the Thebans ordered Locris to levy coin from a city their neighbor Phocis also claimed ownership to. Locris did, and as a result, the Phocians retaliated. They invaded Locris, warred with them, and took the levied funds. In response, the Locrians requested aid from Thebes. The Thebans responded and attacked the Phocians. The Phocians then sent to Sparta for aid. The Spartans enjoyed killing Thebans as much as Persians and were quick to respond. This was what Thebes wanted, justifiable grounds for war with Sparta. To other cities unaware of the inner happenings, it would now seem that Sparta was being too aggressive, and hopefully, these other cities would also rebel and become allies of the Quadruple Alliance.

The Thebans didn't stop there though. They also attacked the Spartan garrison in their city. The Spartans were heavily outnumbered and many Equals fell. The few who did manage to escape, returned to Sparta and informed their countrymen of Thebes's insolence.

Pythagoras and the council ordered two moras for retaliation. King Pausanias was given command of the entire campaign. He ordered Lysander to lead one of the moras and to meet him in Haliartus, Thebes's neighbor, in three days to begin sacking the city. Lysander and his mora reached Phocis on their way north to enlist allies, while Pausanias stopped in Tegea to do the same. By the third day, Pausanias did not show. What Lysander did not realize, was that they had departed Tegea on the second day because the allies were tardy. Additionally, while passing through Corinth, the Corinthians refused Pausanias's orders to join the Spartans in their war against Thebes. The king felt that he could waste no more time and he would have to deal with them later.

Lysander, against his better judgment, delayed his attack to the fourth day to give his king the chance to show, but still, he did not. The legendary warrior of Laconia could no longer wait or he would risk fighting greater numbers. He had been spotted that morning and he would not allow Theban reinforcements to come to their aid before he attacked. He wanted victory. Lysander needed it to heighten his status that much more to have a chance at swaying the council with his constitutional amendments. There was also a benefit to his current predicament. The king was tardy and he had done as ordered. In his mind, this was proof in itself that he was more of a patriot than his own king.

First, he yelled to the people of Haliartus, who were standing on top of their wall, to open the gates and revolt. Lysander was a grand trickster who knew how to persuade men. He sympathized with their fears, which through his career of endless war, did not faze him. The people on the wall began talking among themselves in favor of Lysander's counsel. He was having an effect, but just as quickly, the Boeotians were yanked off the wall by their Theban masters from inside.

A moment passed, and soon after, a Theban popped his head over the wall. "Retreat before you cannot!" he yelled, and then he threw a small stone at Lysander.

Lysander blocked it with his twenty and then he eyed the man on the wall. "Those words you speak require the backing of a city!" he thundered. Then, he immediately ordered his mora to lay siege to the walls.

In typical warfare, besiegers would build a surrounding rock wall around the walled city, but Haliartus was small and so were the number of Lysander's men, respectively. So he ordered the heavy armored troops to form up in a phalanx and wall in the front gates from fifty paces away. They consisted of all five hundred seventy-six Equals and two hundred Phocians, while the remaining one hundred allies were composed of slingers and archers. He ordered these light armored troops around the left, right and rear of Haliartus. When the trumpets sounded, they unleashed endless volleys of rocks and missiles into the city. Meanwhile, the Thebans counterattacked with a similar assault from the inside. Lysander and his wall of men waited it out patiently behind their twenties, as arrowheads and rocks rattled off of them. It would only be a matter of time though, before the Thebans' magazine was depleted and the city dwellers were forced to accept their terms.

The hoplites ended up being stationary for the better portion of the day. They pissed, ate and drank on the spot if they needed to from behind their twenties. Finally, the Thebans' counterattack ended. The sun was now beyond its zenith and Lysander, as well as his men, doubted the king would ever show, until they heard the sound of men on the march from their rear in the unseen distance.

"That's the king boys!" Lysander shouted to liven the men up, as most of them, himself included, were ready to doze off from the boredom of their siege.

The men instantly perked up and shouted their enthusiasm. However, when they all looked back, they spotted a force, consisting of almost two hundred cavalrymen and one thousand heavy armored troops. They were making their charge from a furlong away.

"Turn about! Hold the line!" Lysander ordered. He had never suffered a defeat from any force on land or sea. He was a champion and a master of war who despised death. His victories proved it. He was a living legend, a hero to his people. He would take the Theban reinforcements head-on and devastate them. He knew the cavalry would take fright as soon as they saw the iron points on their eights. He had seen it a thousand times and he still couldn't fathom why men persisted in attempting such foolishness.

The hoplites held the line as they faced the incoming charge, but the slingers and archers became paralyzed with fear. Phobos infected them all and they fled. Lysander glanced at the deserters and then down his line, as the sound of pounding hooves and war crazed Thebans closed the gap. The Equals were the only ones focused, while at the end of each wing, more Phocians took flight. There were about seventy-five allies in all remaining. Lysander's gaze returned to his opposition. The cavalry was no more than forty paces away and their hoplites weren't far behind.

"Back to the wall! Hold the line!" Lysander ordered.

The Phocians on the wings couldn't hear the commands being sent down the line, but they shadowed the Spartans, step for step. Lysander's regiment kept a short gap between their backs and the Haliartus Wall. It was just enough to thrust their eights, when the cavalry came in and then veered hard along their line. The horses whinnied in pain from the jerking maneuver, but it was either that, or run smack into an iron spiked wall. They circled back around behind their own hoplites and Lysander knew they were out of the engagement.

"That's it boys!" Lysander shouted, as the Theban hoplites were six spear lengths away. "Show them reason! Forward!"

The orders went down the line. The Spartans were six men deep, to the Thebans' eight and they were severely outflanked.

"Double!" Lysander commanded.

The mora doubled their file, weakening their columns to outflank the Thebans. The Phocians got mixed up during the shift and they remained at six deep. The Spartan force stepped into the crush and they shoved the Thebans' front line with their twenties. The opposing force didn't budge. The stalemate trapped the Spartans in between two walls, one of stone, the other of bronze. Eventually, Lysander managed to find an opening and he thrust his spear, when a hoplite from the Thebans' third row broke rank, jumped off the shoulders of a fellow trooper to his fore, and drove his spear through Lysander's clavicle upon landing. It was an unconventional tactic and all so sudden. Lysander fell, and with him his conspiracy, but just prior, he pulled his ash back and anchored the butt end to the ground, so that he could take his killer with him. Lysander's ash drove through the Theban's abdomen and out his upper back. There they remained, one on top of the other, spears gripped, battling in death.

It was a symbolic pose, statue-like, which shocked the Equals. The legend of Sparta was gone. The Thebans responded as if they had killed the Spartan king and surged forward. Their ferocity overwhelmed the Spartans and Phocians. Many of them fell in great slaughter by the wall. By the time the Spartans signaled their retreat, their contingent had been halved. They broke to their wings and charged their way around the wall of mangled dead, and then forward behind the exhausted Thebans, who had run in full kit from Thebes to Haliartus, but enemy cavalry still lay ahead.

They chanced it and dashed toward them. Then the Theban cavalry countercharged. They took a few Phocians down, while the Equals yanked a few riders off their mounts to cause confusion during their escape. After they had passed, the Theban cavalry turned about and chased them up a hill, leaving their own hoplites to recover. The uphill terrain proved to be impassable for their horses. The higher they ascended, the more their ride became a climb. Trees, crags, clefts and stones impeded their path, and finally, they were forced to stop their pursuit. When the Spartans saw the enemy cavalry massed together and struggling to turn around in such a difficult place, they unleashed their javelins on them. Every man hit their mark. Then they quickly resorted to rolling down boulders on them and pelted them with stones. Horse and rider took fright. Mounts fell on mounts and crushed the cavalrymen. Theban crowns were fractured from the volleys and the boulders rolled over many. Least to say, they never rode again.

The Spartans and their allies reached the top of the hill after suffering both defeat and victory. They labored for air and craved water, and as they peered down the other side of the hill, they saw Pausanias and his regiment in the far distance. In their minds, if the battle was over, they needed to recover their dead and bury them properly. But if the battle was not over, they wanted to take their dead back by force.

The survivors informed Pausanias of their defeat and they marched with five hundred Greek allies and the king's mora of Equals back to Haliartus. By this time, the Thebans had recovered their dead and sought refuge inside the city. The Spartan army stood in plain view of the wall and the fallen. Somewhere in that bloodied, cleaved mess was Lysander. The Equals vowed to get him back, but as their king surveyed the area in all directions, the front gates opened and the Thebans emerged with the Athenians backing them. A standoff ensued. Pausanias gave no commands, while his army desperately wanted to engage them. The king was thinking of what was best for Sparta, and finally, after much deliberation, he crossed over to the center gap, alone.

The Theban leader defiantly stepped to him. "What? You want to do battle like the champions of old, myself versus you?"

"I seek a truce to collect my dead," Pausanias said reluctantly.

The Theban chuckled. He felt that he had the advantage now. "Take your filthy dead and never set foot in Boeotia again. Then you shall have your truce."

Pausanias felt dejected. He swallowed his arrogance and said, "Done."

Oaths were sworn and a sacrifice was made. The Equals watched it all in disgust. The Athenians and Thebans oversaw the Spartans haul their dead away and they escorted them out of Boeotia. All the while, they shouted insults and threw stones at them until they had gone.

The Equals were vexed by their king's ill decision not to do battle and they kept their heads low, while entering the Five Villages. Night fell upon them, when they arrived at the Shrine of Athena of the Bronze House. The ephors and Elders were there to greet them, as they were anxious to learn of the outcome. When Pythagoras heard what happened, he charged Pausanias with several crimes against the state and he ordered him to appear before the council the next morning.

When the sun rose, Pythagoras planned to hold a public trial in the agora. The Spartan truce was an unacceptable defeat. Pausanias should have used force to retrieve the bodies. He also failed to meet Lysander on the appointed day of battle. These were the charges brought against their king. Pausanias thought the best course of action was not to risk the lives of anymore Equals, but the council was more concerned with Sparta's reputation. The king calculated that he would not be acquitted this time and he would surely be sentenced to death. So he fled in the night, leaving his family behind. Some say he didn't go far, only to Tegea where he died a short while later from sudden illness. Others say he took his own life, but really, he was on his way to Sicily, when three Equals sought him out on the western coast of the Peloponnese. He was attempting to push a small boat out to sea, when they came upon him. Pausanias didn't bother putting up a fight and the Equals dispatched him, dumped his body on the vessel, and sent him on his way.

## Λ

Agesipolis, son of Pausanias, was merely seven years old. He was too young to understand what happened to his father when he ascended the throne. Nonetheless, the boy king now had the honor of representing the weaker Agiad dynasty. He stood next to Pythagoras as they watched the burial of Lysander and the other Equals. The ceremony was informal. No engraved stones to mark the men, just Agesipolis, Pythagoras and ten or so other Equals who wanted to see them off. Even Cynisca approached from a distance, smiled at Lysander's fate, and then she strutted off. While Pythagoras observed the bodies being laid in a hole and the dirt poured over top, he became increasingly concerned with Thebes's insolence and the number of Equals at Sparta's disposal. He could manage the boy king for a short while, but with Sparta's precious men of war rapidly declining before his eyes and something amiss in Greece, he was determined to resolve matters.

# The Great King

Agesilaos's army marched deeper into the interior for two moons, passing Lycaonia and Cappadocia, and finally reaching Media in pursuit of Artaxerxes. The Persians had maintained a seven day lead, then five, and now the Greeks were only two days out. Scouts continued to come in, informing Agesilaos of the Great King's whereabouts. Reports of a million men were confirmed, time and again. The army loved the odds. It made them yearn for war. Every one of them sought retribution for the past two Persian invasions their forefathers suffered. In their minds, it all came down to honoring their ancestors and looting the Great King's riches. If they could put Artaxerxes's head on a stake, melt his golden throne in a fire, and get rich, they will have obtained glory beyond their wildest imaginings.

The march was difficult though. They pushed themselves hard and fast, covering nearly two days' ground in just one day. The dust, sand and scorching sun were their greatest enemy. They took it on—thirsty and dry. Their skin was tanned, burned, cracked and blistered. Many of them were darker than Ethiopians and it made them wonder of their true origins. So to make light of their hardship, they joked of each other's mother being a savage. Oh, they loved to loathe!

Due to Xenophon's knowledge of the land, he was able to lead the army to watercourses by the end of each marching day. They drank their fill and took as many skins with them as possible, drinking them dry before the next morning would end. The men shit once every seven days if Fortune blessed them and they could hardly squeeze a piss out to save their lives. It was a hellish trek, and after two more days, they caught sight of the Great King.

Artaxerxes was three days' march from Ecbatana, his destination. When he saw the Greeks' relentless pursuit, he knew he must face them, then and there, or risk losing his entire empire. The armies settled for the night and they camped with eight furlongs of sand between them. The next morning, they would war.

The allied army readied themselves next to their fires. World glory was just out of their grasp. They could feel it, as they went to sleep under a crisp, clear sky, which hosted a myriad of stars. Agesilaos shared a fire with Xenophon and Cotys. They were about to hunker down for the night, when a runner approached from the western side of camp.

His name was Epicydidas. He was an Equal sent by Pythagoras to deliver a skytale to Agesilaos. There wasn't anybody in Greece, not even a horse, who could run as long and as far as he, except only Sparta knew of his ability. He was kept secret just for this purpose and he was forbidden to compete in the Olympics and in war. Epicydidas could run from dawn to dawn to dusk without stopping, save for a piss. When he arrived in Phrygia, he had missed the army by thirty days. He had run from the Peloponnese to the edge of Thrace, sailed across the Hellespont to Lampsacus, and from there, he ran south and then east to Phrygia. Here, the freed natives, after learning that he sought the king, provided him with twelve horses, forty skins of water and food for both him and his animals. Tracking the army wasn't difficult. Epicydidas just followed the path of debris and the pointing fingers from the natives he passed. The horses were taxed from the demanding pace he required of them. They were inevitably driven into the ground from sheer exhaustion and he was forced to run the last two days in order to reach their camp.

Demaratos approached the king straight away by his fire. "My king, a skytale."

Agesilaos was surprised. "Epicydidas?"

"Yes, my king."

Agesilaos shook his head in amazement. "The man ran to the edge of the world for his country. Bring him to me, at once."

Epicydidas was escorted through the multitude of troops and he handed his king the sand covered skytale. Agesilaos wound it around his staff and then he read in between the bits of grit aloud by the fire. "Sparta, requires, you, at, once." Agesilaos looked at Epicydidas with concern.

"Much has happened, my king. Lysander has fallen. King Pausanias was charged with treason and fled. It's rumored that he took his own life in Tegea. Thebes has rebelled, along with Corinth, Athens and we also believe Argos."

Agesilaos offered him a subtle grin. "Lysander has fallen? Ha!" he thought, and then a scowl formed on his expression. "Thebes rebels?"

"Yes, my king. We learned all too late that they have been funded with coin from the Great King. Before I left, two moras were preparing to march on Corinth to make them see reason. The storms of war are upon us, my king," Epicydidas said gravely.

Agesilaos was in awe. "By Zeus, the entire world is at war! Why did the council delay sending for me?"

"It all happened at once, my king."

Agesilaos swung his head around to glance across the desert plain at the speckled firelight, which glowed throughout the Persians' camp. "Our freedom is under threat. These are grave times, indeed," he thought, and then he looked back at Epicydidas.

The runner was waiting. He was anxious for his response, but the king's consternation said it all. He was at the height of his power and nothing more would please him or his army than to kill the king.

Agesilaos then vented through his nose. "Return at once, and tell them I am directly behind you."

∧

It was unbelievable. The army departed in silence before dawn and they now sailed across the Hellespont in all haste. Artaxerxes woke that morning to a great surprise, when he found that the plain had emptied. He praised Ahuramazda for saving his empire and then he continued on his way to rest and leisure in Ecbatana. Pharnabazus remained in Media with the Persian army as a preventative measure, until they received word from Timocrates that the king's bribe had paid off. He was then sent by the Great King to attack the Spartan navy in Phoenicia. Cotys returned to Paphlagonia. Except for four hundred of Agesilaos's Asiatic Greek cavalrymen, the native troops returned to their respective cities as well. Everyone in Asia Minor, especially those along the coast, were deeply saddened that Agesilaos was leaving for his homeland. They feared slavery would return without his presence, but Agesilaos promised them that he would return if all went well at home. The king had done what he had set out to do and more. The only thing that left a bitter taste in his mouth, was not killing Artaxerxes in pitched battle.

He was below deck with Xenophon, Herippidas, Demaratos and Theras as he held a Persian coin in his hand. He glared at the archer depicted on it. The Spartans despised archers. They considered them cowards, to have to stand from a distance in order to kill someone. Agesilaos then looked to his men. "Thirty thousand archers have routed us," he grumbled. "Could Priam have bought off Agamemnon? I should think not!" he said, and then he tossed the coin on top of his spoils.

The men looked at each other awkwardly and then Demaratos stood up, garnering their attention. "My king, your men think the most of you. There isn't one of us here who wouldn't die for you. A day away from dethroning the Persian king and our orders are to return home. So what did you do, you ordered the army to return home. Not many could say they have done that. For Sparta, my king! We shall make our enemies pay for their insolence!"

Hairs rose up and down their limbs. They all nodded in agreement and sailed the remainder of the way to Thrace in silence.

## ∧

Once they landed, Xenophon offered a voluntary discharge to his Ten Thousand. Twice they ventured to the interior and twice they made it out alive. So many years had gone by that they knew no other way of life. They declined the offer and out of loyalty to their general and King Agesilaos, they stayed on the march.

Agesilaos and his Greek army were received in a friendly manner by all the Thracians as they marched west for home. It was unexpected since Thrace, the most eastern region of Greece, had remained as it had always been, lawless and uncivilized. When they reached the land inhabited by the Trochalians though, they finally received a proper greeting. Here, the local king brought his army of savages up and blocked their path. A messenger from each side met in the center gap. When Agesilaos's messenger returned, he learned that the local king demanded one hundred talents of silver and one hundred women to freely pass.

"Does he not know who we are?" Agesilaos questioned.

"I told him, my king," his messenger said.

"Savage and stupid!" Agesilaos exclaimed. Then he brushed past him and headed toward the center.

The army couldn't wait to see this, as their outraged king strutted across the gap, passed the enemy messenger, and confronted the Trochalian king who was standing with his army.

The Trochalian king stood a head taller than Agesilaos and smirked in a taunting manner at him.

Agesilaos narrowed his gaze as he looked up to meet his eyes. "Why don't you just come and take it?" he asked, and then he marched back over to his men.

The Trochalian king became furious.

Agesilaos ordered his men into battle formation and they met the Trochalians head-on. Great slaughter ensued and the Trochalians were routed. Agesilaos desperately wanted to raze their city and burn their crops, but he was just as desperate to return home.

So they pushed on without stopping after the skirmish and reached Macedonia on the eighteenth day. Again, stupidity struck.

The local king and his army had massed, so as to block the Greeks from passing. Agesilaos couldn't believe it and he had had enough. He ordered his men to hold, his messenger to remain in file, and just like before, he strutted across the gap to confront their king.

The allied army was thoroughly enjoying the spectacle, which was about to arise, because if their king was harmed in anyway, they would lay waste all of Macedonia.

"Let me guess, a hundred talents of silver and a hundred women as the cost of passage," Agesilaos said sarcastically.

"Yes. That is strange. Tell me, how did you know?" the Macedonian king asked, as if he had all day.

Agesilaos couldn't fathom his blatant audacity. It frustrated him greatly that the Macedonians and Thracians did not recognize him as their king. He looked the barbarian up and down and then square in the eye. Then, he leaned in closer. "Why don't you just come and take it?" he asked again.

The Macedonian king hid his surprise. "I will consider it."

"Good! You consider it, while we march on!" Agesilaos said, and he crossed back over to his men.

The Macedonian king's jaw dropped. He couldn't believe the Spartan king's daring.

"Morons, this part of Greece!" Agesilaos said, as he stood at the head of his army. And once again, he ordered his men to march into battle. As the gap diminished to a mere few paces, fear struck the Macedonian king and he ordered his men to step aside.

The Greek army carried on uncontested for another seven days and entered Pharsalus, which was in southern Thessaly and just north of civilization. However, the Thessalians were Theban allies and as the army marched through in their double column, their rear ranks were soon harassed by five hundred cavalrymen. The

Thessalians had long prided themselves as the world's finest riders and they began picking off the men rapidly. The horsemen would charge into their rear, stick them with their javelins, circle back around, and then do it again.

When the screams of terror rose, Xenophon was up front by the king and he was harshly reminded of the horrors he experienced in Persia. He saw that Agesilaos was already contemplating how to respond, so he suggested the hollow square formation since it had worked for him. The king passed the command along and they formed up on the move as Xenophon proposed. It didn't work. So Agesilaos improvised by ordering half of his cavalry, which was at the fore, to go to the rear. With this tactic, he found success. The Thessalians refused to engage them, but they did persist in shadowing the troops. Agesilaos responded swiftly again, and he commanded the remainder of his riders to the rear with orders to engage. They charged them at breakneck speed in a galloping phalanx. They closed the gap so fast that it prevented the Thessalians nearest them from wheeling around in time. They met their deaths from the iron points of the ash, while the remainder of the Thessalians fled. Agesilaos's cavalry pursued them, killing all those who did not reach sanctuary. The hoplites followed up the countercharge to finish off the fallen and the world renowned Thessalians were routed.

Agesilaos earned himself another victory, but this one in particular, was more grand than most. He had trained his own men, who were unrefined from the start to be effective riders and he defeated the so-called masters. He mounted a victory trophy and ordered the men to camp on the field of battle. Save for the Spartans, the men drank hard that night to celebrate their victory, and their return home.

# Λ

The men woke to a gray dawn, scraping for water, while Xenophon joined the Equals for their morning gymnastics. After, they ate a hearty breakfast of melon and barley bread, when Diphradas arrived at their camp. He was a newly elected ephor in Sparta and he was very fond of Agesilaos. He told him of Sparta's victory in Corinth and then he gave him official orders to make war with Thebes. Nothing more could have pleased Agesilaos at that moment, save for killing the Great King. He was still upset about that one, but to have his revenge with the Thebans for vandalizing his sacrifice was good enough. He was informed that the two moras who fought in Corinth would rendezvous with him, just south of the pass, in Thermopylae.

# Leonidas

Night fell and the army camped south of the pass at Thermopylae. It was known as the Hot Gates, the place where their forefathers gave their lives during the second Persian invasion to preserve their freedom, just three generations ago. The atmosphere was intimate as the men huddled together. Their campfires hissed and popped, glowing embers swept up to the heavens, and there was even an eclipsing of the moon.

"I remember a brave king and his three hundred!" one of the Equals announced, as he stood before the men and pointed his finger. "It was right over there that they gave their lives!"

"Leonidas!" the men shouted.

"He gave our country time to prepare, so that we could defeat the Persian horde!"

"Leonidas!" the men shouted again.

"He took many lives before he fell!"

"Leonidas!"

"All our fathers killed a hundred times their lot! And when Leonidas fell, there were few against many!"

"Leonidas!"

"Yet they pushed the enemy back to save his body!"

"Leonidas!" Cheese and Red yelled with everyone, as they sat together with the youngest troops. They were enthralled by the warrior before them, who sang such an alluring tale about the king of old. Leonidas was a legend, but the name also became a term for bravery, respect and sacrifice.

Before Agesilaos had departed Thessaly, he requested from Diphradas fifty volunteers of the youngest age group to campaign with him. Meaning, troops who had successfully completed the agoge and completed at least two years of training the Youths. Cheese and Red were first in line as soon as they heard there was a chance to march with the king. There was no way they were going to miss out on this.

"We shall remind the Thebans of it tomorrow!" the Equal continued. "For all of Greece joined in that fight, but they!"

The Equals and allies shouted their war cry. It shook the ground beneath them and echoed across the sea and land.

Agesilaos was enjoying the bonding of the men, thinking nothing could be better, when Diphradas approached him. All around them, the men continued to sing and praise their forefathers, while the ephor whispered terrible news in the king's ear.

"You are certain?" Agesilaos asked with concern.

Diphradas confirmed. "Yes, my king. The Persians and Athenians have defeated our navy."

"And Peisander?"

Diphradas shook his head.

The king was truly saddened by the death of his brother-in-law while he stared at the moon. Agesilaos perceived the eclipse as a grave omen and then he looked back to Diphradas. "Tell no one."

"Yes, my king. Of course," Diphradas said.

The men became quiet and attentive as soon as Agesilaos rose to his feet. The last thing the king wanted to do was dampen their spirits on the eve of battle. "I've just been informed that our navy was victorious against the Persians, but we have lost our admiral."

Every single one of them stood and raised their eight. "Leonidas!"

# THE BATTLE OF CORONEA

The Quadruple Alliance mustered their army on the colossal plain of Coronea, when reports came in that the Spartans had entered Boeotia. They faced them from a distance of two furlongs away, while the Spartans began their war ritual as usual. However, this time the freed helots and their allies joined them too, as they were all brothers on this day. They began by running around their camp three times. When that was done, they dashed to the far edge of camp and back three times, and then they formed up in columns to begin their gymnastics. They dropped to the ground belly first, placed their twenties upside down on their backs, pushed themselves off the ground, and then lowered back down. They repeated this pushing movement, until they couldn't. On command, they sprang to their feet and lowered their rears with their twenties held out in front, as if they were sitting on chairs, and then they stood back up. They did this, until they couldn't. Next, they dropped their twenties by their feet, bent over, picked them up, and then stood tall with their twenties raised high overhead. Then they lowered their twenties back to the ground and repeated this lifting movement, until they couldn't. Finally, men of similar size paired up. One man rested with his back on the earth, while locking his legs around the standing man's waist. Then, they grabbed hands and the standing man pulled his partner off the ground toward his own chest, and then he lowered him back down. It was just like rowing. They did this, until they couldn't and then they switched up. When their gymnastics were complete, they sat for morning inspection, which was performed by their polemarchs. Afterwards, the helots distributed rations of bread and fruit, and they ate a hearty breakfast.

The Quadruple Alliance did nothing of the kind. It took all their courage just to meet the Spartans in battle. They were already in their kits and fiddling with their lids or shields to occupy their minds before the coming engagement.

Meanwhile, back across the plain, Spartan trumpets sounded off, ordering the men to form up in columns again, while Agesilaos was given a she-goat to make sacrifice. He straddled her between his legs and slit the beast's neck. She buckled to the ground after a bit of bleeding and then Agesilaos proceeded to remove the liver. After discovering the organ was healthy, he nodded to Diphradas and the other ephor standing off to the side of the army, silently telling them all was well. Agesilaos then crossed over to them and he placed the drooping viscus on the fiery spit, as an offering to Zeus and Athena. The remainder of the goat was cut up and also offered to the gods. The legs went to Artemis, Ares and his two sons, Deimos and Phobos. The eyes went to the twin gods, may they both see at the same time. Every bit of the goat was offered, and after completing the ceremony, Agesilaos returned to the fore, eager as a youth. He couldn't wait to kill Thebans. He stood facing his polemarch, as Demaratos and Theras had been ordered back to their original rank of enomotarch. The demotion wasn't punishment at all. They had served the king well in Persia. What it did come down to though, was seniority and experience.

"Pipers," the king ordered.

The polemarch serving the king's mora turned and pointed a finger at the pipers. The pipers began playing, as all other moras followed in suit. Then the king nodded to his polemarch, who responded by barking the same order he had always given the men. "What are you looking at, you worthless dogs? Square your kits! Armor on! Get in file!"

All the way down the line the command was repeated by the other polemarchs. The men responded as if it were a time of leisure, while the helots brought them their oil and combs. They untangled their hair, making sure their locks would fall just right over their crimson cloaks, as crusted grime and bugs fell to the earth beside them. Then, they anointed their bodies from crown to toe in olive oil. The Equals always made themselves beautiful just in case they must pass on to the next world.

On the other side of the field, the Quadruple Alliance was hoping to get on with the engagement and return home before dark. Many of them, save for the Thebans, were becoming demoralized the longer they had to wait. It seemed to them, that every step the Spartans took to prepare for war was a ritual within a ritual, like the meticulous way the Spartans draped their cloaks over their bodies, and the way they shined their twenties, lids and points on their eights. It instilled fear into them, whether they realized it or not. Some were ready to charge straight away, while others were ready to pack up and go home. They could do battle another day, they thought, show up much later, after their enemy had prepared and just got on with it. The wait made them squirm and lean from one foot to the other. Their commanders noticed and they ordered them to remain in formation, but then it happened. A man pissed himself. Then another man vomited. Eventually, waste was being excreted throughout. It was Phobos, son of Ares, sweeping through them like a plague, and all a part of the Spartan plan.

The Equals continued their ritual by placing their wool caps snugly over their crowns, followed by their polished lids. They bore scars and dents from previous campaigns, telling a tale of each man's life as a warrior. Next, they carefully reassembled the leather arm strap on the backside of their twenties. This would allow them to slide their forearm through and secure it to their person. It had to be done just so. And finally, with the sun above the tree line, they were ready.

The pipers were signaled to stop and the Equals ordered their helots to return to the baggage train and guard their property. Then the trumpets sounded off and each man stood at attention. There was one column per enomotiae, which was commanded by one enomotarch. For every mora, there was one polemarch, four lochagi, eight pentecosters and sixteen enomotarchs. When the second signal was given, the enomotiae snapped three abreast, again, and now six. The polemarchs take orders from King Agesilaos, who in turn give commands to their lochagi. They relay the orders to their pentecosters, who command the enomotarchs. The enomotarchs give out the final word to the six columns, standing sixteen men deep behind them.

The Spartan army stood sixty furlongs in breadth and consisted of approximately the following:

1,232 Spartan hoplites
8,600 peltasts and hoplites from the Ten Thousand
6,000 Greek allies, serving as peltasts and hoplites
2,000 freed Helots, serving as hoplites

450 cavalrymen, serving as baggage guards and message bearers for the king

Across the plain, the Quadruple Alliance stood one hundred furlongs in breadth and consisted of approximately the following:

3,600 Theban hoplites
6,000 Athenians, serving as peltasts and hoplites
4,200 hoplites from Argos
5,160 Corinthians, serving as peltasts and hoplites
10,000 Greek allies, serving as peltasts and hoplites
600 cavalrymen, serving as baggage guards and message bearers for their commanders

The armies faced off, ready to commence. The vast field was lush and green. The sky was clear and the sun shined down on their shimmering, bronze armor. The men of Sparta took the right wing, as it was customarily known as the strong side in warfare. Xenophon was honored again to fight alongside Agesilaos and his knights. He was placed in the sixth row directly behind him. Cheese was in the rear of the other Spartan mora, which was to the left of the king's. He was with his age group, along with Red. It was their first campaign. They were nervous and excited. Not only that, they were honored to have their troop leader from the days of the agoge as their enomotarch. Demaratos glanced back to ensure they were in line, when Cheese stepped to the side and caught his eye. They didn't have the chance to speak since his return from Persia, so they pointed their eights at one another. "Never quit, never yield," they mouthed, and then they fell back in line.

The Ten Thousand and the freed helots filled the center. Herippidas was given command of Xenophon's troops. He was still as ugly and terrifying as ever. The Spartans' allies held the left wing. Many of them were Boeotians. They were known as the people of Orchomenus. The Orchomenians were bitter rivals of the Thebans, as the Argives in the Peloponnese were to the Spartans.

The Quadruple Alliance placed the Thebans on their strong side to engage the troops of Orchomenus. The men of Athens, Corinth and their ten thousand allies filled the center, while the Argives held the left wing to face their rivals.

Agesilaos turned away from the enemy to face his men. "Make these insolent wretches, see reason!"

The army bellowed their war cry. It echoed across the field, making the Quadruple Alliance shiver. The Thebans however, remained confident, as they were still roused after defeating Lysander.

"Double!" Agesilaos ordered to match the enemy's breadth.

The polemarchs issued the order to their lochagi, who passed it along to their pentecosters. The enomotarchs received the order and they issued it to their enomotiae. The three step maneuver was executed with perfection. It sounded like three claps of thunder.

"Forward!" Agesilaos ordered.

Even though they were severely outnumbered, the king's army advanced fearlessly to the triumphant song of Castor's Air. Across the field, the Quadruple Alliance was trembling as they proceeded forward to their own hymn. The lines of each army were massive, stretching across the entire plain from tree line to tree line. Pitched battle was upon them. The fate of Greece rested in their hands. Not much farther now, when their songs came to an end.

With less than a furlong to go, the field fell eerily silent. A moment later, the Thebans let out their war cry and they charged their Boeotian rivals. The Athenians did the same, charging the Ten Thousand. The highly trained Spartan army remained unfazed and they kept to their disciplined march. When the gap narrowed to a mere forty paces, Agesilaos ordered Herippidas's regiment and the Spartan allies to countercharge. The orders were sent down the front line and they reached them after six paces. The Spartan allies, which included the men of Orchomenus, met the Thebans in the crush, while the Athenians ran into a ferocious, spiked wall of bronze and iron from the Ten Thousand. They were going to remain undefeated. Half the pitch was now at war, as the other side was about to engage.

"Twenties!" Agesilaos ordered, while he and the remainder of the army followed up the charge.

Directly across from the Spartans, the Argives were struck with fear and they decisively retreated beyond their own camp in the mountains. It was Laconian might at its finest. The Argives never engaged their rivals, and so, they were defeated without a man fell.

"Hold!" Agesilaos ordered, as he glanced to his left. The line was so long, one was unable to see beyond their own mora, let alone the far wing. The Spartans thought they had routed the entire army and they began celebrating with shouts and cheers. Xenophon even kept a garland on his person for when the time came and he presented it to Agesilaos to honor his victory. At first, the king was hesitant to accept it because he couldn't make out what was going on with the rest of his army. He wondered if the clashing sounds of men on the far end were a rout or a defeat. As he didn't want to disappoint his good friend, he began to place the olive wreath on his head, when one of his cavalrymen approached.

"My king, my king!" the cavalryman yelled, as his steed came to an abrupt stop.

Agesilaos looked over and he read the rider's consternation.

"The freed helots have just routed the Corinthians and their allies. The Athenians will be finished soon enough by the Ten Thousand, but the Thebans have turned defeat into victory. They've broken through the Orchomenian lines, my king. They attack the baggage train!"

Agesilaos's eyes went wide as the garland slipped from his clutches. "Ensure the ephors are safe!"

"Yes, my king!" the rider said, as he yanked his mount around hard and rode off at once.

"Square the line! Countermarch!" Agesilaos commanded.

The two Spartan moras formed up and they rotated their square phalanx as one. They now faced their baggage train, while everyone remained in the same relative position.

"Forward!"

They charged at the double toward the Thebans.

"Hold!"

Agesilaos surveyed the happenings with precision from a short measure away. He spotted Diphradas and the other ephor being escorted away on horseback by three hundred riders, while the Thebans were putting the helots to slaughter in an effort to reach safety.

After routing the Orchomenians and the other Spartan allies, the Thebans pushed all the way through, far and wide to the corner of the pitch. At that exact moment, they had received word from their own cavalry that the Argives had retreated to Mount Helicon, which rested behind their own camp. They were trying to do the same in a cohesive manner, but as the plain was bordered by hills and trees, they were forced to wheel around and come up behind the Spartan baggage train in an effort to get there. When the Thebans finally broke through, they yielded and gazed upon a dreadful and terrifying sight. The Spartans were within spear's reach. So as the Thebans had defeated their antagonist and the Spartans had routed theirs, a new rivalry for the ages was underway, one for ultimate rule.

"Twenties!" Agesilaos thundered.

The wall of lambdas was formed. They were going to take them head-on. In typical warfare, the Spartans, or any other Greek army for that matter, would allow the enemy to pass through and then they would attempt to cut them down from behind. This was to prevent their own men from being killed unnecessarily. And there it was, that never before seen thing that men would tell tales of for generations to come.

"Take'em!" Agesilaos ordered, as his men were so close that they already had.

The Equals fed off their king's daring. They yearned to make these insolent wretches see reason. For Lysander. For Agesilaos. And above all, for Sparta. Unparalleled glory was going to be found here, as many men were about to die.

A cacophonous sound rose above the din as shield met shield. The Spartans and Thebans shoved for their lives in an attempt to gain the upper hand. The line was stubborn. It wouldn't budge as both sides were firm in their cause. The stalemate remained this way for a good measure of time.

Cheese and Red were in the rear row, observing their seniors perform their labor. They were more like spectators at the games. They wanted glory, as did any Spartan, but to see war for the first time in their lives, this close, secretly satisfied their hunger. This was why the youngest were placed in the back. It was another lesson to be learned, to continue preparing their minds to willingly make the ultimate sacrifice.

Xenophon was in the sixth row directly behind the king, pushing on the back of an Equal to his fore. His feet dug into the earth, stripping skin and breaking nails. Socrates was right, he thought, I will die on tour with the Spartans. Then his eyes went wide as he glanced at the crush.

The Thebans became desperate. Troopers from their second and third rows began hurling themselves off the backs and shoulders of the men to their fore. They aimed for Agesilaos, spear and head first, just as they did to Lysander. This was against traditional Greek warfare and deemed dishonorable. But if they could kill the king in this manner or any other, they could devastate Sparta's reputation for all time. The weight of their falling bodies broke the Spartans' right front line. Their spears nicked and penetrated the king's limbs next to his age-old scars as they fell and never rose again. They were getting closer. Many of the king's knights gave their lives as they shielded him. Men in the second row stepped forward and replaced their fallen brothers, while Agesilaos remained steadfast during the thick of it. The pain and sight of his own blood made him yearn for victory. "Send these dogs to Hades!" he yelled.

The Equals in the second and third rows put a stop to their enemy's desperation. They shoved the broken line back into place, while skewering the Thebans who fell in their ranks with the butt end of their eights. It was discipline amid total chaos, and they were masters at it. The shoving match resumed, until more enemy troopers resorted to launching themselves in the air, in an attempt to come down on Agesilaos again. The crush was thrown back into confusion. The lines broke on both sides, but the Spartans exploited the gaps and they gained the advantage across the center and left wing of their front.

Shield shove!

Spear thrust!

Forward advance!

Back by the king, great slaughter continued. Thebans and Spartans were killing one another with a feral like ferocity. They were lions battling lions. Men fell. The Thebans trampled over their dead to fill their front in a mad frenzy. Their middle rows were now at their fore. Agesilaos took more hits. He grit his teeth in pain. Several spearheads had punctured his midsection, but he had trained himself to step back and to the side, so as to move with the attack. In this way, his vitals would remain unscathed. It saved his life in the past, and thus, so far. He surged back into the fray, fearless, a true man of Sparta, dismembering his adversaries, while holding the line. The knights around him continued to fall. Xenophon now found himself directly behind his good friend. It was difficult for him just to keep his feet steady on all the mutilated dead, as he himself was one step closer to death.

Elsewhere on the battlefield, the surviving Quadruple Alliance had fled to Mount Helicon, while the other moras were recovering from their exhausting labor. Their hands were on their knees, gasping for air. The fight had gone on for so long that the sun already reached its zenith.

Demaratos and Theras were among the second mora to the left of their king. They were painted red as they neared the rear of the Thebans' right line. Cheese and Red were now getting a taste of what they had trained for all their lives. The youngest troops were driving the iron pointed butts of their eights down as they marched on top of the enemy. Every few paces forward, a trooper's foot would sink up to his calf. He'd pull it out and observe a dark, reddish-brown mixture. The thick, lumpy substance was similar to barley meal and water, but consisted of earth and men.

The second mora eventually routed the Thebans' right wing and they allowed the rear lines of the enemy to flee. The Spartans lost a good number of their men, but they couldn't think about that now. They must press on to ensure victory, so that the deaths of their brothers, cousins, fathers, uncles and friends would not be in vain. The polemarch of the second mora immediately ordered the countermarch. They rotated their phalanx around to the right and flanked the Thebans, where the fighting was still the worst.

Agesilaos continued to fight hard as his body was being pieced off. It was the battle of the ages, greater than the Great War. All around him was gore and screams of men killing men. They were blood stained and speckled with entrails. Bodies lay torn open in all directions. The Equals had broken their eights three times. There were so many in surplus though, that they would just reach down blindly and pick another one up. Xenophon remained behind his friend, thrusting his javelin over Agesilaos's shoulder. They fought relentlessly and desperately to hold the line, but the Thebans just kept throwing their lives away trying to kill the king. Xenophon was deeply concerned, and then it happened. His eyes bulged from his crown as he watched Agesilaos fall backward on to him. There was a gaping, black hole on his thigh. Blood leaked from every contour of his body. All eyes were on them at that moment and then the Thebans erupted with a great roar. They had done it. They had killed the king and they could feel their victory, but then it happened again, that never before seen thing. Above the din, the Spartans shouted their most sacred order, one that every Equal wished to be given, a command to unleash the wrath of Ares and shit on Tartaros if necessary. Thrust your eights. Lay down your life. *Do whatever it takes, damn you, and save your king!*

"Leonidas!"

Nine Equals nearest Agesilaos formed a phalanx within the chaos to shield their king. They drove back nearly two hundred roused Thebans with their own might. It was a Heraklean feat. An instant later, all nine were cut down by the enemy surging inward from their flanks.

"Leonidas!"

More Equals stepped in and held the line. It bought Xenophon the time he needed to drag the king out of the skirmish. The troops behind him opened up a pathway and then he shuffled backward to reach safety.

"Leonidas!"

Herippidas heard the cry from a good measure away as he was returning with his Ten Thousand. The other polemarchs too, heard the call and they shouted the sacred order.

"Leonidas!"

Spartans and men of Greece hit the Thebans, like a wave surging across land. They brought them devastation. The Thebans in the rear lines managed to funnel out from behind the slaughter, before they too fell, and then they retreated around the battle to Mount Helicon.

Many shouted. "Nike!"

Others bragged. "We killed the king!"

Meanwhile, Xenophon had dragged Agesilaos to a wooded area just off the pitch under the cover of shade. "Don't you die on me, Agesilaos!"

The king's eyes opened and weakly rolled around until they spotted his friend. "Ha!" Agesilaos said, and then he fell unconscious.

Xenophon panicked as he gazed at the maimed king. Then he tore his cloak into long strips, but he didn't know where to begin. The blood just wouldn't stop gushing. It was coming from everywhere. The most severe injury seemed to be on his thigh. The wound looked as if a spear came in at an angle, and went through and through, before it retracted. His abdomen had been torn open in three places. The flesh on his arms was shredded. Literally, all save for his neck and crown had been mangled. The king desperately required aid. Xenophon wanted to call for the doctors at the baggage train, but he could not risk drawing enemy attention during the Thebans' retreat. So he tied the wounds up tight, as best he could, and waited in silence for the battle to end. Oh, the joys of war.

∧

The Coronean plain was gruesome. Thousands lay dead, their bodies torn in threes and fours. Shields were shattered. Swords and spears were broken and strewn across the bloodstained earth. The dying and wounded ailed, pleading for aid, or for their end. The Spartan army was gathered at the baggage train to have their wounds tended to. Theodoros made it out alive and unharmed. He was overwhelmed, seeing to everyone he could, as were the other doctors. Severed limbs and puncture wounds had to be cauterized. There were hundreds of them. The youngest troops carried the wounded off the field. For them, it was another lesson in war, to acclimate to the horror of it all. The enemy, they disregarded and let them bleed out.

Agesilaos woke to find his entire body bandaged. He looked like the Egyptian dead. The opening on his leg was burned with hot iron to stop the bleeding. It hurt like hell. His stomach was sewn shut in three places and the remainder of his injuries, after being cleaned and dressed, proved inconsequential. He tried to stand.

"My king, are you mad? Sit down before you fall apart!" Xenophon ordered.

Agesilaos was in grave pain and he yielded his efforts. He didn't realize Xenophon was by his side and then he looked to him with a sense of urgency. "Are we the victors?" he asked with concern.

"Yes, my king. Few Thebans will walk this plain again."

Agesilaos glanced around at all the wounded warriors and then back at Xenophon. "Find a stretcher. I must check on the men."

The Spartan king was carried through the baggage train to witness the aftermath and also to let the men know that he lived. From there, he was carried through the field of battle. He was distraught by all the dead, including his foe, when a cavalryman approached.

"My king, the enemy is in sanctuary on the peak of Mount Helicon."

Agesilaos looked up and found the snout of a horse looming over him. It was too painful for the king to shift his gaze to find the rider's face. So he spoke to the cavalryman, while looking at the horse. "We must show reverence to the gods," he winced. "Escort them to safety, wherever that may be."

"Yes, my king. I am grateful you were spared," he said, and then he rode off.

A polemarch approached immediately after. "Your orders, my king."

Agesilaos winced again. "Collect all the dead. Place them inside our lines."

"Yes, my king. Thank the gods you are still with us," the polemarch said, and then he departed.

By the time dusk neared, two enormous mounds of bodies had been stacked, one friendly, the other foe. Cavalry guards were posted around the entire camp. Fires were lit and the wounded hunkered down for the night, while those who were still capable, began burying the men in masses. Agesilaos slept intermittently from the pain. When he would wake, he would grimace, as if it was his end and then he would fall back asleep. Xenophon remained by Agesilaos's side. He was greatly concerned for his fate. The Equals kept approaching him too. They offered him praise and their thanks for saving the king's life, as he kept an eye on his friend for the duration of the night.

Λ

The next morning when Agesilaos woke up, he found Xenophon asleep by his side. He eyed his friend thoughtfully for a moment. Then he stood up, which caused him to grit his teeth, and he limped away. Xenophon opened his eyes shortly after and he sprang forward, as he was surprised to see Agesilaos standing on his own two feet. Agesilaos heard Xenophon rise, but he didn't turn around to face him so that he could conceal his true anguish. "You're a good friend, Xenophon."

Xenophon smiled in response to his kind words as he watched the king make his way toward the edge of camp, swing his cloak aside, and relieve himself. The former philosopher shook his head in amazement due to his overnight recovery. When the king turned around, the polemarchs ordered the trumpets to sound off and the men woke from their slumber. Xenophon brought Agesilaos a staff and offered him a shoulder to lean on, but the king refused, accepting only the staff. "Square the line," Agesilaos ordered to his polemarchs.

"You heard your king, you worthless dogs! Square your kits! Armor on! Get in file!"

All those still able to serve, threw their lids on, grabbed their twenties and eights, and snapped into file.

Agesilaos could see from wing to wing. It told him he had lost many, as he looked back to his polemarch. "Raise a victory trophy. Everyone is to wear a garland," he said. Then he looked to his army and yelled, "Nike!"

The men shouted back. "Nike!"

Once the victory trophy had been raised and the men fashioned themselves with garlands, they ate their morning meal. A Theban messenger arrived at the edge of camp at this time and he requested to speak with the king. His appeal was granted and he was escorted over to Agesilaos.

"Spartan king, we request a truce to bury our dead," the messenger said.

"Spartan king?" Agesilaos inquired mockingly.

"My king," the Theban restated bitterly. "We request a truce to bury our dead."

Agesilaos looked toward the edge of camp, where the mound of enemy corpses were waiting to be buried. He was grieved by the loss and sighed. "You were given coin from the Persian king to war with me. But together, we could have taken his empire, and you could have had all the coin you wanted."

The messenger silently acknowledged, and then he noticed the victory garlands on the men's crowns. As he looked back at Agesilaos, he lowered his gaze in a defeated manner.

"Truce granted," Agesilaos grumbled, and then he walked off.

After the enemy dead were taken, Agesilaos ordered three hundred Equals, who were to be led by Herippidas, to reinstate the garrison at Thebes and to use any means necessary to do so. The Spartans and their allies finished burying their dead and they were preparing to return home, since their Persian campaign had finally come to an end. They all wondered what they would do now, especially Xenophon.

# Xenophon

Dark, turbulent storm clouds were on the horizon, while Xenophon wore a hooded cloak as he inconspicuously made his way to the Athenian agora. There, he spotted Plato. He remained at a distance and stood behind a Doric column on the far end, while he watched him teach a group of youths. It made him feel like he was choking. He swallowed hard to refrain from crying, but a single tear did escape. It wasn't just Plato, everywhere he looked men were teaching boys to use reason and logic. Some were pointing to the sun as they measured a shadow with their feet. Another teacher was scratching a system of numbers, letters and symbols on the earthen floor, and then he used it to prove a theory. Xenophon's city had changed dramatically, and seemingly, for the best. It was the Athens he longed for, before he had left. It made him wonder so many things. He wondered if Socrates would still be alive had he not left. Or, would so many of his pupils be teaching in public, if Socrates had not been executed. It all became too overwhelming as he stepped back and disappeared into the masses.

By dusk, the rain began to fall at a slow pace. Plato approached Socrates's house with bread, fish and wine. He was going to deliver it to his late teacher's family, as he had done every day since his passing, when Xenophon stepped from the shadows and approached his fellow pupil.

"Plato," Xenophon whispered.

Plato was caught off guard. He thought he was to be beaten and his goods were to be stolen, until Xenophon slid his hood back to reveal himself. "Xenophon? Is that you?"

Xenophon offered a partial grin. "It is."

"You are twice your size! A beard? And you don't even look, like you!" Plato said with surprise.

Xenophon stared at Plato without a word. He was a callous mercenary now and he didn't waste time with idle talk.

Plato realized he had changed on the inside too. "You must be careful. They have banned you from the city," he said, feeling like there was a great distance between them.

"Is it true he died well?" Xenophon asked, as he appeared to be unconcerned for his own safety.

"Yes, it is true. But, I regret I was not strong enough to face him at the time," Plato said.

"Nor would I have been able to," Xenophon replied sympathetically.

A silent moment passed with only stares being exchanged. They each wondered what the other had been through during their years apart.

"We used to be the greatest friends, eh Xenophon?"

"We still are," he said Laconically.

Plato smiled. "I suppose you want to know where he is."

Xenophon nodded.

"Do you recall the hill just inside the city wall, where he would take us when we were young?"

"The one with the three myrtle trees."

"Yes, the grave is unmarked, but you will know it when you see it."

"Thank you, Plato," Xenophon said, and then he slipped his hood over his crown as he took his leave.

A moment passed, when Plato felt the sudden need to call out to him. "Xenophon!" he said desperately.

He turned around from a short measure away.

"He never stopped talking about you."

Xenophon acknowledged without a word and vanished into the night.

## Λ

The rains became heavy as Xenophon approached the secret place where Socrates had been laid to rest. Fond memories came flooding back uncontrollably. "Well, here we are old man," Xenophon said, followed by a rush of tears. Then, he suddenly became weak and dropped to his knees as he cried. "You were right. You were right, Socrates. I should have listened to you." The philosopher in him sobbed like a little boy. He drooled and dripped mucus as he lowered his face to the wet earth. "I'm sorry I wasn't there for you." Xenophon wept harder for another moment and then he abruptly picked his head up. He wiped his face clean after rising back to his feet and stared at the grave one last time. "Off I go again, old friend," Xenophon said, as he swallowed the lump in his throat. "To start a new life, once more."

# Agesilaos

Agesilaos refused to be carried home to allow his wounds to heal. It was his homecoming after all and he wanted to set foot in the Five Villages on his own two feet. He marched in at the head of two moras with his walking staff and entered the agora by the Shrine of Athena of the Bronze House. All of Sparta congregated to greet them upon their arrival. The citizens rallied around their king and they praised him for his Persian and Theban victories, as well as not succumbing to foreign influence while abroad. Meaning, he had returned as he had left.

Mothers who learned they had lost their sons at Coronea inquired to the Equals if they had died bravely. "Where were his wounds?" they would ask. When hearing that the fatal wounds were to the fore, the mothers rejoiced. There were a few however, who learned their sons were struck in the back and so they wept. Clearly, their sons had tried to flee from battle and they died like cowards. There was no other possible explanation in their minds.

Word of Peisander's naval defeat spread throughout as well. It was spoken of directly in front of King Agesilaos, but no one found fault with him for keeping the men's morale up on the eve of war.

It was a joyous time in the Five Villages with everyone back home, but Agesilaos was in a great deal of pain. He excused himself and made his way inside his modest dwelling. He kissed Kleora now that they were in private and then he took a seat at his oaken table. She walked Archidamus over to him and Agesilaos held him in his arms for the very first time. When he met the boy's eyes, he became so overcome with joy that he felt compelled to stand and trophy him around. Kleora watched. She was all smiles despite losing her brother, when all of the sudden, in the midst of holding Archidamus high over his head, Agesilaos felt an immense surge of pain spread throughout his body. He stepped over to Kleora with a heavy foot, passed the boy off to her, and collapsed on the spot. Kleora was shocked. She couldn't comprehend it. Yes, he was covered in wounds, but he was always covered in wounds. Then, after a closer examination, she discovered that the one on his leg had become disfigured.

"Doctor!" the queen yelled. "Doctor!"

Demaratos, Theras, Cheese and Red happened to be walking by outside and they heard her cry. When they stormed inside, they found their king down. Demaratos looked to Cheese and Red. "You know who to get."

"Yes sir," they said, and they departed at once.

"I'll get the doctor," Theras said, and he ran off as well.

Demaratos gazed at the undressed wound. It had become large and round from the burn he was given to stop the bleeding. It was also speckled with some sort of strange, greenish-black, crusted grit and a bloody puss oozed from where it seemed to have reopened. The skin around the wound had an unusual violet hue. It did not look well. Demaratos then looked up and he met his queen's eyes. They were both despondent.

Λ

Theodoros just began examining Agesilaos, when Sparta's finest doctor barged in and pushed him aside. He lowered down to inspect the wound and then he rose back up to his feet. "My queen," he said sullenly. "There is nothing anyone can do, save keep it clean. If I cut the leg off, he will surely die. It is up to his god now. I am truly sorry, for all of Sparta." He glanced at Demaratos, Theras and the boys, and then again back at his queen before he departed. "I will sacrifice a cock to Apollo."

Kleora was distraught and feeling utterly helpless, but after the doctor took his leave, Theodoros performed a more thorough examination and then he looked to her. "My queen, there is one man above all who can cure the king. I'll swear my life, and freedom on it."

"Well, by the gods who?" Kleora asked.

"Hippocrates, my queen."

"But he lives in Kos! That is nearly in Asia!"

"There is still time, my queen," Theodoros insisted.

"You two," Kleora commanded to Demaratos and Theras. "Prepare a ship and leave at once. I will speak to the council on your behalf."

Demaratos and Theras bowed their heads and immediately took their leave. Cheese and Red followed, with Theodoros trailing them.

"Not you!" the queen commanded.

Theodoros turned about.

"See to your king!"

# ʌ

Theras and Demaratos rode their mounts south to Gytheum and enlisted oarsmen. From there, they ventured to Taenarum, the southernmost point of the Peloponnese. The oarsmen funneled their way below deck, sat on their benches, and were ready to row. Demaratos, Theras and twenty other Equals from the local garrison, boarded the ship along with them.

The captain, a hired hand who was known for travelling at great speeds, approached Demaratos. "You say you wanted to go to Kos?"

"Do we have a problem?" Demaratos asked sternly.

"By the gods, no sir," he said in a fearful manner. "It's just—"

"Speak sense!" Demaratos ordered. "This is no time to be idle!"

"Those seeking Kos, are usually seeking Hippocrates," the captain said curiously.

"What of it?"

"He came through, just three days ago. To Olympia, was where he was headed."

Demaratos grabbed the captain by his throat and squeezed. "Do you swear to Poseidon, you speak the truth!"

"Yes, sir," he gagged.

Demaratos looked over to Theras for approval and got it. He then focused back on the captain. "Keep your coin, and look at all these men around you," he said, while letting go of his chokehold.

The captain favored his throat as he gazed at the sinewy, sinister men, wearing their crimson cloaks.

"Consider them your enemy, if I have been deceived."

# Λ

Hippocrates entered the king's bed chamber the next evening. "My king," he said, feeling a bit nervous due to Agesilaos's renowned. "I am Hippocrates."

Agesilaos weakly peered up from his bed and he spotted a man staring into his eyes. He had long white curly hair, a youthful appearance, and unfortunately, an Athenian style beard. Agesilaos suddenly perked up, as he comprehended who he was. His eyes bulged and his belly dropped because he was in awe of the famed doctor. Tales were told that he could cut a man open and repair things on the inside. Others say he wielded dark, magical powers from the underworld. "I am, honored, you have come all this way just for me," Agesilaos said.

Hippocrates spoke nothing of the coercive tactics and blatant abduction, which he was forced to undergo by Demaratos and Theras, as he briefly glanced back at them. "The honor is all mine, my king."

Demaratos and Theras took that as a sign and made for their leave, while Agesilaos gritted his teeth from another surge of pain.

"Where does it hurt, my king?" Hippocrates asked.

"You will speak not a word of this to anyone outside the Five Villages," Agesilaos demanded, as he was concerned for Sparta's reputation.

Hippocrates looked at Agesilaos oddly. "I don't know who has been tending to your health, but I swore an oath to the gods to never speak of such matters, other than to the person I am treating."

"Very well," Agesilaos moaned. He pulled each end of his cloak away. His flesh was riddled with scars and dressed wounds.

Hippocrates was most impressed that a man could take such a thrashing and still be alive to talk about it. "Well, which one is the problem?" he joked.

Agesilaos grinned and became a bit more relaxed in front of the acclaimed doctor, as Hippocrates removed the linen and willow bark treatment, which Theodoros had applied to his stomach and leg. He quickly examined the abdomen and then reapplied the dressing. As for the leg, he pushed and squeezed on the round hump in various places. The king grunted from the excruciating pain it caused. Simultaneously, Hippocrates was grinning, as if he was mad in the head while he performed his magic. It seemed to calm his nerves, while in the presence of royalty. Finally, the trapped fluid erupted and a great deal was released, offering Agesilaos some relief.

"Well, that should do. I've seen much worse, but another couple of days and I would have taken your leg, my king."

Agesilaos was expecting further treatment. "That is it? That is all that was required?" he asked, after noticing the hump had diminished.

"What more would you like me to do?" Hippocrates countered.

"Ha!" Agesilaos exclaimed. "A doctor who can take a joke."

Hippocrates smiled at him in response, while Kleora did not understand what had transpired. She needed reassurance of her husband's well-being. "What is it doctor? What is the problem?" Kleora asked.

"It is the first stage of infection, my queen."

"You will save him?" she asked naively.

"I should think I already have, my queen," Hippocrates said.

She and the council, who was listening in the next chamber, felt tremendous relief.

"But I must ask, merely out of curiosity. Who treated him before I?" Hippocrates inquired.

"Just one of our helots," Agesilaos said. "Why do you ask?"

"His treatment is exactly what I would have done." Hippocrates said. "Now, you need to do several things if you want to keep your leg, so pay close attention. First, where is this helot of yours? Please, bring him in."

"I freed him many years ago," Agesilaos added in.

"I don't doubt you, my king," Hippocrates said sarcastically, which gave them both another laugh.

Meanwhile, Kleora stepped through the main chamber, passing members of the council, and she called for Theodoros from the front door. He was outside, waiting for the outcome with Demaratos, Theras, Cheese and Red, as well as many other worried citizens. He answered her call at once.

"I am Theodoros, sir," he said to the doctor. "You called for me?"

"Yes, your use with the willow is precisely the right method. Three times a day, you are to clean the king's wounds. Apply a light coating of castor oil, continue with the myrrh and willow leaves, and top that with the bark as you have done. Always use clean linens to dress the wounds. That is vital," Hippocrates said.

"Yes, sir," Theodoros replied.

"Additionally, three swallows of the willow's nectar. Ideally, after the king has eaten."

Agesilaos groaned at everything being prescribed to him, as Hippocrates continued. "Let's see, it is the waxing of the moon now...Continue to treat him until the second waning. He should have a full recovery by then." Hippocrates looked back at Agesilaos. "And my king, do stay off your feet until then."

Agesilaos whined. "By the twin gods, doctor! I won't have a chance of staying alive, if I have to do all that!"

Hippocrates briefly chuckled and then he felt it was time to leave. "It has been an honor, my king. I believe your god is Apollo. I shall offer him a cock."

"Thank you, doctor," Agesilaos said.

Next, he turned to Theodoros after rising to his feet. "Come and visit me in Kos, should you be able. There is much there for you to learn."

Theodoros nodded.

Finally, Hippocrates looked to Kleora. "My queen," he said, bowing his head, and then he walked out of the king's house.

Outside, Hippocrates confronted Demaratos and Theras. "I am ready to return to Olympia, and this time I demand to be escorted."

"Ask him," Demaratos said under his breath to Theras, as he nudged him.

Theras hesitated, causing Hippocrates to feel unsure. "Doctor, I apologize for our ill treatment of you, but some of the men are complaining of a, problem," Theras said uncomfortably.

∧

Demaratos, Theras and seven other Equals were in an empty barrack facing Hippocrates. Their expressions were grim.

"How can I be of service?" the doctor asked impatiently.

The Equals were embarrassed to seek aid from the start. They thought it girlish and hesitated as they looked to one another.

"I'm a very busy man, and I must leave sooner rather than later," Hippocrates said sternly. "So it is best to just get on with it."

Theras stepped forward and cleared his throat. "We all have a similar pain, sir, on the inside. It is making life, difficult. It did not used to be so. There is also blood, back in here," he said, motioning to his rear. "When we go."

Hippocrates laughed hysterically. "Welcome to old age, my young sirs!"

The Equals were perplexed.

Hippocrates immediately noticed their confusion. "Oh, never mind it. You are all perfectly healthy. Just cut down on the cheese, eh?"

The Equals still didn't follow.

The doctor realized this, but he didn't waste any more time explaining and just got down to it. "That fire needs stoking. Get it hot. Fetch me some iron, thin and long. The rest of you, lay down on your sides and wait."

The Equals obeyed, as if he was their polemarch.

A short while later, Hippocrates pulled the iron rod from the fire. It was glowing orange, as he walked over to Demaratos. Demaratos's eyes went wide with fear, while Hippocrates spread one side of his rear apart to widen his anus. Theras and the other Equals sat up to see what they were in for and panicked.

"This shouldn't hurt at all," the doctor said. "It seems my abduction has come with a reward, though," Hippocrates mumbled, and with great pleasure, he inserted the fiery iron into Demaratos's rectum, and then he immediately pulled it out.

Demaratos howled in pain.

"Oh hush, you big girl," Hippocrates said, and then he stepped over to perform his surgery on the next Equal, filling him with the utmost terror.

# Book VII
## Man Taming

*An Athenian woman once encountered a Spartan woman. They talked of many things, including their own lives. During their conversation, the Athenian woman expressed how distressed she was because all day she was bound to her home to do her chores and serve her husband. Nor was she permitted out of her own house, unless she was escorted by her husband or another male family member of age. She was miserable and she had no say in any of her own affairs. The Spartan woman scoffed and laughed with the utmost arrogance, explaining that it was quite the opposite where she was from.*

*The Athenian woman became envious. "How is it that you Spartan women can rule your men?" she asked her.*

*The Spartan woman looked her square in the eye and said, "Because we are the only ones who give birth to men."*

# Xenophon

Xenophon wandered through Greece without any true aim. He was at a loss on where to go or what to do, now that he could no longer call Athens home. He drank himself mad for many nights in many villages, as he stumbled along from Attica to the Peloponnese. He woke one morning after too much straight wine. His head screamed at him, but he finally found clarity. It wasn't so much that he missed campaigning, as he did the companionship it offered. It was a bold maneuver to say the least, but he crossed the River Eurotas and stood facing two men of crimson and bronze at the border of the Five Villages. He waited there until a third Equal returned.

"You will stay as the king's guest friend," the third Equal said.

Xenophon couldn't believe it. He thought for sure that Agesilaos would dismiss the notion. He was escorted to Limnae, the nearest village, where he found Agesilaos waiting for him. The king was still on the mend and using a walking staff to get around. He shook Xenophon's hand as he greeted him. All around them, were many onlookers, wondering who the foreigner was. It made Xenophon feel uncomfortable, so he kept his gaze fixed on the king. He told him that he had been banished from Athens and that his family renounced him. Agesilaos sympathized. He promised to have a house built for him near Olympia, and until that time, he would stay as the king's guest friend. Xenophon was not only grateful, but he was about to experience something very few outsiders could ever claim, a tour of Sparta.

Agesilaos walked him through the Five Villages, showing him the famed city without walls. The land was lush, green and mystical, more so than any other in Greece. Shrines of gods, unknown heroes and deities were everywhere he looked. The gymnasium was full of Equals and Youths performing their gymnastics and perfecting their martial capabilities. Xenophon had never seen men sculpt their bodies with machines before. He was beside himself. The entire city was so peaceful and serene. It was no thoroughfare like Athens. There was no hustle and bustle of traders from far and wide. In fact, Xenophon was the only foreigner in the city. There were no foul odors from filth and waste, and everyone and thing seemed to be in its proper place. Sparta bred the finest warriors in the known world and absolutely nothing was as he expected it to be. Least to say, it didn't take long for Xenophon to become seduced by his surroundings.

He was given a guest house all to himself for the duration of his stay. Those who recognized him from their Persian and Coronean campaigns, acknowledged him, but other than that, he wandered the Five Villages like an uncared for hound. He witnessed the Hyacinthia, a festival dedicated to Apollo in the village of Amyclae. He ate their Black Broth and he found it to be repulsive. He observed some of the grueling rigors of the agoge, which impressed him the most because the Youths were so quick to obey their seniors. Not a smidgen of backtalk, like the Athenian boys. There were so many unexplained wonders, he was overwhelmed. He had been enthralled by all the rumors he heard prior to even knowing a Spartan, and now that he was here, some of those mysteries were beginning to unravel.

On the fifth day, when the sun was nearly set, Agesilaos brought him to the Shrine of Artemis Orthia, where the Youths were ordered to run the infamous gauntlet and steal the cheese offered to her. There were Equals armed with wooden clubs, who were scattered about in front of the shrine, while the Youths hid in the surrounding woods.

"What is this, my king?" Xenophon asked.

"You will see."

They waited until night fell and the waning moon lit the clearing. That's when the Youths finally appeared from all directions. There was a small horde of them. Some of them crept in the shadows, while others dashed toward Artemis in plain view of the Equals. The Equals swung their clubs at the Youths and struck many of them down before they had a chance to reach her. Those who did fall, were out of the competition. The Youths who were still standing gave it their all, as they advanced forward, dodging their betters who were taking a swing at them, while they aimed to steal the cheese from Artemis's stone hands. As Xenophon watched with the king, he began to understand what was happening. Finally, there were two Youths who managed to reach the shrine unnoticed. The boys grabbed the cheese and then they raised their hands victoriously. "Nike! Nike!" they cheered.

Xenophon smiled at their success, but then all the Equals fell upon them and beat them into the ground. Even after the Youths fell, the Equals continued to swing. The boys' skulls were smashed and bloodied, their bones broke, and inevitably, they died. Xenophon was appalled as he met the king's eyes.

"It wasn't that they stole, Xenophon. It was that they got caught," Agesilaos said, while motioning for them to take their leave.

"I see," Xenophon said, feeling a bit shook up. He forced himself to shrug it off as he walked away with the king and continued his education of Spartan society.

The next morning, after breakfast at the kings' mess, Xenophon walked through the agora and he observed an Equal, who was scolding a Youth across the way. The Youth seemed to have been caught walking with his hands on the outside of his cloak. It was a minor infraction, which needed to be addressed. The Equal continued by smacking the Youth across his face, like a father to his son. At that moment, another Equal he recognized from Persia passed by. "Is that the boy's father?" Xenophon asked out of curiosity.

"We are all the boy's father," the Equal said and he continued on his way.

Again, Xenophon was baffled and amazed. He fully approved of Sparta's man taming beliefs. So much so, that he felt his future sons should be raised here. He continued to look around the agora at the various people tending to their various duties and his loneliness came back to haunt him. He realized, then and there, that he needed more than friendship to cure him of his illness. Xenophon, needed a wife.

# Agesilaos

Theodoros tended to his king three times a day. Agesilaos was improving so rapidly that he no longer required the aid of a staff. After the doctor's visit this morning, he kissed his son and wife, and departed his house. As he shut the door behind him and faced forward, he found Cynisca standing before him. She was deeply concerned.

"The conspiracy lives, brother," she said.

"Leotychidas?" he asked.

"Lysander," Cynisca said firmly. She had heard it from the women. They had always known more than they should.

A scowl curled across Agesilaos's brow and then he kissed Cynisca on the cheek. "I love you, sister."

"And I, you," she said, as she watched her brother march away, vexed.

He went across the village, stormed straight toward Lysander's abandoned house, and kicked the door off its ancient hinges. He turned the place out, ransacking it. He tore his bed to shreds with his sword and then he flipped the frame over. He was looking for something, anything that could put an end to the internal strife, which had plagued him since his ascension. He threw the oaken bench beneath Lysander's table against the empty cupboard, which was crawling with insects. Dusty amphoras were smashed in the process and the oil they contained spilled across the floor. He gazed around in all directions and then he slammed his fists on the table. There was nothing. He couldn't believe that Lysander was haunting him in death. Agesilaos continued to scan every nook and crevice as he leaned on the table. He still couldn't find anything, but he thought there must be something, when Myron appeared at the door. He had yet to be assigned to a new master and nor did he push for one on his own accord. It made life easy for him during the interim and he figured no one could fault him for continuing to take care of his late master's house.

"Myron!" Agesilaos said, fuming at the mouth.

The helot became very nervous. "Yes, my king."

"What was Lysander up to? Tell me and be truthful, and you shall have your freedom."

A third promise of freedom. His hopes and dreams had been shattered twice now, but three was a godly number, and who better to make it than the king. "What you seek lies under the table, my king."

Agesilaos hastily lifted the table up on its end. There it was. The two pieces of timber nailed to the underside. The king wedged his blade in between the wood and then he pried the outer slab off. Papyrus floated down to his feet. He picked it up while his blade was still in his other hand and he gave it a quick study.

Myron remained in the doorway during that time. He could feel his freedom at last. He knew Agesilaos was a man of honor and he hadn't the slightest doubt that the king would rescind on his offer.

Agesilaos picked his head up and met Myron's eyes. "Well done," he said, and then he strutted away.

The king made his way to the agora, where the Elders and ephors met every morning to discuss affairs of the state. He waited for them to adjourn and then he confronted Pythagoras with Lysander's constitution. Pythagoras thought it was best to discuss the matter in private, so they walked back to the Elder's house. Once inside, Pythagoras strained his eyes as he read the amended laws Lysander was going to propose. His notion of throwing the kingships open to all, was the most dreadful. It could be viewed as highly favorable by many of the citizens, especially those who lost their status of Equal. It struck genuine fear inside the old man's heart. The laws must remain as they always have. It is why Sparta rules all of Greece, he thought. Pythagoras lifted his heavy head. His mouth was agape, while across the oaken table Agesilaos was leaning forward in his seat, unable to contain his anger. "I shall read it before the people, so they know of his treachery," the king said.

Pythagoras swallowed hard to collect himself. "My king, we do not know how far his corruption has spread. Many names have been mentioned here, many names of influence."

"Many indeed and they shall be dealt with."

"Let us keep this between us, and keep these enemies of the state, close at hand."

Agesilaos sighed. He desperately wanted to expose Lysander as a traitor, but as he reflected upon Pythagoras's strategy, he became open to the idea. "What do you propose?"

"We shall kill them," the Elder said, as he still thought things over.

"Yes, of course!" Agesilaos said with enthusiasm.

"With kindness, my king."

"Send some of them abroad for the year. The others, invite to my mess so they can walk with the king. Is that what you are implying?"

"Precisely," Pythagoras said.

"Done," Agesilaos replied, and then he began to take his leave.

"My king, there is one other matter."

Agesilaos spun back around.

"Before you arrived this morning, the council was discussing the possibility of charging you with crimes against the state."

"By the twin gods! What law have I broken now?"

"It seems that many feel there were others more qualified than Peisander to command the navy. They say you wanted to please the queen."

"Pythagoras, I appreciate you forewarning me. However, I have already sent orders for my half-brother Teleutias to take his place. He is just as qualified as Peisander or any of the others. Will you now charge me with crimes for trying to please my stepmother?"

Pythagoras was stunned. "That, that is a matter for the council to decide, my king."

"Good! You decide, while I dissolve this conspiracy once and for all!"

# Raping the Bride

Night felt like it came on fast for Eirene, while Aspasia cut her hair clean to the scalp. It was required of her as part of her initiation, her passage into her new life. She was to become Theras's wife in secret. It was customary in Sparta for the bride to dress like a man and an Equal to take his bride as a mora would take a city, which was why Sparta called their marriages, Raping the Bride. There was no dowry or ceremony like the other cities had and she expected Theras to arrive at any moment to perform his duty. Eirene continued by anointing her naked body in olive oil. Then she placed a crimson cloak around her shoulders and strapped a pair of boots on her feet. With one kiss, Aspasia said farewell to the old Eirene and welcomed her new friend, the bride, before she left her all alone to be taken at Pitana Grove.

Aspasia was also to be taken. She proceeded to her father's farm house as earlier planned with Demaratos. When she arrived, her bridesmaid was there, waiting to aid her, but during the walk over, mixed feelings stirred inside and she began to have a change of heart. Aspasia sent her away and then she sat by the cloak and boots laid out for her. She stared at them, contemplating her decision and thought if she still wanted to marry, she could quickly prepare herself before Demaratos arrived.

Meanwhile, Theras and Demaratos were at their mess having their evening meal. Their minds were filled with excitement, yet they could not talk about their pending marriages with anyone, as it was forbidden. It was also forbidden for an Equal to be seen going to or leaving the company of a woman he was not married to. In fact, no one in Sparta would know of their union until a child was born. Many always noticed of course, that one of their women had been taken from the sight of their bare crowns, but they would not know whom with.

Demaratos slurped his Black Broth in a hurry and then he glanced over at Theras, who was doing the same. They had told each other of their marriages and no one else. Once their evening meals were finished, it was late and the men went to their barracks for sleep. At the first snore, they snuck out to fulfill their duty.

"Where are you to meet her?" Demaratos whispered.

"Pitana Grove. You?" Theras asked.

"Her father's farm house."

"See you after," Theras said, and they went their separate ways.

When Theras arrived at the moonlit grove, where they had first coupled, he found Eirene lying down on the bank of the stream as expected. He had his mind set to be the aggressor, but instead, he caringly picked her up and took her across to a wooded knoll. He just didn't have it in him to be militant toward a woman. After finding a secluded clearing, he went to gently set her back down. That's when she pulled him toward her and slammed him down hard on his back with a wrestling maneuver. She didn't stop her attack there. Eirene drove her nails down his chest and stomach, and tore his flesh. She then caressed his stick with her tongue and hand to ensure his vigor. As she lowered herself down on him, Theras tried to roll her over without harming her so that he could have the advantage, but she shook her head. Theras laughed, as did she. He wasn't surprised at all that he was the one to be raped. However, all his life, he did envision it the other way around.

Demaratos reached the farm house at the appointed time to wed Aspasia, but when he entered, she was not there and he became visibly concerned. They had seen each other in secret on many occasions since his return and he knew all was well between them, or so he thought. He immediately ventured to her house, while her father and mother slept. The wooden shutters were open in her bed chamber and he spied her sleeping all alone in the moonlight. It devastated him. He loved her and he had to know why she backed out of the engagement.

Aspasia woke after the third pebble tapped her crown. Her heavy eyes opened and she spotted her betrothed. "Why would you risk coming here?" she asked softly, yet rudely.

"Tell me why, Aspasia," he said with desperation.

Aspasia grew tired of her predicament quickly. "I love another, now go."

"Tell me who it is. Who is the worthier man?"

Worried, she looked back to see if they had woken her parents. "If I tell you, will you go?"

Demaratos nodded.

"He is the one closest to you," she said. "He serves me like a real man. Unlike you could ever do." When Aspasia heard herself say that, she meant it, but she did not intend to offend Demaratos. She truly had no ill feelings toward him, she just wanted to escape her discomfort.

Nonetheless, it broke Demaratos's heart. He remained silent as he met her scornful glare and then he vanished from her window.

# The Women

Xenophon was constantly astounded by everything he saw during his stay, the women most in particular. Every time he walked through the city, he couldn't help but notice that the women of Sparta spent so much of their day outside. They would eat meals at any time. Their food even looked appealing, as opposed to the men's blood vinegar stew. The women seemed to eat as much as they wanted also, unlike the men's single serving of breakfast and dinner. They would converse and gossip about whatever they desired, which the men were forbidden to do. Their liberties seemed to have no bounds. The women even criticized their young girls, just as the men do to the boys, and the girls accepted it, without taking offense. Mothers also nurtured their young outside, rather than in private. When mothers had to leave the house, their infants were left inside their homes alone. They would inevitably cry, but the mothers insisted their infants remain alone, until they learned not to. Their freedom seemed to even give them powers over the governing body. On one occasion, when Xenophon was heading through the agora, he observed a woman sway the council over some grievance or other with just a glance. To him, everything he witnessed in regards to the women was marvelous and a far cry from Athens. It made him wonder who actually ruled this warrior society.

One of the mysteries Xenophon was able to unravel, was in regards to a rumor. He used to hear in his former city that Spartan women were called thigh flashers, and it was the only rumor that the Athenians had gotten right. Their tunics were short, but their bodies wore them well. This was because of their gymnastics. The women and girls were just as diligent about them, as the men and boys. They would perform them in the nude, just like their male counterparts did, and sometimes they would even do them together, and still, there was no shame in it. The girls too, even ruled the boys. They would point out flaws on their naked bodies at the gymnasium, so as to help them improve their physical appearance. Xenophon found their unprecedented nature irresistible and intoxicating. He kept his enjoyment of gazing at beautiful naked women and girls to himself the best he could. However, it was difficult because he kept catching glimpses of their loins and breasts, even when they wore their tunics.

Many more days had gone by and Xenophon was still determined to find a wife. He made his way from his guest house to the agora, as he had done every morning on his way to the kings' mess for breakfast. He crossed paths with many of the same women along his route. Two of them would always giggle and talk about him as he passed. Their Laconic accents were exceptionally strong and it made them difficult to understand from afar. He figured they were probably insulting him, but he always remained respectful and kept walking. However, this morning he chose to do otherwise. He stopped in midstride across from them as they made their jokes and then he approached them with his hands inside his cloak. "I am Xenophon," he said nervously.

They placed their hands over their mouths, laughing some more. "Yes, we know," the one woman said, and then she looked to her friend with a smile before facing Xenophon again. "You are sculpted like our men, and we are curious to know if you can satisfy us like them too."

Xenophon was surprised, not only by her unwavering confidence and blunt speech, but they were not insulting him as he had thought. He tilted his head as he gazed into her eyes. He was awestruck. "This has got to be a joke," he said to himself.

"Come with me," she said, and she walked away, leaving her friend behind.

Xenophon followed her from three paces back. He was giddy and excited as he watched her wide hips and slender, strong legs lead the way. Maybe I will find a wife, he thought. Could it really be this easy in Sparta?

They passed by many houses, all collected together with more women outside doing their usual, and she led him into the last house on the left. When she entered, she dropped her tunic from her shoulders and allowed it to fall to the floor. Then she turned around and faced the Athenian completely naked.

Xenophon was beside himself, because she was a Helen.

"Well, are you going to take me or not?" she asked.

And so bold, he thought, as he quickly tossed his dress to the side. He hadn't been with a woman since his Persian debacle and he couldn't even remember what to do.

The woman realized this and took control of the entire affair. She motioned for him to join her in bed and he did. Then she grabbed his stick and placed it inside of her. She was amused by his shyness, while Xenophon allowed her to take full advantage of him.

"You are doing well, Athenian," she said, as she rode upon him.

"Uh, thank you, my lady."

"Warn me when you are going to seed," she insisted.

"Yes, my lady. I believe, I believe, right now," he said in a blissful state.

She abruptly ended the engagement and aimed his stick away from her. She would not allow his seed to touch her, for fear of weakening her future sons. "Very well," she said, concluding the affair. "We are done."

Xenophon sat up, feeling excited, relaxed and a bit abused. "Uh, yes of course, my lady," he said. The last thing he wanted to do was offend anyone in the Five Villages.

They both stood up and stared at one another for a brief moment.

"That means leave," she said.

"Yes, of course," he said again. Then he threw his tunic on and placed his cloak around his shoulders. "It's just, I never learned your name, my lady."

She responded by opening the door without any dress on and gestured for Xenophon to leave. The other women were outside, cheering and laughing at them. She smiled and waved to acknowledge her fellow women across the way and then she rolled her eyes at Xenophon before shutting him out.

Xenophon couldn't comprehend what just happened as he faced the wooden door and then slowly turned around to all the women, who were laughing at him. He was embarrassed and confused, but not for the reasons he should have been. He did not realize that if he were an Equal, he would have been mortified to have been seen leaving a woman's house. This was why they liked him. He walked by them all as he had no other choice. He kept his head down during his retreat, until another woman stepped in his path. It was another Helen. How could this be? How is every woman in Sparta so strikingly gorgeous? He had no time to ponder it, as she was ordering him inside her home.

Xenophon hesitated and then he looked across at all the women, who were watching him. It was as if he was the most amusing person of the ages. He was Sparta's Aristophanes, and so, Xenophon complied. He stepped inside and she had her way with him. Just as before, the woman wouldn't allow his seed to touch her skin and she immediately ended the engagement. He left when he was commanded to and he did not bother with any idle chatter. By the time Xenophon made it back to the agora, he had been with three additional women.

He arrived at the entrance to the kings' mess very late and bewildered. Agesilaos had already taken his leave and six polemarchs were on their way out.

"Enjoy yourself, Athenian," one of the polemarchs said, which caused the rest of the Equals to laugh.

Xenophon looked at him questioningly. He wondered how they could have known what he was up to in such a short amount of time.

The polemarch read his consternation, while offering a cunning smile. "A secret isn't a secret, unless the Five Villages knows about it." Then he turned gravely serious. "And be mindful, those are wives of Equals you couple with."

Xenophon panicked. "Have I angered a great many?"

The polemarch hesitated. "By the gods, no!" he said, bursting into laughter. "That is not possible in Sparta," he concluded, and then he took his leave, as he continued to laugh with his men.

Xenophon was astounded again. How could the men not become envious? He sat down inside the mess and found that the king had honored him with his second meal. Xenophon picked up his spoon and ate his breakfast all alone. After a bit of reflection, he smiled because he came to the conclusion that the most fearsome military society in the known world was not only ruled by women, but it was a sexual utopia.

"By all the gods on Olympus!"

# Agesilaos

Agesilaos walked with his entourage of councilmen and polemarchs to his mess for their morning meal. He had Myron executed for treason the night prior. And so at last, the helot got his freedom. The king also sent three of the six men, who were mentioned in Lysander's constitution, away. They were Equals and he gave them annual positions abroad at some of their garrisons on the Asiatic coast. It was a high mark of distinction to be chosen for this and it was the last thing they expected, so they felt obligated to prove their loyalty to their king. The other three were council members and they walked with him now. They wore their new cloaks Agesilaos gave to them, when he invited them to his mess. They were quick to show their gratitude, and when they were to return home later in the day, they would also find an ox for each of them to use on their farms. Agesilaos knew how to pour the honey on top and the conspirators began to see the advantages of walking with their king.

These three councilmen were also the ones who proposed the notion of criminal charges against Agesilaos and they assured him that the allegations would be dismissed. They calculated that Agesilaos's decision, as paradoxical as it was, to replace Peisander with his half-brother Teleutias as the naval commander, erased any notion of favoritism toward his family over Sparta. Agesilaos killed the conspirators with kindness, and by doing so, he dissolved the conspiracy once and for all. Word even came in that the Spartans defeated the Persians at sea after Peisander's death, and all was seemingly well in the Spartan Empire.

When the men arrived at the mess, Xenophon was already there, standing at the door. He couldn't fathom wasting another day in paradise, being passed around like some slave. He realized all too late that he had embarrassed himself to a ridiculous extent, when he allowed the women to manipulate him. So he came early to avoid further abuse and humiliation.

Agesilaos grinned. "Good of you to join us," he said to Xenophon.

"My king," Xenophon said, while he avoided his gaze. He then followed the entourage inside and took the seat on the end, opposite the king. Meals of barley porridge were served and the helots were dismissed. The slop was bland and the portions were large, so Xenophon learned to put it down fast.

While everyone slurped their meals, Agesilaos glanced at his guest friend. He was completely humored by his visit. "Xenophon," he called, garnering everyone's attention.

Xenophon picked his head up and looked at the king with uncertainty.

"I've received word that your house is nearly complete, a day or two more at most."

"Yes, my king. But, would it be possible to stay a while longer, till the next moon perhaps?"

Everyone at the table laughed and joked.

"He likes it here, my king," one of the polemarchs said.

"Your wife must have him by the balls!" another polemarch countered.

"An Athenian, who knows a good thing? By Zeus, what is happening in this world of ours?" a councilman questioned.

Xenophon blushed and smiled, as he finally felt accepted.

"And he can take a joke," Agesilaos said, calming everyone down. Then he offered one of the conspirators his second meal, as he looked to Xenophon. "We depart in three days' time. Herippidas informs me that the Thebans and their allies have rallied in Corinth. The vile wretches block our passage out of the Peloponnese."

# The Men

After their morning gymnastics, the king ordered six moras to hold mock battles. It was three against three. Their eights were fitted with a dense linen cover to prevent injury and death. It didn't always work. Agesilaos had made a full recovery by this time and the Youths watched their king lead the moras into the fray with great enthusiasm from the side of the pitch. Xenophon did as well. Pythagoras arrived with Agesipolis toward the end of their training, as anti-Theban aggression ran rampant among the troops. The Elder's mind was elsewhere though. He was considering a suitable regent to act in Agesipolis's stead, until the boy king was of age.

By sundown, the army convened at the gymnasium for a second round of gymnastics. Torch fire lit the sands, pitch and athlitika. Thousands were there, honing their skills in speed, strength and hand-to-hand combat. Xenophon accompanied the king to the athlitika to use the machines. Passing through the masses, was a marvelous sight. He could think of nothing more patriotic and honorable, than a city which dedicated itself to their city.

Meanwhile, Demaratos and Theras were at the sands as they began to box. Cheese and Red were nearby doing the same. Everything in Theras's life was in place. He was feeling good, while Demaratos was coming in hard with blows of uncontrollable aggression toward his friend.

"What bothers you?" Theras asked, dodging his strikes.

"I am to lose my status," Demaratos said sharply.

Theras punched him, making light contact. "You will find someone, I assure you."

Then Demaratos countered by giving Theras two devastating blows to his midsection. "It had best be soon!"

Theras stumbled back, recovered, and stepped forward with his guard up. "You know, Eirene talks of you all the time. It gives me quite the pain across my brow," he said, hitting Demaratos on his shoulder and then again on his jaw.

The last strike infuriated Demaratos, and just as he was about to counterattack, he yielded. "What are you saying, Theras?"

Theras dropped his guard. "We can double if you like. I'm sure she will not object."

"You do not mind?"

"I was thinking of having Aspasia too. She is much more enjoyable."

Demaratos was surprised. He thought Aspasia lied to him, only to be free of her commitment. "Have you coupled with her since our return?"

"I have," Theras said, putting his guard back up.

"What does Eirene say?" Demaratos questioned, as he raised his fists.

"She speaks of you."

Demaratos dropped his guard again. "Double you say?"

"She will be both of ours."

Demaratos burst into an unexpected smile. "Done," he said, and he hugged his best friend for saving his reputation from ruin.

"Good. Now stop hitting me like a girl and box," Theras said and he shoved him away.

They laughed and resumed their sparring, while across from them, on the other side of Cheese and Red, a large crowd was forming around two Youths who had just squared off in a pankration match.

"Cheese, have a look at your prodigy!" Demaratos yelled.

Cheese glanced over, while his scarred back told the difficult tale of his upbringing. The fight was evenly matched, until the one Youth put the other Youth into a familiar arm lock, which Cheese and Red knew all too well. Everyone around them was yelling for the boy to yield, so he wouldn't lose the use of his arm, but he refused to listen.

"By the twin gods, when is he going to learn?" Cheese asked Red in frustration.

The boy dominating the match looked over to them, as they were now the Youths' trainers. Cheese and Red gave him a nod to proceed with his technique. The Youth did and the other boy's shoulder snapped. Cheese winced, remembering how it felt, and then he looked over at Red.

"You're it," they both said at once.

# Agesilaos

On the third day, the men were given the day off before they would embark on their campaign. Agesilaos wasn't sure how long he would be gone, but he felt confident that he had subdued all elements of corruption from within the state. However, he wanted to be sure. So he decided to invite the three councilmen to go on a morning hunt.

They ventured south toward the Taygetus Mountains, where the hunting was good. They were going about it in the old fashion. Meaning, they left their hounds at home. Fortune blessed them the moment they reached the base of the mountain, when they discovered boar tracks. They followed the trail in total silence up the thick wooded face. They went up a good ways, keeping their eights at the ready, when they finally saw the beast foraging near a fallen tree from ages ago. Agesilaos gave a hand signal for the men to go around and force the boar back to him. The boar was a massive male. He spread as long and as thick as a lion. Its horns were long and curved. One was broken in fact and left jagged, probably from warring with one of his own kind.

Agesilaos waited for the beast to take fright. He was kneeling in heavy brush, while the three councilmen took their separate routes. One was to flank the boar from the left, another from his right, and the third councilman was moving beyond the boar, opposite of

Agesilaos. Everyone was waiting for the latter man to get into position and everyone required the other's trust. Finally, he was in place and he broke into a charge, ash first. The boar's ears twitched. He glanced at the predator trying to take his life and then he ran toward the king. Agesilaos remained hidden for a moment longer, so as to deceive the boar, and then he stepped out of the brush. The boar barreled toward him in a mad fury. Many men had died attempting this, even if they did manage to stick the beast. Those who had seen it, say that a boar can run in death. The king stood his ground though, firm and fearless, his eight clutched, ready to kill. All it would take, was for one of those horns or the weight of the beast to fall on him and the king would be no more. It was reckless. As the ten pace gap narrowed between boar and king, the councilmen charged with their javelins aimed at Agesilaos. The king's eyes went wide. The hunt had brought out their treachery, he thought. They could simply say the king fell, as so many had before and Sparta would be plagued with endless corruption until her death.

The five lethal points charged toward him, but Agesilaos despised death, so he took his chances. As the boar came in, Agesilaos struck him in his fore, gouging his grizzly neck. He held his eight steady, but the ashen shaft snapped from the force of the charge. He shut his eyes, resolving to die, and in that uncertain moment, where he had expected to find himself sailing down the River Styx, he did not. When the king opened his eyes, he found the boar by his feet, skewered on all four sides. The councilmen had done their duty and passed the king's trial. Sparta, would endure.

# Xenophon

Xenophon woke to find Agesilaos standing in the doorway of his guest house. It was time to go. He felt relieved and saddened by his departure. The night before, while Agesilaos offered the boar to his gods in preparation for his Corinthian campaign, Xenophon spent his last evening with a woman of similar age. He told himself that he was going to stay away from the women, but he could not help himself. She was a Helen without a doubt and he had fallen in love with her. She was fond of him as well, despite their three day long relationship, and she decided that he should no longer be shared with the others. So last night, he told her that he was to leave and he proposed that she become his wife and live with him at his new home. Hysterical laughter erupted. She had devastated him in the most Laconic of ways. Really, she, like every other citizen, was property of the state, and therefore, she had no authority to make such a decision. As Xenophon marched with Agesilaos out of Laconia, he chuckled. He thought to love a Spartan woman was far too easy, but to corrupt their bloodline with foreign seed was impossible. He decided not to take it to heart and found the king eyeing him as he mumbled to himself.

Xenophon learned from Agesilaos that he was going to execute a complete massacre at Corinth. To war against the same people again and again is not only folly, but against the Laws of Lycurgus, the king explained. So everyone there was to die. Their city would be reduced and their land would be consumed in fire. It was to remind the rest of their enemies who was in charge, and for once, Xenophon was glad he would not be taking part. He had had enough of war.

By nearly day's end, the army arrived at Xenophon's new house. The philosopher was in shock. His lot stretched as far as the eye could see and his house was made of oak and stone. It spanned fifty paces in breadth. He was supplied with horses, chickens, goats, pigs and crops. "I, I don't know what to say, my king."

"Say nothing and quit calling me your king, you fool," Agesilaos said.

Xenophon faced him in a brotherly way. "What is it the gods want from us, Agesilaos? How is it, they have paired us?"

The king smiled. "I have been wondering the same thing."

"You are a good friend to me. I pledge my undying devotion to you, and Sparta for as long as there is a breath inside of me."

"I hope that I can call on you then, when the time comes."

"Of course," Xenophon said wholeheartedly. "But how can I repay you, to show you my gratitude?"

"I assure you it is nothing, Xenophon. I take great pleasure in helping friends."

Xenophon remained speechless, while he watched his king march toward a golden, cloud covered horizon with his bronze and crimson men. They were beautiful as gods, he thought, as they headed off to war.

When Xenophon walked into his house, he found it was full of furnishings and provisions. He crossed through the main quarter and entered his bed chamber. Then he fell asleep on his new bed and he woke up days later, unsure what to do with himself. Once again, he was all alone. Many more nights passed, until finally, the full moon returned and he realized what he must do. He was going to write his history, of his time with the king, his two campaigns in Persia, a treatise on Spartan society and a lengthy piece of work dedicated to Socrates's greatness. It all came at him so fast. He wanted it to last for the ages. He was so excited and overwhelmed to just get it down on papyrus that he wrote chaotically at first. One moment, he wrote of Cyrus's war against his brother. The next, he found himself writing about a conversation he had with Socrates. He would then toss those aside and scribble something noteworthy about Agesilaos. After a few days, he realized that he was getting nowhere and he knew it was because he desired a wife and sons. His quiet surroundings were of no help either. There was no one within earshot of him. He did travel into the city one time and had a message sent to his father. Another moon came and went without any reply. He knew his father had renounced him, but he thought the old man could at least send word back to him, to let him know that he was alive. Xenophon was hurting, but finally, after so much self-pity and self-loathing, he embraced his isolation and found his focus. He began again, writing his history first. He decided it was best to start after the Great War and write every single event from then until now. He went for days without stopping and made excellent progress, when suddenly he heard a woman curse from afar. He looked up and all was quiet, not a sight or sound from anyone. He shrugged it off and then he resumed his labor, before the temptation to take pity on himself returned. A page later and there was a knock at the door. It was unexpected. He felt alarmed and excited to have a visitor. It didn't matter who it was. He dropped his pen, sprang from his seat, and went to answer the door. When he opened it, he found a young woman, who was around twenty-five years of age, standing before him. She was covered in mud and grime from crown to toe, but he looked beyond that. He envisioned her after a bath. She had dark silky hair which fell beyond her shoulders, tanned skin which glistened with oil, and green-brown eyes which could peer into his soul. She was perfect, he thought. And before either of them spoke, their eyes locked in a way that brought comfort to the other, as if the gods had put them under a spell.

"Could you please help me, sir?" she asked. She was flustered, but she forced herself to smile. "I have broken down."

"I have as well, for far too long," Xenophon thought. Then, he looked at her wagon in the far distance. It was on a stony dirt path, which the rains had turned to mud. Xenophon saw that one of her wheels had snapped in two. Then he peered back into her majestic eyes, which kept him in a trance. "I will do all that I can for you and more, my lady."

# Author's Afterword

Strife plagued Sparta relentlessly for the next twenty-three years and she held firm, ruling all of Greece. During that time, Thebes never saw reason, and in the year 371 BC at the Battle of Leuctra, they defeated the Spartans. It was a decisive victory. Sparta's fearsome reputation was shattered. Her population of Equals was decimated. They would never recover, and thus, the Oracle's prophecy of a crippled kingship proved true. Agesilaos ruled for another eleven years during Sparta's fall from power and lived until the age of eighty-four, where he died on the shores of Libya as a hired mercenary while attempting to refill Sparta's coffer.

Xenophon died shortly after his friend's death in the year 354 BC. Fortune blessed him with two sons and they were given the high honor of being raised in Sparta. He also completed his histories, writing many lengthy works, as well as several short treatises. Many of them have survived to this day, which gives us our small insight into Spartan society. Whether Xenophon's birth name was in fact Xenophon or it was a name given to him by the Spartans, we will never know. However, as he was an Athenian writer who was devoted to Sparta, it was quite fitting because Xenophon's name translates to "foreign voice."

Not much is known about Cynisca, other than the fact that she did return to the Olympics in 392 BC and repeated her victory. She is also the only woman recorded in Spartan history to have a hero shrine built in her dedication after her death.

Such extraordinary lives...This book begins in approximately the year 401-400 BC and concludes around 394-393 BC. By comparison to our own present day lives, I am astounded by what these men and women accomplished. Not only was it during a short period of time, but it was under such a very different set of circumstances.

# Acknowledgments

This book could not have been attempted without the surviving histories of Pausanias, Plato, Plutarch and my favorite author, Xenophon. Thank the gods for them.

Done

# ABOUT THE AUTHOR

Dimetrios C. Manolatos is the author of the novel The Sons of Herakles and The Assassin's Pitch. He has also penned 47 Ronin, The Athenian Job and several short stories.

Printed in Great Britain
by Amazon